Depths of Paradise

Vance Albright

LIGHT AND DARK NOVELIZATIONS

Cover Designer: Brandi Doane McCann. https://www.ebook-coverdesigns.com

Developmental Editor: Savannah Gilbo. https://www.savannahgilbo.com

Spelling and Grammar Editor: Sara Kelly. https://reedsy.com/sara-kelly

ISBNS

E-book: 978-1-7340628-0-9

Paperback: 978-1-7340628-2-3

CONTACT

Vance Albright can be contacted at the following links.

Website:

https://lightanddarknovelizations.com

Business E-mail:

lightanddarknovelizations@gmail.com

Facebook:

https://www.facebook.com/lightanddarknovelizations

PROLOGUE

Prologue: The Creation of Niihau Base

On January 17, 2020, the Japanese government purchased the privately owned Hawaiian Island Niihau. The smallest of the Hawaiian Islands, Niihau covers an area of seventy miles. Officially, the land and the surrounding waters were purchased to train dolphins and other marine life for usage in water parks across America and Japan. Unofficially, the island's true purpose is to train attack dolphins to locate and destroy any hostile marine threats that threaten the Japanese islands.

Land Construction

To make project Niihau a reality, a small airfield and boat dock were created to provide work crews with transportation to and from the island. Next, important buildings like work crew shelters, warehouses, and a hangar were built to hold vehicles and months of supplies. Niihau was known to experience long periods of drought. To combat this, large water distillation tanks were assembled to convert the local sea water into drinkable water. For the island's permanent staff, a housing unit was built that could hold up to seven people. The outside of the house had the appearance of a simple one-story home. What was simple on the outside was state-of-the-art on the inside. The inside of the house had top-of-the-line private quarters, kitchen, living room, and medical supply room. The basement of the house held a state-of-the-art laboratory and recreation area.

To further aid in hiding the island's true purpose, the large areas of land not used for storage or housing were converted to a wildlife refuge for critically endangered species. The public was informed the wildlife was tracked by a network of ground sensors, equipped with HD cameras installed across the island. Photos of flora and fauna could be found on the Niihau wildlife preservation website. The deception worked, hiding the sensors' true purpose of locating any intruders on the island.

Fencing

A massive network of underwater fencing was constructed half a mile from shore. It stood seven feet above the water line and surrounded the entire island. The fencing served a dual purpose. Primarily, it would act as the dolphin's habitat; secondarily, it acted as a barrier to keep unwanted vessels from entering the area. The fencing also played a role in the dolphins' intelligence testing. Bottle nose dolphins can leap fifteen feet. The test was to determine which dolphins learned they could easily clear the fence. Occasionally, the dolphins that learned this would escape and go for a swim outside the training zone. Dolphins that failed to return on command or by themselves shortly after leaving were tracked down by GPS and removed from the program. Failed dolphins were sold to zoos or marine aquariums across the world.

It took a year of nonstop work from hardworking Japanese and American contractors, but in early 2021, the job was finished. Now, the facility at Niihau was ready to create the first wave of the new Japanese marine defense force.

CHAPTER 1

10:17 PM 4/7/2021 HST

The Japanese fishing trawler Lucky Dragon sailed thirty-two miles off the coast of Maui. The Lucky Dragon was a sixty-foot-long vessel that held a crew of four: a captain, a helmsman, and two deckhands. Captain Fumio Kudo sat in his cabin reading a Hawaiian newspaper. Whenever the Lucky Dragon docked for supplies, he picked up a newspaper at the port. He enjoyed reading about the news events from different countries, and how those countries perceived and reported on world events. Fumio was an older man in his early sixties, who had worked around fishing vessels since he was a teenager. His reading was interrupted by a beeping sound, which alerted the crew a fish was on one of the lines. He smiled.

Another catch, he thought to himself. He could hear the sound of the fishing line getting reeled in. Music to his ears. The ship's freezer was filled with large yellowfin tuna and marlins. In a few days, the Lucky Dragon would begin sailing back to Japan. Ready to cash in on a big payday. *A successful trip.* The thought brought a smile to Fumio's face as he went back to his reading. A few moments later, a deckhand's voice came over the ship's intercom.

"Captain Kudo, please come on deck right away!" The voice had a confused and slightly worried sound to it, which made Fumio wonder what was going on above him. He opened his cabin door, walked through the sleeping cabins, up a set of stairs, and onto the main deck. The bright ship's lights made him squint. He looked out at the dark ocean to let his eyes adjust. Clouds covered the moon, making the water surrounding him nearly invisible. He walked over to his two deckhands who were standing around the recently caught fish.

"What is the problem?" he asked.

"Look, Captain!" one of the men said, pointing at the seven-foot tuna. The entire bottom and middle portions of the tuna had been removed. Only the head, tail, and a few pieces of flesh hung from the tuna's still intact spine.

"This is unfortunate," he replied, looking at the mangled fish. "What did it? A shark?" Fumio asked.

"I don't think so. Not with a bite like this!" one of the deckhands replied nervously.

"Captain, come to the main cabin right away!" the helmsman shouted over the intercom. Fumio quickly ran into the main cabin where the helmsman was glued to the radar screen. "Captain, a large object started circling us several minutes ago!" Fumio looked at the radar screen, which showed a large blip fourteen feet in front of the boat. The blip started moving towards the Lucky Dragon. The radio also showed it was rising towards the water's surface. Fumio pressed the intercom button and spoke.

"Turn on the spotlight now." He then turned to the helmsman and ordered him to cease engines. The object was most likely nothing more than a whale, but after seeing that half-eaten fish, Captain Kudo was taking no chances.

He watched as a deckhand rushed to the assigned position. The ship had a single spotlight mounted on the front of the ship that could be rotated three hundred and sixty degrees. The other deckhand walked up to the spotlight holding a shotgun. The spotlight's first scan showed nothing but the dark ocean. Just before the deckhand started the second scan, the helmsman's voice screamed over the intercom.

"The object just surfaced on the starboard side." The light and shotgun barrel turned right. The spotlight illuminated a large fast-moving wake heading right towards them. In rapid succession, three slugs left the shotgun. Small ripples formed on top of the wake as the bullets pierced the water. Nerves filled both men as the wake's speed increased. The deckhand holding the shotgun got ready to unload another volley. Suddenly the sound of a thunderclap filled the area, and the spotlight went out. Some of the crew scanned the skies, looking for the source, while others looked at the deckhand operating the spotlight. He was shouting in confusion, trying to get the light back on. Alarms started going off in the main cabin as the boat was violently shaken, nearly knocking Captain Kudo and the helmsman off their feet.

"What's happening?" Captain Kudo demanded to know.

"We're taking on water!" the helmsman shouted as he tried to start the ship's engines. "The engines are not responding! The engine room must be flooded!" he screamed in a panicked voice. Although nervous, Captain Kudo managed to keep his composure. He ordered the helmsman to send out an S.O.S.; then he ran outside and began shouting orders to the deckhands.

"One of you go below and see how much damage we have taken! The rest of us will ready the life raft!" Before the men could move, the boat was struck again. The deckhand with the shotgun screamed and fired his gun as he fell over the boat's railing. "Man overboard!" Kudo shouted.

"Captain, the spotlight is not working. I don't know what's wrong with it," the remaining deckhand shouted, rushing to the middle of the boat. Kudo handed him a flashlight.

"Come on. We must try to locate him." Kudo and the deckhand rushed to the spot they saw Ryu fall overboard. The beams from the flashlights revealed nothing.

"Ryu! Ryu!" both men cried, hoping to hear a response. Abruptly a loud splash occurred, followed by the sound of shattering wood and glass. The boat started to turn to the right, knocking both men off their feet. A scream from the helmsman filled both men's ears, which was followed by another splash. Kudo got to his feet, struggling to stand on the increasing vertical deck. He looked at the main cabin. The right side was completely destroyed.

My God, what is this thing? he thought to himself.

"Captain, what do we do?" the deckhand screamed.

"Into the life raft! Abandon ship!" Kudo ordered, snapping out of his shock. He and the deckhand tossed the life raft into the water. Kudo and the deckhand jumped off the boat into the circular life raft. Both men sat in disbelief as the ship slowly sank beneath the ocean. For the moment, the sea was silent. The only sound came from the water softly hitting the raft. Neither man wanted to speak, nor could they explain what just happened. Kudo opened the emergency supply kit and started going through it. The silence was broken by an eerie moan, followed by another splash.

"It's a Kappa," the deckhand said, frightened. Normally, Kudo would have lectured the man for suggesting such a thing, but now he was unsure what to believe. Hesitating, Kudo turned on his flashlight and started to search the waters around them. Suddenly, the loud hissing of breaking rubber occurred. Both men let out a final scream as the sides of the life raft started to enclose around them. Kudo felt water touch his body as the raft sank beneath the surface.

***

It was late afternoon in Tokyo, Japan. Commander Okada Takahashi sat in his office, located in building A of the Japanese Ministry of Defense complex. The defense complex had five main building lettered A to E. He intently looked over the latest reports on the progress of the Japanese Marine Defense Force dolphin training drills. Okada Takahashi was in his mid-thirties. He was tall for a Japanese man, standing at six feet with a muscular build. He had black hair and brown eyes. He spoke in a thick authoritative Japanese accent. When on duty, his face always had a serious look on it. He also had a strong reputation for always having a serious no-nonsense attitude. His mere presence in a room intimidated most people. A perfectly cleaned and pressed Japanese military uniform covered his body. A knock on the door made Okada's eyes rise from his papers.

"Enter," he said. His personal assistant, Saburo Nakamura, entered the room and bowed deeply. Saburo was a thin built man with short brown hair. Unlike the intimidating presence Takahashi gave off, Saburo had a much more professional business presence to him. His professional suit, small glasses, and polite smile added to the aura.

"Sir, I just received a report from the American Coast Guard," Saburo said.

"Concerning what?" Okada asked.

"Thirty-two miles off the Hawaiian mainland, at exactly ten seventeen Hawaiian Standard Time, the Japanese fishing vessel Lucky Dragon was attacked and sunk," Saburo replied.

"Attacked by what?" Okada asked, expecting Saburo to say "pirates." Saburo paused for a few seconds, trying to find the right words.

"Well . . . I know this is going to be hard to believe, but the ship reported it was under attack by a large unidentified sea creature." Okada looked straight ahead with an unreadable stare on his face.

"Have any crew members been recovered?"

"Not that I know of, sir. The American Coast Guard is conducting a rescue operation as we speak."

"Bring me the full report as soon as you receive it, and make travel arrangements for me. I'm going to join my team on Niihau and personally look into this situation," Okada ordered.

"Yes, sir," Saburo replied. He bowed and started to leave the room. He stopped and turned to the commander. "Sir, may I ask something?" Okada shook his head yes. "Are you taking this sea monster report seriously?"

"I'm not making any assumptions until I have more information," he replied.

"Sir, what if the Lucky Dragon truly was sunk by a sea monster?" Saburo asked, concerned. "If the legends are true, then more ships may meet the same fate."

"I am confident my team and I can discover what truly happened to the Lucky Dragon. Once the truth is revealed, we will take appropriate action." Saburo smiled, satisfied with the answer, and left the room.

CHAPTER 2

4:43 PM 4/8/2021 HST

Mya Kendig nervously stood near the baggage claim belt of Kahului Airport. When her flight landed, she had received a text from her sister Jade stating she was going to be late picking her up from the airport. That was the last thing she needed. This was her first time flying, and her first time traveling alone. Thoughts started to fill her head as she waited for her suitcase. She had no idea where to go or where Jade was going to meet her. To make matters worse, Jade was not responding to her return texts. She hoped this was because she was driving to the airport. She spotted a large black suitcase with a stuffed dragon tied to it. She reached over and grabbed it off the rack.

Mya Kendig was in her mid-twenties. She had long dark brown hair, with large streaks of it dyed purple. She had a thin build, with pale skin. Mya scanned the crowds of people, hoping to locate her sister's face. Mya checked her phone again; still nothing. Still nervous about the situation, Mya took a deep breath and headed for the airport entrance. After a short walk, Mya sat at a bench near the entrance door and anxiously waited for her sister. The half hour that went by felt like an eternity to Mya.

What if she forgot I was coming? Mya thought, staring at her phone. Finally, her phone's ring tone went off.

"Jade," Mya said.

"Hey, I'm so sorry I'm late. The diving tour took longer than expected and then the traffic was terrible."

"It's fine," Mya replied in relief. "I'm just glad to hear your voice."

"Where are you?" Jade asked.

"Sitting at a bench right near the airport entrance."

"Did you go outside yet?" Jade asked.

"No," Mya answered.

"Good; don't go out until I get there. Criminals wait around to grab unsuspecting tourists."

"What?" Mya asked nervously as her eyes scrutinized the crowds of people.

"I'm kidding," a voice said next to her. Mya jumped up, startled only to see her older sister standing a few yards from her. Jade was a few inches taller than Mya and in her late twenties. She had long light brown hair and matching brown eyes. She had an athletic build, and what some would call perfectly tanned skin. A smile formed on Mya's face as the two sisters hugged. "It's so great to see you! Over a year is too long," Jade said.

"Yeah, I'm happy to see you too!" Mya replied.

Jade released the hug and said, "How are you holding up?"

Mya put her head down. "As well as can be expected," she replied, trying to hide the pain in her voice. A few seconds later she perked up and said with a smile, "But I'm in Hawaii for a week and ready to have fun!"

She noticed Jade was keeping one hand hidden behind her back. "Jade, what are you hiding?" Jade leisurely brought her arm forward and placed a bright pink Hawaiian Lei around Mya's neck. Mya looked at it with an annoyed expression, which made Jade laugh.

"Welcome to Hawaii!"

"Just what I always wanted," Mya said sarcastically. "Can I take this off now?"

"Not until we get to the car," Jade replied. "I want you to get the full Hawaiian experience. How was your flight, anyway?"

"After a six-hour flight, I'm jet lagged and hungry. When can we go eat?" Mya asked.

"You're such a dork," Jade said. Lifting up the small green dragon on her suitcase, she pointed to the black shirt with multiple Chinese dragons on it she was wearing.

"That's puff, my traveling buddy from Legendary Quests and Creatures." Jade rolled her eyes, never understanding why Mya preferred fantasy adventures to the ones in the real world. Mya pulled the handle of the suitcase up and started to wheel it across the floor.

"I can take that. You had a long flight," Jade offered.

"Thanks," Mya replied, handing it off to her. When the two sisters exited the airport, Mya took a deep breath as she was introduced to the pleasant Hawaiian temperature for the first time. In front of her, she saw the waves from the crystal blue ocean crashing against the shore. She turned and saw several forest-covered mountains with clouds hovering over their peaks. "Wow." she said softly.

"I wanted to be with you when you saw it for the first time. Don't worry; we will be seeing all of that," Jade said, moving her hands across the mountains in the distance. She and Mya walked over to her newly bought blue convertible.

"I still cannot believe you bought this car," Mya said, taking off her backpack and placing it next to her suitcase in the back seat. Instead of opening the car door, Mya put both hands on the door and leaped in.

"Mya! Do you know how much this car cost?" Jade asked, surprised.

"More than I could ever afford," she replied. "What's the plan for today, anyway?" Jade started the engine and began to drive.

"Today, we'll go home and get you settled in. Tomorrow is when the adventure begins," Jade replied.

"How long of a drive is it to your house?" Mya asked.

"It's about half an hour drive to Makena. We're drop your stuff off at the house, then go out to eat."

"Sounds good," Mya replied in a generic voice. Her full focus was on the scenery surrounding her. "What did you have planned for tomorrow?"

"My gosh, Mya, you're still wearing the Lei!" Jade said. In the excitement, Mya had forgotten about the ugly pink flowers around her neck. She pulled them off and tossed them on the floor.

"Anyway, about tomorrow?"

"Tomorrow we are getting up very early and going to spend the day scuba diving!" An excited look formed on Mya's face.

"Really? Where at?" she asked.

"You'll find out tomorrow," Jade replied.

"Now I'm going to be up all night wondering. Just promise it's not some kiddie pool for new divers."

"No, we're going to a magical place you will never forget," Jade answered. Mya leaned back in the car seat and smiled.

CHAPTER 3

6:22 PM 4/8/2021 HST

At the south end of Niihau near Kawaihoa Point, Liz Tayler laid prone on the ocean floor. The ocean depth in the area was seventeen meters. Both her hands grasped a spear gun. She tensely examined the area as she waited for her prey. She glanced above her. It was late evening, and the surface light was fading fast. The water visibility was not perfect, but good enough. To her left she saw a shadow moving at the edge of her vision.

"There you are," she said as her target swam circles around her. Each time, the circling creature got a little closer. "Not this time!" she said. Liz got on one knee and aimed her spear gun. Her mind started focusing on the speed of the current and how fast her target was moving. Her intense focus was broken when she was struck hard from behind. The force of the strike sent her face first into the ground.

"Dam it!" she screamed in annoyance. She kicked her feet, righting herself. She glared at the two bottlenose dolphins swimming around her. They were making playful clicking noises. Most likely, they were pleased with the win.

"That's another kill for the dolphins. That makes five kills for them and one for you," Max Varian said, amused.

"Shut up. They just got lucky," Liz replied, not wanting to admit defeat. She hated losing but she loved working with the dolphins and deep down even had respect for them. She was about to demand a rematch when her oxygen gauge started beeping. "Nearly out of air; coming up," she said.

***

"We're nearly out of daylight anyway. Let's call it quits for the day," Max said, getting up from the table sitting on the dock. Max Varian was a biologist and animal trainer who had great success training attack and bomb dogs while contracted with the American military. His success was noticed by the Japanese government who hired him to work on the attack dolphin project. In appearance, Max was 6'1" with a muscular build. He had light skin and short light black hair. Max blew two short bursts from his whistle, which was the signal for the dolphins to return to him. Moments later, both dolphins broke the surface of the water in front of him. Their front flippers rested on the dock, as they clicked loudly, pleased with their work.

"Great work, Seafin, Aquatail," he complimented. He tossed both dolphins a small squid as a reward for a successful training day. Seafin was the largest of the seven military dolphins Max was training. Seafin, Aquatail, Atragon, Harpoon, Tsunami, Torpedo, Atlantis, and Depth Charge made up the pod. All seven of the dolphins were male. The decision to use only male dolphins was due to the male dolphin's larger size and weight. Liz emerged from the water. She climbed onto the dock and ripped off the diving mask.

"Okay, I admit it. Max Varian and the seven dolphins beat me," she complimented.

"That's the idea," he replied as both dolphins disappeared beneath the waves. "These last tests showed they're learning to work as a team and can coordinate attacks."

"I feel sorry for any diver or sub that comes across these fish once they're ready for military usage," Liz said, impressed by what had occurred.

"They're mammals," Max pointed out.

"Forgive me," Liz replied sarcastically, not really caring about her error. The far-off sound of a helicopter engine caught their ears. Max typed a command in his data-collecting laptop. The sound of a long whistle blow started playing over the underwater microphones; this told the dolphins that the patrol training was over and they could return to doing whatever they wanted. One by one, dolphins broke the water's surface near the dock. Wanting a reward for their efforts. Max handed out treats as the Japanese rising sun on the bottom of the helicopter became clear. It was Okada Takahashi's personal helicopter.

"Wonder what this unscheduled trip is about?" Max said.

"All he told me was something happened and he would explain the details in person." Liz shrugged her shoulders. "Let's get back to the house and see what he wants." Liz Tayler was 5'11" and had an athletic build. She had light skin and short black hair that extended to the bottom of her neck. Liz grew up in the Navy life. Her father was stationed on an American Navy base in Japan. He met Liz's mother during his regular leaves to Tokyo. After high school, she followed in her father's footsteps and joined the Navy. During combat training, she became known for her aggressive attitude and natural weapon skills. This caught the attention of one of Japan's greatest commanders, Admiral Tetsuya Takahashi. At age twenty-two, she was placed under his command and became a Navy diver. A few years after entering his service, she began dating his son, Okada Takahashi. Having dual citizenship, Liz was ordered to oversee and assist with the dolphin project on behalf of the Japanese government. During that time, Max and she had grown close, forming a tight brother and sister bond.

Minutes later, Max pushed the front door open, which entered into a living room. The kitchen was located behind it. To the right of the living room was a short hall that held Max and Liz's personal rooms. Each room had a bathroom and the entertainment they enjoyed. Two other rooms held double bunk beds for when visitors from Japan came to inspect or assist in the work. The left of the living room mirrored the right side. One of the rooms was a medical facility, equipped to treat minor injuries. The remaining rooms were used as office and storage areas. Liz handed Max her training spear gun.

"I'm going to get dressed. Can you put that away for me?"

"Can do," he replied. He walked into the kitchen and opened the door to the basement where his laboratory and the combat training center were located. He walked to the training center and placed the spear gun in the weapons locker. The locker mainly held spear guns, but also had a few assault rifles, just in case hostile intruders came ashore.

Returning to the top floor, he said, "Liz, I'm leaving to pick up Okada." Max exited the house and walked out to the large warehouse, which was located a few hundred yards away. He looked up as the chopper flew overhead before pulling a set of keys from his pocket. He unlocked the warehouse door and climbed into the all-terrain Jeep. Max started the engine and drove towards the airfield, which was located half a mile to the west of the living area. The small airfield had a runway, refueling area, and two hangars. One hangar held the team's personal chopper, while the other was used to store visiting aircraft. Max stopped the Jeep in front of the landed helicopter. Okada was getting his gear out of the passenger seat. Max got out of the Jeep. Both men stared at each other and bowed slightly. Max was used to shaking hands as a form of greeting, but he always bowed to Okada as a sign of respect.

"It is good to see you, my friend," Okada said.

"Good to see you too," Max replied. "Liz is at the house. We just finished a successful dolphin training session."

"I'm pleased to hear the program is going well; however, that is not why I am here," Okada replied.

"I figured that out," Max said, knowing the next dolphin training demonstrations were not scheduled for another two weeks. "So, what's the situation?" Max asked.

"I will explain everything back at the house," Okada replied as he and Max got into the Jeep.

Liz was sitting on the porch when the Jeep returned to its spot in the warehouse. She knew by the Okada military uniform that he was here on business and not for pleasure. Even though they were a couple, during business or military operations, Okada treated her like any other person under his command. Liz appreciated this. She did not want or need special treatment or privileges from her commanding officer.

"What happened?" Liz asked, knowing by Okada's walk and demeanor that something was wrong. Okada waited a few seconds until Max arrived. He sat down before he spoke.

"Last night, a Japanese fishing vessel was sunk off the Hawaiian coast."

"What does that have to do with us?" Max asked.

"The report states the vessel was sunk by a large unidentified sea creature." Max and Liz looked at each other for a second. Okada pulled out his military-issued smartphone. "Here is the radio signal the Hawaiian Coast Guard received." Okada pressed the play button. A panicked voice spoke quickly and loudly.

"This is the fishing vessel Lucky Dragon. We are thirty-two miles west of Maui. Latitude is..." The radio went silent for a moment. "We need help! A large unknown object is ramming us! The vessel is taking on water!" The dialogue again went silent for a few seconds. "We have just been rammed again! One of the crew has fallen overboard! Send help right away!" For the next minute, the message of the Lucky Dragon's location was repeated, this time with the longitude and latitude coordinates. As the panicked man was explaining the vessel's situation, his voice suddenly went silent. Heavy breathing could still be heard, followed by a large crashing sound. "Monsuta!" he screamed in Japanese; then the radio went dead.

"That transmission occurred early last night," Okada said.

"Has the ship been located, and are there any survivors?" Liz asked.

"Yes, the Lucky Dragon has been found by the Coast Guard, but no survivors have been located. I have requested that all dive teams stand by, so we can investigate the wreckage personally."

"Why do you want us to investigate the wreckage?" Max asked.

"You are both experienced divers. Liz will recognize weapon damage and markings. While you can. . ." Okada paused for a moment. His face showed he was trying to think of the right words to say. "Recognize if the damage was caused by a large unknown animal."

"You want me to see if the ship was attacked by a sea serpent?" Max asked, convinced he had not heard Okada right.

"That is correct," Okada said, not believing he had just given that command.

"What about our work here?" Max asked, thinking of the dolphin program.

"The investigation will only last one day. After it is completed, you will return to your normal duties," Okada replied.

"And if a sea monster did cause the ship to sink?" Liz inquired. Okada gave her a look that told her he was not counting on that happening.

"When do we leave?" Max asked, convinced his presence on the mission was going to be a waste of time.

"Gather any supplies you will need and get some rest," Okada ordered. "We depart at first light."

CHAPTER 4

2:09 AM 4/9/2021 HST

Kelsey Young lay next to her husband in one of the underwater rooms at the Nautilus hotel. The Nautilus was a luxurious hotel located near Kaanapali beach. The ceiling and walls of the room were made of tempered glass. Marble floors sat beneath the king size water bed. Kelsey started to quickly drift into dream land. The night of drinking and dancing made it easy, despite Lyle's snoring. Kelsey shifted to her side of the bed and wrapped the pillow around her head, trying to filter out the sound. She took pressure off the pillow when she heard an unpleasant scraping sound coming from above her. It sounded like something was clawing the glass ceiling above her. She slowly turned her weight to lay on her back, terrified of what she might see above her. From inside the room, the underwater world was beautiful during the day, but at night the world was transformed to a world of sheer darkness. The hotel had dim LED lights around the rooms, but those only illuminated a few feet at most. Kelsey shook Lyle as the scraping continued. He grunted and turned around.

"Lyle," she said softly. A feeling of relief came over her when the noise abruptly stopped. Still freaked out by the experience, she shook him again, this time waking him.

"What time is it?" he asked in a slightly drunken voice.

"I don't know," she answered. "I heard something above us."

"I didn't hear anything. What did it sound like?" he replied, turning towards her.

"Like clawing or something scraping against the glass," Kelsey replied, beginning to think she had imagined the entire thing.

"Are you sure you weren't dreaming?" he asked, trying to get this over with quickly so he could go back to sleep.

"Yes." She paused for a moment. "Well, maybe . . . I don't know." He smiled and kissed her.

"Go back to sleep, dear." Kelsey lay back down. Everything was quiet for several minutes. Kelsey quickly sat up, when she heard a large banging noise above them. She turned to see Lyle sitting up as well.

"What the devil was that?" Lyle screamed. The sound was followed by several *clings* on the floor. Kelsey hugged her pillow tightly when a continuous dripping noise started. Lyle turned on the bedside rotating wall lamp and shined it across the room. A look of horror formed on Kelsey's face. Water was dripped from the darkness above. Lyle turned the light upward, which revealed a massive crack in the glass ceiling.

"How did that happen?" Kelsey screamed.

"Just run!" he replied. Both of them ran for the door across the room. The ceiling was struck again. This time a portion of the glass ruptured. Kelsey clutched Lyle's shoulder area with both hands as he fell, to avoid the shards of glass raining down in front of him. The room started to rapidly fill with water. The bedside lamp shorted out, leaving them in complete darkness. As she whimpered, Kelsey could hear Lyle cursing. He had cut his foot on the broken glass. She could feel the water levels rising. It was now at her ankles.

"Lyle," she sobbed. Above her, she could hear the sound of bending steel and more glass breaking. The breaking glass sounded like raindrops as they hit the water.

"It's okay," Lyle said, breathing heavily. She felt his hand gently move to her face. "We have to wait for the water to rise to the ceiling and swim to the surface."

"Why can't we use the stairs like we did to get down here?" she asked in a near hysteric voice.

"There's no way we could open it with that much water pressure pushing against it. Our only chance is to wait and swim to the surface."

"Can you please just try to open the door?" Kelsey begged.

"We're only sixty feet underwater. We can easily make it to the surface," Lyle said in a reassuring voice. Kelsey tightly gripped his hand. Hearing the confidence in his voice helped calm the panic that was overwhelming her. The seconds felt like hours as the water level brought them closer to the surface. The pitch blackness faded as their eyes adjusted to the darkness. The outline of the roof started to become clear. Finally, the water levels rose high enough that they could reach the ceiling. Lyle saw the left side of the roof was the portion that had been damaged.

Kelsey watched him gingerly grip one of the supporting steel beams. When he felt no glass, he tightened his grip and looked down at her.

"Kelsey." She looked right at him. "I'm going through the hole, then I'll pull you through."

"I'm scared," she replied.

"So am I. I love you. Now take a deep breath and hold on." Kelsey gave a frightened smile, took a deep breath, and closed her eyes.

Just imagine you're having fun in the pool, she said to herself. She extended her arms, expecting Lyle to grab her hand. She moved them around, trying to find it. A feeling of warmth came to her when she grabbed her husband's hand. She tightened her grip and pulled on it. The arm effortlessly came towards her. She opened her eyes. Air bubbles shot out of her mouth at the sight of Lyle's severed arm. The sight of the severed limb with the twitching fingers sent her into a full-blown panic attack. She released the limb and started swimming hastily. She felt her head slam into something hard. She threw her hands out and realized it was the hotel room wall. She swam in the direction she thought was up. She felt another barrier in front of her.

I have to get out of here. Need air, she said in response to the pain in her lungs. She started swimming, searching for the escape hole. Her arm brushed a soft object. She soon identified it as her bed. She looked around for the roof, not knowing up from down. She was completely disoriented. Her lungs were now burning for air. She took a deep long breath to satisfy them. Her senses started to fade. She hardly felt the teeth working their way into her stomach. She closed her eyes for a final time and was gone.

CHAPTER 5

5:30 AM 4/9/2021 HST

The Hawaiian sun began to rise over Niihau. Okada, Max, and Liz had just finished a quick breakfast and were getting ready to head out. Okada walked out to the Jeep to look over the gear that had been loaded the previous night. In his experience, the most unnecessary mission failures were caused by missing or faulty equipment. He was strict about double- or even triple-checking mission equipment. Max and Liz changed into their wetsuits. One less thing to do when they got to the mission site. After a final search for forgotten equipment, Max headed out the door. Liz grabbed two cups of coffee and joined him.

Okada was sitting in the driver seat with the engine running. Max climbed into the back seat. Liz got into the passenger seat and handed a coffee cup to Okada. He thanked her and put his foot on the gas pedal.

"What do you think attacked the ship?" Liz asked, turning around to look at Max.

"I honestly don't know," he replied. "I highly doubt it was a whale or a shark. So right now, my prime suspect is Nessie," he said in a joking voice.

"Cute," Liz replied. Okada stopped the Jeep next to the X-7. The previous night it had been fueled up and towed from the hangar.

"My turn to fly," Liz said. She climbed into the cockpit and got the X-7 ready for takeoff. Okada and Max loaded the gear and entered the helicopter. The X-7's trio of blades began to spin, and soon they were airborne.

The X-7 was a silver hybrid helicopter. In addition to the normal overhead blade, the X-7 had two forward-facing propellers that were attached to short-span fixed aircraft wings. This allowed the X-7 to reach top speeds of two hundred and ninety-three miles an hour. At that speed it could reach the farthest Hawaiian island in only a few hours. Visitors from Japan arrived by commercial airlines and needed to be transported to Niihau. By using the argument of less travel time, this meant more work could be accomplished. Liz convinced the military leaders in charge of the operation to purchase the fastest helicopter available: the X-7. Off duty, the X-7 had become Max and Liz's personal island hopper. Bulk supplies were transported to the island monthly; however, Max and Liz preferred to gather smaller supplies themselves. Living on an isolated island made them enjoy trips to the other islands. Even if it was for simple things like groceries or housing supplies.

Half an hour later, the X-7 landed on a U.S. Coast Guard offshore patrol cutter that was stationed above the wreckage of the Lucky Dragon. The ship's commander and a few crew members approached to greet them.

"Commander Takahashi, I'm Vice Admiral Thomson. Welcome aboard the Sea Eagle."

"Thank you, Vice Admiral," Okada replied. He briefly motioned to Max and Liz. "My team, Lieutenant Liz Tayler and Max Varian, a civilian biologist." The two momentarily stopped unloading their deep sea diving gear to shake the Vice Admiral's hand. "Thank you for your Government's assistance and cooperation during this tragic disaster," Okada continued.

"Of course. We're all allies here," Vice Admiral Thomson replied. "I have received orders from Governor Fatu to let you and your team run the show from here on out."

"I hope that will not be a problem for you or your crew," Okada said, not wanting the Vice Admiral to feel like they were taking over the ship.

"No problem at all. I'm honestly grateful. You're taking a load off my plate. Monitoring and coordinating the crew recovery efforts gives me enough to worry about."

"Have you located any survivors or bodies?" Okada asked.

"No," Vice Admiral Thomson replied in a puzzled voice. "We have been searching the surrounding waters for over a day and not a trace. We're about to expand the search grid a few hundred miles. If that brings up nothing. . ." Thomson paused for a moment. "Well, I'm afraid we will have to call off the search."

"I understand," Okada replied, fully understanding the difficult decision the Vice Admiral needed to make.

"Have you had any unusual sonar readings?" Max asked.

"None that I'm aware of," Vice Admiral Thomson answered.

"What depths is the wreckage at?" Okada asked.

"Our sonar shows the ship is resting just under one hundred seventy-five feet. Are all three of you going down?" Thomson inquired.

"I'm staying on board to monitor the situation from the control room," Okada replied.

"The ship's sonar has a longer range then the small sonar devices we use. During deep sea operations, we have two divers and one sonar operator," Liz added as she and Max put on their rebreathers.

"Okay; before you go down. Equipment check list," Okada said. Max and Liz both stated their equipment.

"Rebreathers check, diving transceiver check, underwater camera and tools check, spear guns and extra spears check, diving knifes check, Pontus system check." The Pontus system was a small sonar and tactical GPS device. Liz normally used the Pontus, while Max took care of the photography.

"Very good," Okada said as Max and Liz put on their diving masks.

"Before you ask. The diving transceivers work," Liz said smartly.

"I'm glad they do," Okada answered, seemingly not enjoying the joke. "I'm heading up to the ship's control room. Keep in radio contact." The transceivers they used had two channels. One for the divers to talk to each other, and one for communicating with a ship.

"Let us know if the sonar picks up anything . . . strange," Max reminded, not wanting to use the words "sea monster."

"Way before it reaches us," Liz added. Okada motioned that he understood. Max and Liz fell backwards into the water and disappeared beneath the surface.

"What do you hope to find down there?" Thomson asked. He wondered what Max meant by strange sonar readings.

"Answers," Okada replied.

***

Max pointed at the wreck.

"There," he said, pointing towards the ship resting on its side. "Well, to state the obvious, the entire right portion of the bridge is caved in," Max said.

"That doesn't make any sense. The ship must have hit a rock while sinking," Liz said. Max took photos of the damage.

"Okada." Max said.

"I'm here," Okada replied.

"Does the ship's sonar show any large rocks or terrain changes around the wreckage?"

"No," Okada confirmed. That was the answer he did not want to hear. The closer they got, the more it looked like the damage was caused by something massive ramming into the ship.

"Here's the plan. I'll stand guard. You explore the wreckage," Liz suggested.

"Okay with me. You wouldn't know what to look for anyway," Max teased.

"And you couldn't hit a two-hundred-foot sea monster right in front of you," Liz added. The comment sent a feeling of uneasiness through both of them.

Neither of them thought they would run into something like that, but the dark waters around them caused the thought to linger in the back of their minds. Whatever had sunk the ship could still be lurking, somewhere in the darkness. When they arrived at the wreckage, Liz stood up and rested her back on what was left of the bridge cabin. Her eyes moved between the sonar and her surroundings. With Liz standing guard, Max went inside the ship to search for answers. Even with a powerful flashlight, at this depth, the examination process was difficult. He was only able to see small portions of the ship at a time.

Ten or so minutes had passed when Liz asked, "Max. How's the search coming?"

"Slow. I'm heading to the engine room now. I found another damage site," he said a few seconds later. Max studied the large hole in the side of the ship. What he found unnerving was the wood on the right and left sides of the hole were covered in scrapes.

"Max, is the new damage site what caused the ship to sink?" Okada asked.

"It's definitely large enough. These marks are just odd. It looks like something was trying to claw its way through the hole," he replied. After saying that, his radio went silent.

"Max, you okay?" Liz asked, concerned.

"Yeah," he answered. This sent a feeling of relief through her body. "I cannot believe I'm saying this, but there are claw marks on the inside of the ship," Max continued. He wished he could see the damaged portion of the ship from the outside. Unfortunately, it was blocked by the ocean bottom.

"Claw marks?" Liz said, wondering if she heard right. Her finger moved to the trigger of the spear gun.

"That's what it looks like. I'm going to finish up here and head out," he replied, wanting to leave the area as much as Liz did. The room was starting to become claustrophobic. The machinery inside the room was starting to become the sea monsters of the deep. The levers and switches began to resemble teeth and claws. Max shook off the feeling and focused on the task at hand. He measured the side of the hole and photographed the damage. The hole was three feet around, and the claw marks were half an inch deep.

Liz moved inside the damaged bridge. She saw the light from Max's flashlight. She waved her light to show him her new location.

"Get too scary out in the open?" Max joked.

"Of course not," Liz scoffed. "I was getting the ship's VDR. It's possible we can still learn something from it." Liz pulled the voyage data recorder out of the ship's control panel. "Ready to head back up?" she asked.

"In a minute. I want to check the cabin for claw marks." Having two lights in the small space made the search much easier. In a few seconds, Max spotted what he was looking for. "There," he said.

"What?" Liz inquired, not seeing anything of interest. Max pointed to the cabin floor. Four small holes were carved into the bottom.

"That's where our friend placed one of his limbs. Remember what the helmsman said right before the radio cut off?" Max asked.

"Monster," Liz replied. Her head looked down at the sonar. She jumped when the flash from Max's camera went off.

"Now, if I'm right, another set of holes should be over here," Max said to himself. Liz watched him. She was about to ask how she could help when she noticed the number of bubbles coming out of his rebreather suddenly increase. "Liz, give me your knife!" he shouted in a voice filled with nervousness and excitement.

"What did you find?" Liz asked as she handed him the knife. Her eyes grew wide when she saw what he was looking at. On the end of another set of four small holes was a large claw. The tip of it was sunk at least an inch into the floor. Max carefully dug the knife into the floor and forced the claw out. The claw was white with a large curve on the front of it. On the end of the claw, small pieces of flesh danced in the ocean water. Max was mesmerized by what he was looking at.

"Please tell me you know what animal has a claw like that," Liz said.

"Are you kidding? I have no idea," Max replied in a stunned voice. The tension was broken when Okada's voice came over the radio.

"Max, Liz, we had another possible attack. Return to the surface at once."

"What do you mean? What happened?" Liz asked.

"We just received a report that an underwater hotel room in Kaanapali was found flooded early this morning."

"Why are we just hearing about this now?" Liz continued.

"The hotel thought the accident was caused by structural failure. They sent divers down to retrieve the bodies of the two guests staying there. The divers reported they found no bodies, and what's left of the glass dome had strange markings all over it."

"What type of markings?" Max asked.

"The divers reported they appeared to be claw marks," Okada answered.

"Tell them not to touch anything until we have a chance to look over the damage," Max said.

"As we speak, Vice Admiral Thomson is ordering the area to be sealed off. The Coast Guard and rescue units in the area have been ordered to stand down until we arrive."

Max pulled out a plastic bag and placed the claw inside.

"Liz, let's head back. I want to examine that hotel as soon as possible," Max said. His heart was racing. A day ago, the idea of a real-life sea monster was nonsense. Now, it seemed like the possibility was growing.

"You don't have to tell me twice," Liz replied.

Okada stood on the deck of the Sea Eagle and waited. He knew Max and Liz needed to make decompression stops on the way up. This annoyed him because, although necessary, it also wasted time. An hour had passed when Max and Liz finally broke the surface. Liz held up a large pink snapper she had shot on one of her decompression stops.

"Dinner," she said to Okada.

"Looking forward to it," he replied as he helped Liz on to the ship. Once Liz was on board, he offered his hand to Max. "I assume you brought the claw with you?" Max opened one of his diving suit pockets and pulled the bag out. Okada stared intently at the claw for a moment.

"Place that in the cold storage container, and both of you be ready to fly in ten minutes," Okada ordered.

"No point changing. We're going to be back in the water soon," Liz said. She pulled off her rebreather and placed it in an unused seat of the X-7.

"Agreed," Max said. He opened the cold storage container that sat in one of the helicopter's side compartments. Smoke from the dry ice rose over the container. He was about to drop the claw in when Liz's fish flopped into the container. "Really! You could contaminate the sample," Max shouted. He carefully placed the claw in a corner the fish was not touching.

"The claw's still in the bag," Liz reminded, climbing into the X-7.

"Only you would use a high-tech cold storage unit as a fish freezer," Max said, joining her in the back seat. Okada walked over to Vice Admiral Thomson, who was approaching the X-7.

"Vice Admiral. Thank you for your cooperation and aid."

"No trouble at all, young man. I hope your team found something useful on the dive," he replied.

"They did. Please keep us informed of any new developments."

"Don't worry; you can count on the U.S. Coast Guard to do everything we can to locate your missing sailors."

"Myself and the Japanese government thank you again," Okada replied. Both men shook hands, and then Okada got aboard the X-7. Vice Admiral Thomson and several crew members gave final waves as the X-7 lifted off and headed east.

CHAPTER 6

Mya Kendig rinsed the toothpaste from her mouth, still not believing Jade had woken her up at five-thirty in the morning.

"Hurry up, sleepy head. I want to be on the boat by six," Jade said in an excited voice as she lightly pounded on the door.

"I don't even get up this early on work days," Mya replied in a tired voice. When she opened the bathroom door, a fully awake Jade spoke.

"I get up at five every day and go for a relaxing swim." Mya gave her a look that said she would never dream of getting up that early. The one thing she hated about Jade was that she was a morning person. "Why are you so tired, anyway?"

"I couldn't sleep so I stayed up watching TV until eleven," Jade laughed.

"Watching what?"

"Some paranormal program about Native American legends," Mya replied as they got in the car.

"Learn about anything we need to look out for?" Jade asked in a creepy voice.

"Only the Ogopogo, and some half cat, half dragon that lives in Great Lakes called the water panther."

"What? You're making that up," Jade said, giggling. Loving the stories her sister came up with.

"No, apparently some people believe in it," Mya said, laughing a little herself.

"Let me guess: it swims around the lakes eating people?"

"No, it guards copper and battles thunder birds, and then it eats people. Jeez, get your facts right," Mya said with a serious face. They were stopped at a red light so Jade gave her an annoyed glare. After a few seconds, both sisters burst out in laughter. Jade put an arm around her younger sister's shoulder.

"I'm so glad I get to spend a week with you." Mya gave her a tired smile that said the feeling was mutual. Around fifteen minutes later, Mya groggily followed her sister on to the boat dock. She looked at a fully awake Jade, still wondering how she could be so active at six in the morning. The pleasant salty smell of the sea and the sound of the sea gulls flying overhead lessened the major annoyance she felt having to be this active, this early.

"Come on, sleepy head. We want to get an early start to the day," Jade said happily, whistling a tune Mya did not recognize.

Jade pointed to the first of four boats tied to the dock. "Here's our boat." The sight of the thirty-six-foot power boat sent away any feelings of grogginess Mya was feeling. The boat was ocean blue with several species of fish painted on the lower sides. The bright yellow words "The Maui Diving Experience" stretched across the front and top middle section of the boat.

"Do you own that boat?" Mya asked, stunned by what she was seeing.

"No, it belongs to the company I work for. However, since I'm the lead diver, during nonbusiness hours I get to use it whenever I want," Jade said, raising both her eyebrows.

"Lucky you," Mya said in a slightly jealous voice. Mya grabbed her gear and got aboard. "What kind of boat is this?" she asked as she looked at the controls under the large blue bimini top.

"A 2020 Nevada 36," Jade replied. She handed her diving gear to Mya and unhooked the ropes that held the boat to the dock.

"Where's the kitchen and sleeping area?" Mya joked.

"It's not that fancy, but it does have this little feature." Jade walked over to the side of the control panel and opened a small hatch in the floor. "Here," Jade said, handing Mya a champagne glass.

"You're not," Mya said with a smile.

"Yes, I am," Jade replied as she opened a bottle of champagne. Some sea gulls flew off the pier, startled by the cork's loud popping sound.

"Take my glass, quick!" Jade said, laughing. Suds started to spill over the boat. Mya grabbed Jade's glass and put both under the opened bottle. Jade filled both glasses and set the bottle down.

"Now a toast. To Mya's first boat ride and dive. A day we will never forget."

"To a day we will never forget," Mya replied. The sisters clanged the glasses together and drank. After the glasses were empty, Jade put them and the champagne bottle away.

"We can finish the rest of the bottle at dinner tonight," Jade said. "Now one more thing before we go." Jade pulled out her HD diving camera. She flipped the screen and put her arm around Mya and smiled. Mya stuck out her tongue and made the peace sign.

"Got it! The first of many pictures this week," Jade said. She turned to Mya. "You ready to get this adventure started?"

"Yes!" Mya replied, eager to get started. Jade started the engine and pulled away from the dock. "Oh, Mya, I heard something strange on the news this morning."

"What?" Mya asked. Jade gunned the engine forward. Mya grabbed onto the bimini top support beam, slightly losing her balance.

"There's this hotel called the Nautilus. It has underwater hotel rooms."

"Okay," Mya said, wondering where Jade was going with this.

"One of the underwater rooms flooded last night."

"What? How did that happen?"

"They don't know yet," Jade replied.

"It would be cool to see it," Mya said, hoping Jade would get the message.

"You want to?" Jade asked.

"Can we really?" Mya replied with an excited smile.

"Sure. It will only take us an hour to get to Kaanapali."

"Do you think the owners will let us dive down there?" Mya asked.

"No, best case scenario is we can see the wreckage from the boat. Worst case is the area is blocked off and we need to turn around," Jade replied. "We can stop there after breakfast."

"Sounds good." Mya said, enjoying the salty air striking her face.

"That's the Nautilus up ahead," Jade said a few hours later.

"That place looks fancy. We should have eaten here," Mya replied, staring at the five-story hotel and thinking about the average-at-best French toast she had eaten at a local beach side breakfast café. Mya's thought went off the hotel when she noticed two small patrol boats stationed in front of them. "Jade, are you sure it's okay that we're here?" she asked. One of the men started waving his arms, motioning for them to stop. Jade started to reduce speed and brought the boat to a stop a few yards from the patrol craft.

"Good morning," Jade said, moving her sunglasses to her forehead.

"Ma'am, I'm sorry. These waters are currently restricted and unsafe. You're going to need to turn this vessel around," the man replied in an authoritative tone. The sight of the shotgun he was holding made Mya uneasy.

"Come on, Jade. Let's go," Mya said, not wanting any trouble. Jade ignored her. Mya knew that meant she was curious to see what had happened herself.

"My name's Jade Kendig. I'm the lead diver with the Maui Diving Experience. In the past, I have helped the Coast Guard with diving rescue operations. I'd like to offer to help with the Nautilus disaster."

"Thank you for the offer. However, we have orders not to let any divers in these waters until further notice. Even Coast Guard divers have been ordered to stand down," the man replied.

"What! Who on earth ordered Coast Guard divers to stand down?" Jade asked, stunned.

"Look, like I said before, these waters are restricted," the man said, getting visibly frustrated with her. "Please leave the area now; otherwise, I'm going to have to place both of you under arrest." Mya swallowed.

"Jade, please, let's go! I don't need to see the damaged hotel room." Jade was upset about the situation but got the message.

"Okay, okay," Jade said, putting her hands up. "I just wanted to offer my help. Sorry to trouble you." The man was too busy listening to a message over his radio to notice what she said. Jade turned the boat and headed away from the restricted zone. Mya looked up, noticing the soft roar of a helicopter engine in the distance.

"I cannot believe what he just told us," Jade said, angered. She had the boat moving at a crawl while staring back at the disaster site.

"What has you so worked up?" Mya asked.

"The Coast Guard should have multiple dive teams down there searching for bodies and trying to figure out what caused the structural failure." Jade paused and took a deep breath. "I don't understand why anyone would ever order dive teams to stand down."

"Maybe he was lying so we would leave," Mya suggested.

"Well, nothing we can do about it either way," Jade said. She turned her head around just in time to see a low-flying helicopter flyover. "Jeez!" she screamed in alarm.

Mya ducked down. The helicopter was a good twenty feet above them, but it felt like they could have touched the wheels. The winds the chopper blades created briefly stirred up the sea around them.

"Mya, are you okay?" Jade asked.

"Yes," Mya replied, a little shaken. "Are helicopters allowed to fly that low?"

"No! It's probably the billionaire hotel owner who thinks he can do whatever he wants." Mya watched as the chopper's back door opened and two divers dove into the water.

"Oh, no divers are allowed in the water!" Jade yelled in annoyance.

"They left the back door open," Mya said, trying to lighten the mood. They watched as the X-7 landed on the nearby shore. "What kind of helicopter is that?" Mya asked, looking at the propellers on the side wings.

"I have no idea, but I've seen that helicopter flying around before," Jade replied in a very annoyed voice. Having seen enough, she gunned the engine. "I know one thing. I'm looking into this issue the minute we get back."

"Why is this bothering you so much?" Mya asked. Normally, she was the one who got annoyed easily, and Jade was the calm one.

"Because, Mya, what if people are waiting to be rescued down there and die because of that stupid no divers order, or what if that low-flying helicopter caused you to fall off the boat when it scared you?" Jade pulled her sunglasses back over her eyes. "That's what I have issues with."

"How long until we get to the dive site?" Mya asked, trying to get Jade's mind off the issue.

"About an hour," she replied. She turned to Mya and smiled. "Don't worry. I'll be over it by then."

CHAPTER 7

"We're nearly over the Nautilus site," Okada said, bringing the X-7 to a hover.

"Go." Liz opened the X-7's side door. Max tossed the rebreathers and diving fins out. Max brought his arms to his chest in an X shape and jumped. Seconds later, Liz did the same. Max and Liz put on their equipment and advanced towards the destroyed room. The sunlight lit up the clean water, making the visibility excellent. A large portion of the dome facing them was destroyed. The remaining glass around the destroyed area was covered in white streaks.

"Do those markings look familiar?" Liz asked.

"Yes, they're just like the marks I saw inside the Lucky Dragon," Max agreed. He moved to the remaining glass to closely examine the marks. "Okay, this is definitely the same creature that attacked the Lucky Dragon."

"What makes you say that?" Liz inquired. She was not doubting what he was saying. She was more curious to learn what he was seeing that she wasn't. Max swam next to her.

"Liz, look at that set of claw markings. What do you see?"

"Four straight claw marks that go out from the hole about seven feet."

"Okay, now look at those markings to the left," Max said.

"That set only has three streaks." Liz's eyes lit up and a feeling of excitement came over her. She had figured it out.

"The claw we found on the Lucky Dragon!"

"Bingo," Max replied. He handed her the dive camera. "Get some wide shots of the dome. I want to examine the hole." Max swam inside the room and looked at the hole from the inside. The steel bars that held the glass in place had been broken, and the remaining sections were bent inward, revealing that something had forced its way into the room from the outside.

Liz finished with the pictures and joined him. Max pulled a measuring tape from his dive pocket. "Liz, go to the other end of the hole." Max said, handing her the end of the measuring tape. "We'll measure side to side and then top to bottom." The size of the hole was thirty-three feet wide, fifty-seven feet high.

"Okay, professor, how big is this thing?" Liz asked.

"All I know for certain is the animal caused the damage. The question is was the hole created by the creature's head or the entire creature?"

"I hope it's the latter," Liz stated, not wanting to imagine a creature with a head that large.

"Look around the room for small markings like the ones we found in the Lucky Dragon," Max said. The two of them started a thorough search of the room.

"How much do you think it costs to stay in one of these rooms?" Liz pondered as she scanned the floor.

"I would imagine a lot," Max replied. "What I want to know is why the hotel staff did not notice anything until this morning." A slight movement from above caught Liz's eye. She looked up and spotted something odd drifting through the water above her. She swam a few feet up from the floor.

"Max, I found one of our missing tourists." Max looked up to see Liz waving a severed arm at him.

"Great, bag it up," Max said, laughing inside at her dark sense of humor. Max continued to scan the floor until he saw what he was expecting to see.

"Liz, I found more claw marks," Max said and pointed to the four claw markings in the marble floor. They were barely visible, but there was no doubt what they were.

"Great, tag em," Liz said as she scanned the area for more body parts. Max placed a red block down to tag the location. "And if I'm guessing correctly, I should find another set here," Max said to himself. He moved several inches to his left and found a set of three claw marks in the floor. Max put another block down and continued to think out loud. "At least half its body was in the room. Now I wonder." He tried to imagine the creature standing in front of him; he swam to the location he thought the back legs would be. A moment later he yelled. "Liz, the entire animal was in the room! I just found claw marks from its back legs." Liz swam down to look at the new claw imprints Max was tagging. She put her fist out for a bump. Max smacked it. "Now we can get a rough estimate of how big this thing is." Max and Liz measured the length between the front and back claw marks.

"How many feet?" Max asked.

Liz looked right at him then said in a serious, slightly frightened voice, "This thing is at least twenty-eight feet."

***

Okada sat at the hotel's conference room table across from Jeremy, the hotel's chief security guard, and Carlos, the senior hotel manager. Okada's face had an emotionless expression. Jeremy was visibly annoyed by the continuous questioning. Carlos was showing clear signs of nervousness. Questions from the Coast Guard and hotel ownership were expected, but why was he getting questioned by this stone-faced Japanese military officer?

"If I'm reading this correctly. The blueprints for the underwater room states there are four different sensors placed around each dome," Okada said, staring at a computer screen and pointing to the area he was talking about. "The sensors will alert the hotels front offices if any cracks or leaks occur." Okada paused. "Is that correct?"

"Yes, sir. The sensors are supposed to alert us if even a small crack occurs in the glass," Carlos replied anxiously.

"When did the sensors alert you to the problem?" Okada asked, leaning forward. Sweat started to seep through Carlos's white suit.

"Well, sir... they didn't. We were not even aware any damage had occurred until this morning when guests in the adjacent rooms reported it."

"So, all four of the sensors failed?" Okada said, returning to an upright position. Carlos tried to form words as he thought of an answer.

"I don't know how it happened, but yes; however, all the sensors in the other rooms are working."

"How can you be sure?" Okada asked. Carlos motioned to Jeremy. Who pulled up a screen on an iPad.

"You see here? All sensors in the four remaining rooms are working. The screen showed that sixteen of the twenty sensors were working."

"How often is this system checked?" Okada asked.

"Once every twenty-four hours. It was last checked at eight-thirteen last night," Jeremy replied.

"What about underwater security cameras?" Jeremy said, slightly looking towards Carlos.

"I advised we set up an underwater camera network. However, with the sensors in place, management thought it was not worth the cost."

"That's not true!" Carlos snapped. "The reason we decided not to place cameras around the rooms is we felt that it would make the guest feel uncomfortable. With the glass domes and all."

"Why were one-way windows not installed when creating the domes?" Okada questioned.

"Our research and management teams felt the mirrors' reflections would have a negative effect on wildlife, which could result in bad business." Okada's cell phone rang. He motioned for them to wait and answered it.

"Hello," He said. He started tapping his index finger against the table as he listened to the person on the other line. "Good work... I'm in the conference room.... Bring it inside." Okada put the phone down. He looked right at Jeremy.

"I thought the room had been searched by rescue divers?"

"It was searched by our underwater technicians."

"Did your divers find something?" Carlos asked. Okada slightly moved his head up and down. Jeremy cleared his throat and spoke.

"Sir, if I may ask a question?" Okada showed no sign of objection, so he continued. "Why is the Japanese government interested in a damaged American hotel room?" Before Okada could answer, Liz walked in and slammed the severed arm on the table. Carlos fell out of his seat, screaming in horror.

"Yeah, lawsuits," Liz said. Jeremy had a look of disgust on his face. Knowing it was coming, Okada was unfazed.

"Is that all you found?"

"Of human remains, yes. Max found more evidence of our friend down there." Okada stood up and looked down at the horrified Carlos.

"I suggest you close down all your underwater rooms until further notice," Okada said and walked out.

"Happy to lend a hand," Liz added and closed the conference room door.

"Liz, I need to make a call. I'll meet you and Max at the helicopter." After Liz left, Okada pulled out his phone and called Saburo.

"Yes, Okada?" he answered.

"Saburo, we completed the investigation of the Lucky Dragon wreckage."

"Did you determine a cause?" he replied inquisitively.

"Max strongly believes the wreckage was caused by an unknown marine organism. His theory was reinforced by a large unidentified claw found at the wreckage." There was a slight moment of silence. Saburo could not believe that

Commander Okada Takahashi had just all but confirmed he was hunting a sea monster.

The only words Saburo managed to form were, "Sir, what is your next move?"

"I am creating a task force to gather more information on this creature and, when the time comes, destroy it. Max, Liz, and I are returning to Tokyo. I must personally speak to the Japanese Self-Defense Force high command."

"I will make the travel arrangements," Saburo confirmed.

"As you do, get two tickets for yourself and Akio. The two of you will fly to America to personally recruit the two new members of the task force."

"Sir? Two new members?" Saburo asked, surprised.

"I am adding two new members to assist our current team," Okada replied.

"Understood. I assume you already have candidates in mind?" Okada sent Saburo an email that contained information on the two candidates. "Ashly Cross, an expert in field equipment, computers, and robotics. Samuel Richards is a leading expert in the field of cryptozoology," Saburo read out loud. "Sir, if you don't mind me asking, is there a reason we are taking them to Tokyo and not Niihau?"

"If they decide not to accept becoming members of the team, base security will not be compromised."

"Understood, sir. I will be on the next flight to the American mainland."

CHAPTER 8

9:28 AM 4/9/2021 HST

Mya clumsily tried to fit into her wetsuit. The closer they got to the dive site, the greater the nervous knot in her stomach became. The idea of going diving sounded great when she arrived. Now that she was actually about to do it, she started to feel uneasy.

"What's wrong?" Jade asked. Noticing the expression on her sister's face.

"I'm just nervous," Mya replied as she pulled to get her leg through the wetsuit. She hated how tight it fit to her body.

"About what?" Mya did not answer right away. She knew Jade would laugh at what was making her nervous.

"I'm worried my equipment will fail and I'll run out of air miles below the surface." She waited for Jade to laugh. To her surprise, she didn't.

"I hear that at least once a week. Don't worry; since you're a newbie, we're sticking to the shallows for the first dive," Jade replied, then said in a joking voice, "That way when you do mess up, you won't drown."

"Well, I'm sorry if I'm a professional cosplayer, not a professional diver," Mya shot back. She grunted in frustration as she pulled the wetsuit up her body. Jade stopped the boat and went over to help her sister.

"Here: this will make it easier," Jade said, holding up the arm portions of the suit. Mya pushed her left arm through the neoprene, wondering how Jade had effortlessly put her wetsuit on. Mya breathed in relief when both her arms were through the suit.

"There, you did it," Jade said, zipping the wetsuit up.

"Thanks, but you didn't need to stop the boat to help me," Mya replied, feeling embarrassed.

"I stopped the boat because we're here, silly." You didn't notice the island?" Mya shook her head and started to turn to the front of the boat. "Hold on. I don't want you to see it from here," Jade said, then clamped her hands around Mya's eyes.

"Don't push me in the water," Mya said, expecting her sister to do just that.

"I'm not that mean," Jade replied as she guided Mya to the front of the boat. "Okay, now look." She lifted her hands off Mya's eyes. In front of her was a small crescent-shaped island. Patches of grass made it look like someone had painted green lines on the rocky shore. She looked over the edge of the boat. The crystal blue water was so clear that she could see the ocean floor. Several species of fish swam amongst the rainbows of coral. Mya's nervous feelings were replaced with awe and excitement. Molokini Crater was more stunning then she'd ever dreamed.

"This place is beautiful," Mya said in awe. "You get to go here every day?" Mya asked, with slight jealousy in her voice.

"No, just once, maybe twice a week," Jade replied, pleased to see Mya this thrilled.

"Okay, I'm jealous," Mya admitted.

"Well, it's not always fun," Jade said. Mya looked at her skeptically. "Most of the time I have to keep dumb tourists from killing themselves, but on occasion I do get some hot guys with dive skills." A frown formed on Mya's face. "Sorry, I... wasn't thinking," Jade said in a remorseful voice.

"It's okay. I just don't want to think about that cheat," Mya answered in a bitter voice. "Well, let's get this dive underway." She continued trying to remove the negative thoughts from her head. While Mya continued to admire the view, Jade grabbed the oxygen tanks and diving flippers.

"Here," Jade said, handing Mya an oxygen tank. Jade effortlessly put her tank on. Mya fumbled with hers until Jade intervened.

"Okay, I can get my diving fins on myself. I can do this," Mya said, reassuring herself. Jade dropped the boat ladder. She saw Mya struggling with the diving fins. She waited a few moments to see if Mya could do it herself.

"It's official. I suck at this," Mya said, frustrated, tossing the diving fin on the ground.

"No, it's completely normal for people to struggle their first time," Jade replied. She picked up the fin and held the back of it open. Mya slid her foot through. Once Mya had both fins on, Jade spoke again.

"Hold on. I have another surprise."

"Can't be better than the island," Mya replied.

"It's not, but it will make the dive more enjoyable," Jade said, handing Mya a diving mask. Mya gave her an enthusiastic look. "These are full-face diving masks," Jade continued, putting hers on. "These will give us greater visibility than a normal mask, plus we can talk to each other underwater."

"Awesome," Mya said as she placed the mask over her face.

"Testing, testing," Jade said into the mask's mic. Jade pointed to the button Mya needed to press to speak.

"I read you loud and clear, commander," Mya replied in a serious voice. Both sisters giggled. Mya stood up.

"Mya, don't walk around in the diving fins. You'll fall," Jade said while putting her own fins on. She motioned for Mya to sit next to her on the side of the boat.

"Just one last thing before we jump in," Jade said. Mya turned to listen. "If you see a shark. Swim as fast as you can back to the boat." A look of concern formed on Mya's face. Before she could speak, Jade pushed her into the water. Mya screamed as she fell backwards. Jade let out a happy whoop and fell backwards into the water.

"I can't believe you did that," Mya said in a playful, surprised voice.

"You brought it up earlier," Jade replied as she swam laps around Mya. "Come on, we'll start at Reef's End and make our way to Enenue."

"Were you serious about the sharks?" Mya asked, needing to know this before she could enjoy herself.

"No, there are no dangerous species in this area. Farther out to sea, you may get chomped, though. Now, let's get underwater!" Jade said eagerly.

"You pulled the boat ladder down before you dove in, right?" Mya asked. Jade brought her hands to her mouth.

"Oh my god, I forgot!" Jade yelled. Mya felt a feeling of anxiety come over her. She quickly swam over to the side of the boat; the ladder was on. She smacked the water when she saw the ladder dangling in the water. Jade had got her again.

"You satisfied, Mya the worrier?"

"Forgive me for not wanting to be stranded out here," Mya replied and splashed some water at Jade.

Jade splashed some back and said, "Mya, people at the Maui Diving Experience know where we are, and around what time we are supposed to return. If we don't return, the Coast Guard will send a rescue ship." A look of annoyance briefly formed on Jade's face. "That is, if they can spare some of their boats currently guarding luxury hotels." Jade put both hands on Mya's shoulders. "Are you done worrying?" Jade's voice got pumped up. "Are you ready to have fun and explore the reefs?"

"Yes!" Mya said in a matching voice. Both sisters giggled and dove under water.

For the next two hours, Jade and Mya conducted several dives, exploring the different reefs in the area. Jade had seen each reef dozens of times, but seeing them with Mya was different. Seeing her sister marvel at the beautiful fish and coral made everything fresh and new. The highlight for Mya was when Jade found a small octopus and showed her how to handle it. Mya was following a school of yellow tang when Jade spoke.

"We're at 50 bar. We need to head up."

"Again?" Mya said in disappointment.

"Unfortunately, yes; we're going to take an early lunch break, and after that we have enough tanks for one last dive." The two headed to the surface. Mya swam to Molokini Crater. Jade swam back to the boat for the lunch box and joined her. She handed Mya a sandwich, apple, and a bottle of vanilla soda.

"My favorite," Mya said as she took the soda, setting it next to the other items. For several minutes, Jade and Mya ate and exchanged small talk. Mya looked out at the ocean and happily sighed at the sound of birds chirping, and the waves crashing against the shore.

"Jade, thanks for inviting me to spend time with you. I know I was hesitant to come, but this is really helping me keep my mind off things."

"Hey, any excuse to go diving," Jade replied sarcastically. Jade looked down, thinking of what to say next. "Look, Mya. What happened with Brandon wasn't your fault."

"I know," Mya replied. Her face turned cold. This was a subject she really did not want to talk about, but she knew she had to sooner or later. "I mean, it's bad enough I found out he was sleeping with another girl; then when I confront him about it, he just says, 'Too bad you caught us. I had big plans for you. Now, get out of my house. Having two girlfriends was fun, but I'm done with you.'" A look of anger and bitterness formed on Mya's face as a tear rolled down her cheek.

"I thought I finally found a guy who loved me....Turns out he was just using me!" Jade gently put her arm around Mya's shoulder.

"You planning on moving back in with Mom and Dad?"

"No. After my vacation here, I guess I'll get an apartment and start over," Mya answered as she tossed a small rock into the ocean.

"Look, Mya, it can get lonely on my days off, and you know I have a two bedroom condo. Why don't you live with me for a while?" A small look of happiness replaced Mya's bitter expression. It felt good to get those bottled up feelings off her chest.

"I'd love that," she said softly. "There's nothing left for me back in San Diego anyway." The two sisters shared a hug. "I'll just have to fly back, get my stuff. Cancel or transfer some of my cosplay photo shoots, and then you're stuck with your little sister."

"Leave Brandon in the trash where he belongs," Jade said, delighted Mya accepted her offer. "Well, enough talk. Time for our last dive of the day!"

"Where to?" Mya asked, tossing her trash into the lunch box.

"The edge of the world," Jade replied.

Around an hour later, Jade and Mya approached the edge of the world reef. Despite the deeper dive, Mya's feelings of apprehension were completely gone. From a distance she was even hoping to catch a glimpse of a shark.

"Mya, over here, I want to show you something," Jade said. She grabbed Mya's hand and led her to a small reef that sat on a plateau just above the depths of the edge of the world. On the plateau, the light from the surface shined brightly. Mya looked down. Her eyes widened with astonishment, the light revealing about fifty feet of the plateau wall, then turned to total darkness. "Welcome to the edge of the world," Jade said, presenting it in the voice of a showgirl. Mya snickered, then looked around her, not believing she was in this magical place.

"I've never seen anything like that!" Mya said in an awestruck voice. "How far down does that go?"

"Around two hundred feet," Jade replied.

"Are we going to explore it?" Mya asked excited.

"No, Explorer Mya," Jade teased. "It's too deep for a new diver, and we don't have the proper equipment for a technical dive." Jade looked at her diving gauge. It read seventy-two feet, forty-five minutes of air left. She checked Mya's air gauge, which had a similar reading. The two sisters took some time to explore the plateau. Mya found a flat area and lay down. She looked up at the water above her. It was the most beautiful sight she had ever seen. The light blue color that surrounded her was shared by fish of all shapes and colors. At the surface she could see a small yellow circle whose yellow beams gently pierced the water.

"Better than one of your fantasy worlds?" Jade asked, lying next to her.

"I feel like I'm in one," Mya replied. Jade noticed something out of the corner of her eye.

"Look, seals!" Jade said in excitement. The herd of seals swam directly over them. Several members of the herd started sniffing around the plateau reef.

"What kind are they?" Mya asked.

"Hawaiian Monk Seals. An endangered species," Jade answered. She turned to Mya. "We're lucky to see them." For the next few minutes, they watched the seals swim and even eat some fish. One curious seal came over to sniff the strange new creatures. Mya reached out to touch it. Her eyes were glowing as she gently stroked its skin. Suddenly, the seal cried in alarm and raced out of sight.

"I didn't mean to scare it," Mya said, feeling bad.

"I don't know if that was you," Jade said, trying not to sound worried. As they watched the seals flee the area, a muffled clap of thunder filled their ears. Now even the fish started to disappear from the surrounding waters. A strong feeling of fear came over both of them.

"What's that? Why am I hearing thunder, Jade?" Mya asked in a concerned voice. Her legs and arms felt heavy. She was having to work hard just to move them.

"It was probably a small rock slide," Jade replied. She tried to sound convincing, but she was unnerved as well. Despite her best efforts, she couldn't understand where this sudden feeling of terror was coming from. Before Mya could speak, a small amount of turbulence hit them. It was nothing strong, but enough to be noticeable. At the same moment, the visibility in the water started to cloud up. It was like something had stirred up the sediment around them.

"Jade, let's go back up," Mya begged. She could feel her heart racing. She may be new to this underwater world, but she could tell something was very wrong. Mya looked at Jade, who was standing still facing to her left.

"Jade?" Mya said. She felt herself starting to panic, wondering why her sister was not responding.

"Jade," Mya repeated, swimming over to her. Mya froze when she saw the look in her sister's eyes. A look she never thought she'd see. A look of pure fear. Suddenly, Jade started to scream, which made Mya jerk back in fright. Before Mya could comprehend what was going on, she was struck hard from behind. The force of the impact sent her falling forward into a large mound of coral. Jade's screams were cut short when a large set of jaws enclosed around her waist. Mya moaned in pain as she got to her hands and knees. Unsure of what had happened, she tried to get her bearings and locate Jade. Her heart sank when she saw a large cloud of red water a few yards from her. At the top of the cloud, a large tail thrashed side to side. Mya's eyes filled with tears when the front of Jade's body weakly crawled out of the red cloud.

***

Through blurred vision, Jade stared out at the familiar ocean, but nothing was registering.

Where am I? How did I get here? She thought. She could still move her hands. She tried to move her legs but nothing happened. Her body was in so much pain, she did not know where it was originating from. Jade reached down to her stomach area.

Was it supposed to feel squishy? she tried to remember. She kept hearing someone calling her name.

"Jade! Jade, please answer me!" Hearing her sister's voice made her regain her senses. She had to help Mya get out of here. Get away from that thing. Jade used the last of her strength to speak, but her efforts only managed a low whisper.

"Mya, if...if you...can hear me... get out of here...I lov...." Before she could finish, a front leg slammed onto her back and neck.

***

Mya's body became paralyzed with fear. Long claws extended from the foot and dug into her sister, pulling her back into the red cloud. Mya tried to move, but her body was still frozen in place. She could hear ripping and tearing sounds from inside the now dispersing cloud of her sister's blood. She was terrified of what she was going to see inside.

Mya closed her eyes and launched herself upward. Now that she was moving, she opened her eyes and frantically started swimming to the surface. Her mind filled with images of monstrous jaws right below her. Ready to drag her down into the abyss. Adrenaline filled her body and she swam faster than she thought was possible. She broke the surface right near Molokini Crater and desperately swam towards it. Seconds later, she pulled herself onto the rocky shore. She turned around, hyperventilating, praying nothing would break the surface. For a brief moment she thought she saw a large shadow moving under the water. She pulled off her diving tank and mask, then started walking up the Crater, trying to get as much distance between herself and the water as possible. With her adrenaline rush fading, the shock of what happened started to return, which was too much for her system. Mya felt her legs get weak; then she hit the ground and closed her eyes.

CHAPTER 9

10:24 AM 4/10/2021 EST

Ashly Cross sat at a workbench in her two bedroom apartment located on the outskirts of Greenville, North Carolina. Computer parts were laid neatly across the workbench. Shelves full of small bins adorned the wall in front of it. Two large tables flanked the right and left side of the workbench. The table on the left had three computers, each complete with its own monitor and keyboard. One monitor showed robotic diagrams, one showed a computer code, and the third showed the feed from six different security cameras. The table to the right had a state-of-the-art gaming computer for her entertainment. Ashly adjusted the magnifying glasses on her head visor as she carefully attached two wires inside one of her newest projects. Her concentration was broken by a knock on the door.

"Who could that be?" she wondered. Ashly was average height and had a healthy build. She had fair skin and long brown hair she always kept in a braid. She pushed back on the workbench and launched her blue and black office chair towards her control center. She looked at the security camera that covered the door. A Japanese man dressed in a business suit stood at the door. She watched as he knocked again. She noticed he was holding a brown briefcase. Ashly hit a button on the keyboard in front of her.

"Whatever you're selling, I'm not interested," she said. Unfazed by the voice system that normally alarmed unwanted guests, he spoke.

"I am not a salesman. I am a member of the Japanese Self-Defense Force," he replied, holding up a badge to the camera. "I have important information I need to discuss with you." Ashly changed the camera setting to detect metal items. She was looking for a gun or, more importantly, handcuffs. The detector found nothing that would alarm her.

"Okay, I'll be there in a few seconds," she replied. She quickly moved over to the second keyboard and punched in a few commands, then walked over and opened the door.

"What can I do for the Japanese Self-Defense Force?" she asked. *Just play it cool. You don't know if he knows anything*, she thought to herself.

"I am here to discuss a job opportunity with you. May I come in and give you the details?" That was not the response Ashly was expecting. She moved to the left of the doorway and motioned for him to come in.

"Take a seat on the living room couch," she said. She grabbed a chair from the kitchen table and sat a few feet in front of him. The Japanese man stood up and introduced himself.

"I'm Saburo Nakamura," he said, slightly bowing.

"Hi, I'm Ashly Cross," she replied, staying seated, "but you obviously knew that already. Now, mind if I ask what the Japanese Self-Defense Force wants with me?"

Saburo sat down and opened his briefcase, ready to get the meeting underway. "Mrs. Cross," he started to say.

"Just call me Ashly. I never liked formalities."

"Okay," he continued. "An unusual situation is occurring in the waters around the Hawaiian Islands. Commander Okada Takahashi has ordered the creation of a specialized team to handle the situation." He handed Ashly a ten-page packet divided into two sections. Ashly raised an eyebrow in interest as she skimmed over it. The first section was titled: Suijin Squad. It contained brief information on Commander Takahashi, herself, and three other people. The second section showed locations around Hawaii, and information on two accidents that had occurred there. She found it odd that no information about the causes of the accidents was present.

"Why is there no information about what caused these two accidents?" Ashly asked.

"That is why the team is being formed. To discover the cause of the accidents," Saburo answered.

"Okay, second question. Why me? Why not get a member of the Japanese Security Council or the Japanese army to handle this?"

"For a relatively unknown person in your field, we have found your expertise in robotics and computer usage to be some of the finest in the world. That is why you have been chosen to join the task force," Saburo complimented.

"I'm flattered, but no thanks. I already make a good living creating and modifying computer codes," Ashly said, handing the packet back to Saburo. "Now, if you don't mind, I'm a busy girl, and I have better things to do then worry about accidents in Hawaii." Ashly motioned towards the door. Saburo frowned and reached into the briefcase. He pulled out a sheet of paper. It was time to enact his second plan.

"In addition to making sixty thousand a year creating software, our records show that, strangely, every month, money is taken from the accounts of rich Kuwait business men and placed into yours." Ashly kept her poker face but was getting worried. "These amounts range from five to ten thousand dollars." Saburo handed that paper to Ashly and pulled out another one. "This paper proves that you continuously hack other player's accounts in online games. The people that were hacked reported stolen in-game items and currency."

"I don't think I should say anything more without a lawyer," she replied. She was trying to sound unaffected by the information, but inside it was killing her. How did they find this information? She had covered her tracks so well. She had already thought of two possible escape plans when Saburo took back both papers.

"Don't worry. I am not here to arrest you. I am here to recruit you. With your cooperation, we can make the information on these papers disappear." He smiled at her and ripped up both pages. Ashly sat back in the chair, relaxed.

"When do I start?" she asked.

CHAPTER 10

11:13 AM 4/10/2021 EST

PhD Zoologist Leo Hoffburger stood on stage in front of an audience of around three hundred people in a lecture hall at the University of Pittsburgh. After fifteen minutes of insults and arguing, he was red in the face and almost frothing at the mouth.

"How dare you speak of my theory that way!" he yelled. Samuel Richards sat on the end of the third row with a satisfied grin on his face. Samuel Richards was in his mid-thirties. He was six feet with an average build. He had blond hair that stopped just below his ear-line. A short blond beard covered his face. In public, Samuel Richards always wore the same outfit: khaki shorts and a brown t-shirt, which was covered by a field vest.

"I speak ill of your theory, because how do I put it? It's a pathetic theory that only a fool would dream up," Samuel replied with a slight British accent. Samuel's response caused a majority of the crowd to laugh. Professor Leo Hoffburger had just presented a theory that stated every large land animal had been discovered, and in as little as four years, every land animal would be discovered.

"Well, let's look at what you believe in!" Leo snapped back. He exited out of his PowerPoint presentation and opened an internet browser. In a few moments he was on Samuel Richards's Cryptozoology website, which was titled "The Complete Guide to Cryptids Across the Globe." Samuel Richards was well known in the lower scientific community for believing in the existence of unknown animals. He was also infamous for the enjoyment he got out of humiliating those who mocked his ideas.

"As you can see, this man believes that creatures like Bigfoot roam our woodlands, a monster lives at the bottom of Loch Ness, and aliens are flying though the sky," Leo Hoffburger said in an educated voice, trying his best to humiliate Samuel Richards. A serious look formed on Professor Hoffburger's face as he looked right at the audience. "Is this the type of person you want speaking at universities? Someone who believes in myths and fairytales?"

"What are you? Some kind of nut?" Samuel suddenly shouted. "I cannot believe what I just heard."

Professor Hoffburger looked at him in shock.

"I believe you are the one who believes in myths and fairytales. I believe in documented science." Samuel smiled and started to laugh.

"Yes, of course I believe in undiscovered animals, but everyone knows aliens don't exist," Samuel said while making a mocking face. Laughter started to fill the room, which made the rage Professor Hoffburger was feeling increase. "I mean, think about it. Advanced extraterrestrial aliens travel thousands of miles to this planet, only to lose control and crash."

"What about Bigfoot and Nessie? Would you like to explain to the people here why they are real?" Professor Hoffburger shouted as his finger moved across the audience. "Even though there's no solid evidence out there to support the existence of either creature."

Without any hesitation, Samuel gave his answer. "Just because we don't have evidence for something at the moment does not mean it doesn't exist. People disappear in national parks all the time; maybe those are the people that have come across Bigfoot."

"So, you're admitting you believe Bigfoot is living in our national parks abducting people?" Professor Hoffburger said again in a mocking voice. He was hoping he could get the audience to turn on Samuel Richards. He was outraged when his response only got a few minute cheers.

"No, I'm saying it's a possibility," Samuel corrected. "I believe we don't know everything about this world and need to be open to the idea that unknown and prehistoric animals may still live in the present day." Samuel stopped speaking and pointed at Professor Hoffburger. "If everyone was as pompous as you are, America would never have been discovered, airplanes would have never been invented, and we probably would still be living in the dark ages." Laughter and cheers filled the room. While Samuel basked in the cheers, Leo Hoffburger had had enough.

"Congratulations, Mr. Richards. You have ended this lecture and cheated these students out of learning valuable information," Professor Hoffburger said in a low bitter voice.

"Cheated them out of valuable information? Most people came here to sleep!" Everyone started to laugh again. Professor Leo Hoffburger gave the room one last angry look before storming out the exit door, which closed with a slam. Soon the students started to leave the lecture hall, while Samuel Richards remained seated. He wanted to see if Leo Hoffburger would return with security. In the past, a few lecturers he had driven out in a rage had returned with event security. Although he doubted Professor Leo Hoffburger was in the state of mind to think of that. He was most likely boiling in the safety of his office or had surrounded himself with like-minded people who were informing him how right his theory was. While he waited, a Japanese man holding a brown file folder walked over and sat next to him.

"Samuel Richards. My name is Akio Ikeda."

"Nice to meet you," Samuel said. To Akio's surprise, Samuel grabbed the folder from his lap.

"You spell your name A-K-I-O?" Samuel asked as he started to sign the folder.

"I am not here for your autograph, sir," Akio replied. In a lightning-fast movement, he snatched the folder back.

"Then why are you here?" Samuel asked, impressed by Akio's fast reflexes. "You're not event security, are you?"

"No, sir. I am a member of the Japanese Self-Defense Force under the command of Commander Okada Takahashi," Akio replied, showing Samuel his ID.

"Why are you sitting in a lecture hall in Pittsburgh speaking to me?" Samuel questioned.

"A situation is occurring around the Hawaiian Islands that requires your expertise."

"Really, what type of situation?" Samuel asked, interested.

"During the past few days, several unexplained accidents have occurred around the Hawaiian Islands. We suspect the cause of these accidents is cryptozoological in nature." Akio opened the folder and handed the briefing packet to Samuel. "We are currently creating a task force to handle the situation."

Samuel quickly went through the first section but spent nearly twenty minutes carefully looking over the second section. The main piece of information that intrigued him was a photo of claw marks inside a ship's hull.

"Yes, these could have been caused by a sea monster, possibly a mystery saurian," Samuel said, talking to himself. "What depths were these photos taken at?"

"We can discuss more details on the way, sir. Commander Takahashi would like us to travel to Tokyo as soon as possible. I need to know if you're interested in the position?" Samuel Richards looked over the packet again. Everything looked official and there were no signs that this was some sort of joke. This was the chance he had been waiting for; the chance to finally prove to all the Professors and other people that had mocked him that he was right. He looked right at Akio.

"Sir, you now have the best cryptozoologist in the world on your team."

"That is great to hear," Akio replied, handing Samuel a plane ticket. "Our flight for Tokyo leaves in five hours. I suggest you head home and pack anything you will need for a several-day trip."

"I'll be there," Samuel said. He got up and started walking out of the lecture hall. "So, one of you has finally started to see humans as prey?" he said to himself.

"Oh, there is one other thing," Akio said. Samuel stopped and turned around. If Akio was about to admit this whole thing was a hoax, he was the best actor and forger in the world.

"Both the Japanese and American Governments want this information kept secret, so do not speak to anyone or post any of the information I showed you on your website." Samuel Richards nodded his head he understood, and both men parted ways.

CHAPTER 11

2:17 AM 4/10/2021 HST

Mya Kendig swam through the ocean, desperately trying to reach the surface. Nothing but blackness surrounded her. She swam upwards for what seemed like an eternity, until she saw a faint flicker of surface light. Suddenly, ghostly cries from what sounded like hundreds of souls wailing in pain filled her ears. Mya covered them and tried to locate the source of the screams that seemed to be coming from all around her. In the darkness she could make out the ghostly green silhouettes of swimming spirits. The human-shaped spirits circled her, their mouths occasionally opening as they screamed their ghostly cries. Mya swam faster towards the light. Her only way out of this nightmare. Mya froze in fear when the wailing from the spirits stopped and the sound of a thunderclap came from below her. Mya tried to swim but was not moving. She looked down to see glowing red eyes and a large blood-filled open mouth coming towards her. Mya's eyes opened and she sat up screaming.

"Ms. Kendig, it's alright!" a nurse said, rushing into the room. Sweat covered Mya's face and hair; she breathed heavily as she looked around the room. A large window was to her right, along with a recliner chair. A TV and digital clock were mounted on the wall in front of her. The time was two forty-seven A.M. To the left was the room entrance and the door to the bathroom. The nurse pushed a button on the IV pole to stop it from beeping. "Ms. Kendig, it's okay. You're at the Kula Hospital on Maui." Thoughts started racing through Mya's head as she tried to figure out how she got here. Soon the horrible truth started to come back to her.

"Jade." Mya's head turned to the nurse. "Jade! Where's Jade?" Mya asked in a panicked voice. Deep down she already knew the answer, but she was still clinging to the slim hope that by some miracle, Jade was rescued and safe in the hospital with her.

"Ms. Kendig." The nurse paused for a moment. The look on her face told Mya the answer she was dreading. "You were the only one the rescue team brought to the hospital. You were found unconscious on Molokini Crater." Mya let out a tearful scream. The nurse sat on the bed and placed a hand on her back, trying to calm her down. Mya put her head down and broke down into tears. It was mid-morning. Mya had just finished her breakfast of hospital eggs and toast. Physically she felt fine, but inside she felt sorrow and guilt, helpless and alone. A few weeks ago, she had lost her boyfriend, and now she had lost her only sister. The person she looked up to all her life was gone. *What am I going to do?* she thought to herself. To this point in her life, she had always had someone to lean on and help her make decisions, but now she was alone and had no idea how she was going to go on. She knew she would have to stay in Hawaii for at least a week for Jade's funeral and to sort her belongings, but what then? She looked out the hospital window; it was a nice day outside, puffy white clouds filled the sky. Her thoughts carried her back to when she was a young girl, when Jade and she would lie in their backyard and find shapes in the clouds. Mya's eyes turned towards the door when a gentle knock struck it. When it opened, a doctor followed by a man in a suit and tie entered. She was glad to see them; she wanted answers. Since regaining consciousness, she still had no idea now she got to the hospital or what had happened to the creature that attacked her. She thought she remembered the nurse mentioning something about a rescue team, but she was unsure of anything she heard last night. The doctor moved to the bedside while the other man took a seat in the recliner.

"Hello, Mya. I'm Doctor Gordon," he said, introducing himself. Doctor Gordon was a middle-aged Hawaiian native with balding hair. "How are you feeling?" Mya shrugged her shoulders.

"As well as can be expected, I guess. When can I leave?" Mya asked, wanting to get out of the hospital.

"Hopefully as early as this afternoon," he answered. He then motioned to the man sitting down. "This is Detective Browner of the Maui Police Department."

"Hello, Mya," he said. Detective Browner was a strong-built Polynesian man who looked to be in his early fifties.

"How did I get here?" she asked.

"When you and your sister failed to return or failed to respond to any radio communications, a rescue vessel was sent to Molokini Crater. The rescuers found you unconscious on the crater," Browner replied.

"What about Jade! Did you find her?" Mya asked quickly. She knew her sister was dead, but knowing her body had been recovered would help her get some form of closure. Detective Browner said nothing. He pulled a light brown detective case file out from under his arm and opened it. He removed a blank sheet of police statement paper and a pen. Mya rolled her eyes in annoyance when he started writing something on the paper. She turned to Dr. Gordon.

"Is anything wrong with me?"

"You're suffering from severe psychological shock, and a slight case of the bends," Doctor Gordon replied. He was about to explain in greater detail when Detective Browner cut in.

"Sorry, Doctor, but I need to ask Mya some important questions."

"Now you have time to talk." Mya said to herself; she was starting not to like Browner. She could tell what kind of person he was, the kind that expected everyone to come at his call and wait until he was ready for them.

"Ms. Kendig, we have no idea what happened to you and your sister. I need you to fill out this statement paper, and then answer some questions." Mya looked at the paper; it had written instructions for her to write down what happened as truthfully and honestly as she could recall. Mya moved her breakfast tray to the side of the overbed table. She lay back into the upright mattress and started writing.

"I can answer questions and write at the same time. It's called multitasking," Mya said in a sarcastic tone. Detective Browner expression showed he did not like her tone at all. He reached into his pocket and pulled out a police notepad.

"What were you and your sister doing at Molokini Crater?" Browner already knew the truth, but he wanted to be sure Mya's story matched it.

"We were spending the day diving," Mya replied.

"Was this your first time diving?" Mya looked up and shook her head yes.

"Where is Jade Kendig now?" Mya stopped writing. Her breathing rate increased as she tried to hold back tears.

"She's." Mya paused as a tear rolled down her cheek then said in a low sad voice. "She's dead."

"What happened?" Browner asked in a serious voice. Mya tried to speak, but she only managed a soft murmur. She closed her eyes and cleared her throat, then managed to blurt out. "We were diving near that place called the edge of the world. Some type of sea creature attacked us." She tried to think about something funny, wanting to get that memory out of her head as quickly as possible.

"So, you're stating it was a shark attack?" Browner asked as he wrote. Mya paused for a few seconds, thinking of the right words to say. A person with Browner's personality would not have been her first choice to explain her encounter to, but he was the only one she knew at the moment who could do something to stop the creature.

"I know this is going to sound crazy, but it was not a shark. It was." Again, Mya paused before finding the courage to say. "It was some type of giant sea creature."

Mya knew saying "sea monster" was a bad idea. So, she worked hard to avoid saying it. Browner stopped looking at his notepad and stared right at her.

"I'm warning you. This is no time for games," he said in a firm voice. "Now I'm going to repeat what you just told me. You're stating on record that a sea monster attacked and killed your sister?" he asked, firmness in his voice.

"No, I'm not. I just know it was not a shark or any type of fish. I saw a long tail and a clawed arm, or leg, or something," Mya replied in an almost hysteric voice. She knew how crazy her story sounded. Browner could tell she was about to break down; then he would get nothing out of her. So, for the moment, he changed the subject.

"Ms. Kendig, I did not mention this earlier. Divers were sent down to search the area around the boat. The divers recovered some torn-up pieces of a diving suit." A slight glimmer of hope formed in Mya's eyes.

"What about the body! Did you find it?" A feeling of pleasure came over Browner. His plan to prevent Mya from breaking down had worked. He only needed to ask one more question to confirm what he was beginning to suspect. His expression changed to very serious.

"Did you have any reason or desire to harm your sister?" Mya's expression instantly turned to anger.

"Look, let me make this nice and clear!" she yelled, sitting straight up, her eyes holding an angry glare. "I did not kill my sister, and don't ask me any questions like that again!" Doctor Gordon cut in to defuse the situation.

"Detective Browner, may I speak with you for a moment" Browner got up and walked to the end of the room with the doctor. Despite the two men speaking in a low tone, Mya was able to eavesdrop.

"Great emotional shock can greatly affect a person's memory of a traumatic incident. It is even possible that a traumatized mind may experience hallucinations."

"Are you saying she imagined the attack?" Browner asked, not buying the doctor's statement as an explanation.

"No, I'm stating that during the attack, it is possible the mind could have caused pieces of the surrounding environment, like a shark, to appear as something else." That Browner could believe, although his suspicions about Mya were not totally gone.

"For the record, in your professional opinion, the Molokini Crater incident was a shark attack, not a murder?"

"Yes, that is what I believe. Jade Kendig was killed by a shark," Dr. Gordon said confidently.

"What species of shark do you think is responsible for the attack?" Browner asked.

"I'm not a biologist, but my best guess would be a tiger or great white shark." Hearing the conclusion the two men had come to made Mya clench her fists in anger.

"It was not a shark that killed Jade!" she snapped, which slightly startled both men. Doctor Gordon walked over to her.

"Ms. Kendig, please relax and just listen to what I have to say."

"No, you listen! You didn't see the look of fear in Jade's eyes right before that thing attacked her!" Mya yelled. Seeing the look on both men's faces made Mya realize that screaming was only going to do more harm than good. She took a few moments to calm herself, then said, "Jade loved these waters and knew about any sea creatures living in them. Nothing that was supposed to be there would have scared her like that."

"Ms. Kendig, I'm going to be honest with you," Detective Browner said, approaching the bed. Doctor Gordon moved back and stood a few feet from the bed, but Browner stood right next to it, intentionally invading Mya's personal space. "I'm not convinced you saw anything but a shark." Mya was about to speak when Browner motioned for her to stay quiet. "And I'm going to take the word of an experienced doctor over the word of an inexperienced diver who is suffering from shock. His statement is the only reason you're not coming down to the police station under suspicion for murder." He patted her on the shoulder. "So, consider yourself lucky." Mya raised the middle finger of her hand that was under the blankets. Browner did not see it, but it made her feel better.

"Here. This explains how I survived a nightmare," Mya said, handing Browner her written statement. "Is that all you need from me?"

"Yes, Doctor Gordon's statement was acceptable to the investigation." Mya was relieved when he started to leave the room. The feeling was short-lived when he turned around and said, "Are you planning on staying in Maui?" Under her breath, Mya huffed in frustration; she just wanted him gone.

"At least until the funeral is over and I get Jade's things sorted out," Mya replied.

"We will call you if we discover any new leads. I'm sorry for your loss and hope you recover soon." His words were more robotic then caring.

"Thanks," Mya replied, smiling not at his words, but because he walked out the door.

CHAPTER 12

Max Varian entered building D of the Japanese Ministry of Defense Complex. Building D was dedicated to research and development. After a short elevator ride and walk, he entered the biological research laboratory. To his left were shelves full of boxes, books, and unused lab equipment. The middle of the room had several tables with lab equipment and computers. The right of the room had two large work stations with a sink separating them. A young girl in her early twenties was working at the sink washing used test tubes. Her white lab coat had several water stains from the fast-paced washing.

"In a hurry, Sora?" Max said. She gasped and turned around.

"Sorry, Max, you startled me," she replied with a smile. "I did not know you were coming to Tokyo."

"Neither did I. Is Dr. Yamaguchi around?"

"No, I'm afraid he has gone home for the night. Can I help you with anything?"

"Yes, I need a DNA test conducted on an unknown tissue sample I collected."
He handed a plastic bag to her. She looked at the large claw, puzzled.

"Where did you get this?"

"Inside the wreckage of the Lucky Dragon." A concerned expression formed
on Sora's face.

"Nothing happened to the dolphins, right?"

"No, the dolphins are fine," Max said reassuringly. Sora and Dr. Yamaguchi
had been to the Niihau complex several times to assist with the dolphin research.
During that time, Sora had gotten really attached to them, especially Aquatail.
"When can I expect the test results?"

"Tomorrow afternoon," she replied.

"Okay, see you then." Just then, Max's phone vibrated. He looked at the text
from Okada that read: *Come to my office. Another attack may have occurred.*

Max rushed to Building A and shortly opened the door to Okada's office.
Okada was sitting at his desk with Liz seated at the right side of the desk. Okada's
office was a twenty-foot room. The commander's desk was located at the back of
the room. A large TV was mounted on the wall adjacent to the desk. The right
and left of the room had several display stands. One display stand was larger than
the rest and had a glass covering. That stand held his grandfather's flight suit and
a model of the fighter he piloted during World War II.

Max entered the room and bowed. Okada acknowledged the respectful gesture. "What happened?"

"A report has come in that a Hawaiian news network is about to run a story on
a supposed sea monster attack," Okada answered. He motioned to the remaining

seat next to Liz. "Please take a seat." Max sat down and looked at the screen. The news was currently reporting on the Hawaiian weather.

"Nothing like watching the ten p.m. news broadcast eighteen hours in the future," Liz joked.

"That's because we're nineteen hours ahead of Hawaii. The news is still new," Max added, correcting her in a joking voice.

"Like I said, we're so ahead of our time," Liz replied.

"Max, when can we expect the results of the claw analyzation?" Okada asked.

"Tomorrow afternoon. By the way. When are our new teammates supposed to arrive?"

"They are scheduled to arrive tomorrow morning." Max turned his attention back to the news broadcast, which was on a commercial break.

"I hate that show," Liz said.

"So do I," Max agreed.

***

In Hawaii, Mya laid under a blanket on the couch in Jade's condo. Her eyes were heavy from the long painful day she had. After getting released from the hospital, she spent several unpleasant hours getting Jade's house and car keys from the local authorities. The drive to Jade's house felt like an eternity. It felt so wrong driving Jade's car and living in her home without her. When she arrived there, things got worse. She had to conduct the unpleasant task of calling family members, mainly her parents, with whom she already had a rocky relationship, to inform them Jade had died. What hurt her the most was she could not even tell them the truth about what happened. She didn't dare after what happened at the hospital. She looked at the piles of papers on the coffee table in front of her, knowing the grueling tasks of making the arrangements for Jade's funeral, creating an obituary for the paper, and then sending that information to family members was waiting for her tomorrow. She didn't know any of Jade's friends, but she figured they would learn about her death from the news. She tried to numb the emotional pain she was feeling by watching online videos she enjoyed.

While browsing, she went to a local news stations' website and saw a section of the ten o'clock broadcast was going to cover Jade's death. Despite not wanting to relive the encounter, she decided to watch it anyway. Maybe other people had seen or lost loved ones to that creature. Those were the type of people she could talk to. People who would believe her. Mya's emotions grew when the commercials ended. A middle-aged man and woman appeared on the screen. The man cleared his throat and spoke.

"When most people think of Hawaii, they think of pleasant weather and beautiful beaches. This is the normal Hawaiian scene, but unfortunately sometimes tragedy strikes these beautiful islands. Yesterday afternoon, a diving accident occurred around Molokini Crater that led to the death of an experienced diver, Jade Kendig." A picture of Jade's face appeared on the right side of the screen. "Diving accidents are a rare occurrence, but this one has an odd twist to it. Right, Cathy?" he said, turning to the women sitting next to him.

"That's right, Craig. What's odd about this accident is that Jade Kendig's sister and dive partner, Mya Kendig, claims that her sister was killed by a sea monster." A picture of Mya appeared on screen. A feeling of dread filled Mya's body.

***

Seeing Mya's picture caused a look of attraction to briefly form on Max's face.

"Yeah, I know she's hot. I thought you work too much to have time for girls?" Liz teased. Max glared at Liz. He was annoyed that she caught the few seconds of lust in his eyes. A glance from Okada was all that was needed to get them refocused.

"Really. What makes her think it was a sea monster?" Craig replied in a surprised voice.

"Well, in her police statement she claimed that she saw a sea monster's tail and front leg. Both reporters maintained straight faces, but it was clear they were trying not to laugh. "To better explore this claim, we are going to be joined by Marine Biologist Dr. George Sherwood." Max scoffed under his breath.

"Friend of yours?" Liz asked.

"I don't know him personally, but from the articles he has written, I can tell he's very narrow-minded."

"Thank you for joining us, Dr. Sherwood."

"Thank you for having me, Cathy," he replied.

"Now, Dr. Sherwood, first off, all three of us can agree that what happened to Jade Kendig was a terrible tragedy," Craig said. Then his voice turned slightly humorous. "But I'm sure we can also agree that there is no such thing as sea monsters." All three people laughed slightly.

"Yes, it's still safe to go out and enjoy the water," Cathy cut in.

"What a bunch of idiots," Liz stated.

"Dr. Sherwood, what do you think really happened down there?" Craig asked in a serious voice.

"Well, Craig, my best guess would be a shark attack. If you look at the evidence, shark attacks are rare, but they do occur."

"Dr. Sherwood, if this was a shark attack, then why did Jade's sister claim she saw a sea monster?" Craig asked.

"Probably because to her it was," Dr. Sherwood replied. "Mya Kendig was an inexperienced diver that witnessed her sister getting attacked by a shark. Her day job." Dr. Sherwood paused for a moment. "If you can call it that, is a cosplayer. That probably assisted in creating the sea monster illusion."

"For those of you that don't know, a cosplayer is someone who dresses up as a superhero or videogame character at conventions," Cathy added.

"I wish they would stick to important topics," Okada said under his breath. Max and Liz looked at each other and giggled.

"Now why do you believe that her occupation as a cosplayer caused her to believe she saw a sea monster?" Craig asked.

"Dressing up like superheroes is something children do," Dr. Sherwood answered in a disgusted voice. "The fact that she does this leads me to believe she possesses a weak mind. The shock and trauma of the attack caused her weak mind to go into fantasy land and imagine a sea monster in front of her."

***

Mya sat up clenching her fists. She wanted to punch him so bad.

"You weren't there! You don't know what I saw or what it was like!" Mya yelled.

"Dr. Sherwood, what precautions should the public take until this potentially dangerous shark is removed?" Craig asked.

"Simple things like staying near groups of people, don't enter the water with open wounds, don't swim at night." Dr. Sherwood replied. "I'm sure the Hawaiian Division of Conservation and Resources Enforcement will handle this dangerous shark very soon."

"You heard it from the expert, ladies and gentlemen. The waters are safe," Cathy said. "Dr. Sherwood, thank you for joining us." Dr. Sherwood thanked them and ended the interview. Mya stood up, threw an empty plastic glass against the wall, and then flipped the coffee table in front of her. She knew family and Jade's friends were most likely watching the broadcast. She started pacing around the room.

"They're going to think I'm crazy. They're going to think I'm crazy," she said to herself out loud. The last thing she needed at the funeral was having to explain to people why she told the police Jade was killed by a sea monster. Mya grabbed a picture of her and Jade she had found in Jade's office. She held it close to her chest, went up against a wall, slowly fell down, and burst into tears.

"The remains of the diving suit worn by Jade Kendig have been recovered. Unfortunately, we cannot say the same of her body," Cathy said. "That is our final story of the night. Goodnight, Hawaii." Cathy and Craig both waved goodbye. Okada shut off the TV.

"What do you think?" he asked, turning to Max.

"He wants to talk to Mya. In some video game café," Liz said, knowing full well her friend's favorite hobby was video gaming.

"Shut up," Max said. "I wish I could get a look at the remains of that diving suit." He tried his best to change the subject.

"That can be arranged," Okada said. He picked up his phone and dialed Saburo's number.

"Yes, sir," Saburo answered.

"Saburo, sorry for waking you. Where are you at this moment?" he asked.

"Ashly Cross and I are in Dallas. We had an unexpected overnight delay due to aircraft malfunction. I am currently at the airport waiting to board a four a.m. flight."

"Saburo, I need you to get in contact with the Hawaiian Governor. Ask him to have the Maui Police department send everything from the Jade Kendig case to my office for study."

"I will take care of that right away, sir," Saburo replied and ended the call.

CHAPTER 13

4:49 AM 4/11/2021 HST

Off the Maui coast near Opana Point, the sky was cloudless and the full moon was just beginning to set. Emma Clark and Dylan Patterson lay asleep in their fifty-foot yacht.

Dylan was a marketing executive who had just closed a major deal for his company. To celebrate, he and his girlfriend Emma decided to take a week's vacation sailing around the Hawaiian Islands. Both had blonde hair and the physical appearance of models. The young couple was abruptly awoken by the boat shaking violently. The collision caused both of them to fly a few inches into the air.

"What was that?" Emma asked in a freaked-out voice.

"Something must have hit us," Dylan replied in a shocked voice. The adrenaline rush caused by the experience had fully awakened both of them.

"Another boat?" Emma suggested.

"I don't know," Dylan replied in a confused voice. He put on a blue and white flannel shirt and grabbed a flashlight. "Wait here."

"Be careful," Emma replied. She watched Dylan's dark figure walk through the living area and disappear up the steps that led to the outside. Emma waited, thinking about what could have caused the boat to shake. Images of pirates leaping from their ship to raid hers started filling her head. *Don't be ridiculous,* she told herself.

After a few minutes had passed, she called out, "Dylan." After hearing no reply, she called out again. "Dylan!" Still silence. Worried, she threw on a white tank top and headed from the front sleeping area to the rear of the boat.

When she reached the top of the steps, she said, "Dylan," this time in a worried tone. She looked out past the boat motor compartment into the dark ocean. Terrible thoughts started to fill her head. What if he had fallen overboard? What if pirates really were attacking the boat? She screamed when a light was shined in her face.

"Hey, it's just me," Dylan said, putting his arm around her shoulder. She pushed him off in annoyance and walked over to the driver's seat. She sat down and looked at him, annoyed.

"Why didn't you answer me? I thought you were dead or something!"

"Sorry, I did not hear you until I was near the door."

"Well, please answer next time. I was worried," she replied in a calmer voice. "Did you figure out what we hit?"

"No, I suppose it could have been a rough wave or a whale that bumped us." Not satisfied with the answer, Emma got up and stood on the motor compartment. She looked out at the ocean. Seeing nothing at the rear of the ship, she grabbed on to the ship's guard rail and walked over to the bow of the ship. She held on to the guard rail and looked down at the ocean, scanning for anything unusual. The moonlight gave off just enough light to show the small waves striking the boat. Dylan started to walk over to Emma with the intention of getting her to come back to bed. He paused when a splash was followed by a loud thunderclap. A feeling of uneasiness and fear came over both of them.

"Dylan, start the boat. I want to get out of here," Emma said, looking towards him.

"That's a good idea," Dylan agreed, trying to fight the sudden feelings of dread. He looked around. He saw nothing threatening, just the calm ocean, but the skies were clean with no sign of an approaching storm. Abruptly, he saw a ghostly apparition out of the corner of his left eye. He quickly turned to see what it was. Nothing was there. He shook his head. "You're losing it, man." Suddenly, Emma let out a scream of terror that was followed by a large splash.

"Baby!" he screamed in horror. He ran over to the bow of the ship. He steadied his shaking hand and shined the flashlight towards the water. His eyes widened with terror at the sight of a large scaled tail sinking beneath the surface. The tail was replaced by an expanding pool of red water. Dylan fell down screaming.

"Oh god! I did not just see that!" he screamed in hysteria. After a few seconds of screaming, he managed to pull himself up. He nearly fell down again by a sudden feeling of vertigo. He vomited as he stumbled below deck. He reached the bedroom and grabbed his cell phone. The phone stayed on long enough to show a dead battery icon.

"No! No! No!" he cried. He tossed the phone on the ground and grabbed Emma's phone. He smashed his head in frustration, trying to remember her password. When it came to him, he smashed it in, only to have a low battery icon briefly appear before her phone went dead. "How is this possible?" he screamed. He threw the phone against the wall. A slim feeling of hope returned when he saw the boat key.

He grabbed the key off the rack and ran above deck to the main cabin. He glanced at the ocean to check for anything in the water behind him. Seeing nothing, he sat in the driver's seat and started the engine. The engine only sputtered, then failed. Dylan turned the key again as the boat was once again shaken. He hammered the wheel in frustration when he noticed the front of the boat tilting slightly upward. The hair on the back of his neck stood up when a warm breath blew on it. He felt another breath, and the realization that he was not alone hit him.

He slowly turned around to see a large head with large yellow eyes staring back at him. He shouted in terror when the head came down and enclosed on his head and upper body. Dylan screamed and pounded at the creature's teeth and mouth, struggling to break the vice-like grip, but to no avail. He let out a cry of pain as he was violently pulled from the driver's seat. Dylan's arms and feet were trying to latch on to anything as he was pulled backwards. In a final struggle, Dylan tried to find the creature's eyes, but it was hopeless. The inside of the creature's mouth started filling with water. Dylan let out a final gurgled scream as the teeth sank into his upper chest, separating it from the body.

CHAPTER 14

9:17 AM 4/11/2021 HST

Mya Kendig groggily opened her eyes. She looked up at the wall-mounted clock across the room. A look of surprise formed on her face when she saw the clock read nine seventeen.

"Alright, Jade, I'm up," she said, smiling. She sat up on the couch and turned around, expecting her fully awake sister to be sitting at the kitchen table about to give her a lecture on how she slept the entire day away. A feeling of pain returned to her as she looked at the empty kitchen and hallway that led to the two bedrooms.

With a heartbroken sigh, Mya got up, grabbed a bagel, and made herself some coffee. She took her breakfast on to the condo's balcony and sat on one of the outdoor chairs. The balcony also had an arch-shaped pool that overlooked the island. Mya gradually ate while she gazed into the pool. Her thoughts went back to the night she arrived, to how much fun she and Jade had in that pool just a day ago. A warm feeling briefly came over her. She could almost hear and see the two of them splashing and laughing. "Jade, I miss you," she said, sadly looking up towards the sky. Mya finished eating, then started what she knew was going to be an unpleasant day.

An hour later, Mya walked into the Maui Police Department. A Hawaiian women about her age was sitting at the entrance desk. Mya walked up to the desk and lightly tapped on the glass that created a wall between them.

The desk officer looked up from her typing and said, "Hello, how my I help you?"

"Hi, my name is Mya Kendig. Recently, my sister and I were involved in an underwater accident." Mya paused for a moment to hold back her emotions. "That my sister did not come back from."

"You're referring to Jade Kendig? The shark attack case?" Mya said nothing, just shook her head up and down. She was in no mood to argue over the fact that it was not a shark. "I'm truly sorry for your loss. What can I help you with?"

"Some of my sister's diving suit was recovered. Since Jade's body has not been found, I was hoping to place the pieces of the suit in the casket."

"One moment," the desk officer said. She got up and went through the door behind her. Mya waited eagerly for her to return. A few minutes later, the desk officer returned and sat back down. She looked at Mya and said sympathetically, "Ms. Kendig, I'm sorry, but we no longer have anything related to the Jade Kendig case."

"What?" Mya yelled, not believing what she was hearing. "Why don't you? What happened to it?" The desk officer did not reply. Mya could tell by her face she was trying to make a mental decision.

"I probably should not be telling you this, but last night we were ordered to send all evidence from the Jade Kendig case to Tokyo, Japan." Mya just stood frozen. Her eyes were wide with disbelief. She could not understand why the Japanese government would want her sister's diving gear. She was about to ask some more questions when a door opened. Her look of shock turned to a slight glare when Detective Browner walked into the lobby. When he spotted Mya, he huffed in annoyance.

"Jeez. This is just what I need." Mya didn't look at him or say anything, hoping he would keep walking. Unfortunately, he walked over to the desk officer. "Is she talking about a sea monster?" he asked.

"No, I'm not," Mya replied.

"Was I talking to you?" he snapped.

"No, sir," the desk officer replied. "She was just asking if she could have her sister's recovered items." Mya wanted to slam Browner against the wall and demand he tell her why he sent her sister's items to Japan. However, she knew how that would end.

"What did the Japanese want with my sister's case items?" Mya asked.

"How do you know about that?" Browner asked, surprised. He glanced at the desk officer. Mya repeated the question. This time her tone had a lot more seriousness and attitude to it.

"That's none of your business," Browner answered. Then his attention turned back to the desk officer. He pointed his finger right at her face and said, "Don't you ever give information like that out to a civilian again."

"Yes, sir," the desk officer replied in a frightened voice.

"She was my sister! I have every right to know what is being done with her things!" Mya shouted back. Browner closed in on Mya's personal space and looked down at her. Mya did not move back or look away. The two just exchanged glares. Finally, Browner spoke in a serious, authoritative voice.

"Right now, you have two options, Ms. Kendig. Option one, you can leave now and never mention the sea monster again. I already told you someone will notify you when the shark that attacked your sister is killed." Mya rolled her eyes slightly, which increased Browner's already irritated state. "Option two is, at best, I place you under arrest right now for public disturbance or, at worst, have you committed to a mental hospital...Now tell me right now: which option do you choose?"

"Fine, you win," Mya replied.

"I didn't ask you that. I asked which option. Option one or option two?" An angered look formed on Mya's face. She started to move her lips. "Think carefully about what you say next," Browner said with a slight smirk. He knew he was in complete control of the situation and Mya could do nothing but take whatever he threw at her.

"Option one," Mya said in a soft bitter voice.

"What?" Browner said, crossing his arms.

"Option one," Mya repeated in a louder tone. Inside she was burning up, but knew she was powerless to do anything.

"Smart," he replied. "Now, if you will excuse me, I have to go investigate two missing sailors." Browner brushed pass Mya and headed for the exit.

"I suppose you think I killed them too," Mya said sarcastically. She knew she should have kept her mouth shut, but she was so angry she acted against her better judgment. Browner abruptly turned around.

"Desk officer, write Ms. Kendig up for disorderly conduct and issue her a fine."

I hope you choke on a donut, Mya said, this time in her head. She turned to face the desk officer, who looked upset by the event that had just occurred. "Let's get this over with."

"Sorry, you had to go through that," she said while writing out the fine slip.

"Any chance you can report him for abuse of power?" Mya asked. She did not know how the desk officer would respond, but she seemed to be taking her side.

"Unfortunately, no. A person acting like a jerk is not abuse of power." She looked around the room to make sure no one was in earshot. "But between you and me, no one here likes him either," she said, handing Mya the fine slip.

"I can't imagine why," Mya said, taking it. She looked down at the amount owed, which was one dollar. Mya looked at the desk officer surprise.

"Hey, he never said how much to fine you." Mya grinned and pulled out her wallet.

"Thanks. You just made my crappy day a little better," she said gratefully, handing the desk officer five dollars. "Keep the change. Buy yourself a coffee or something." The desk officer smiled back at Mya.

"I hope you find closure soon."

"So do I," Mya replied and left the station.

CHAPTER 15

11:00 AM 4/12/2021 JST

Max and Liz entered the conference room located behind Okada's office. They approached the front of the wooden conference table and sat down directly across from each other. A middle-aged man and a young woman were already seated at the midsection of the table. Samuel Richards was lying back in his chair, resting his feet on the chair next to him. Ashly Cross was eating a bowl of Soba noodle salad and a large slice of teriyaki salmon. Samuel Richards had arrived in Tokyo yesterday. He had ample time to eat, sleep, and get settled. Ashly Cross's traveling experience was not as pleasant. Due to the flight delay, she had arrived in Tokyo early that morning. When she arrived at her hotel room, she used what little time she had to get a few hours of sleep before the meeting.

"Hi. You must be Max, and Liz. I'm Ashly Cross," she said, smiling. The two of them returned the greeting.

"You're the computer and technical expert, right?" Liz said. Ashly's mouth was full of noodles, so she shook her head yes.

"Have you even seen someone that thin eat so fast?" Samuel added with a snicker.

"Like I already told you, all I've eaten in about a day was the crackers the flight attendant gave me on the airplane. Getting here was not fun," Ashly replied in an annoyed voice.

"We heard you had travel delays," Max cut in to stop an argument before it got started.

"Yeah, not fun," Ashly answered. Her attention turned back to Samuel. "You might want to be polite and introduce yourself to the team."

"I was getting to that," he replied. "I'm Samuel Richards, your expert in the Cryptozoological field. I'm looking forward to working with all of you and would love to know your skills sets."

"Did you not read the briefing material they gave us?" Ashly asked. The fact that he may have neglected to look over the material shocked her. She had only just met him and already she thought he was an arrogant fool.

"Only the parts I was interested in. In my experience, it's not worth wasting valuable time reading information about my teammates when I can talk to them in person," Samuel replied. Ashly gave him a look of displeasure.

"Our new teammates already seem to be best friends," Max said softly to Liz.

"Need a bonding day," Liz replied as she looked towards Samuel and Ashly and said, "I'm Liz Tayler, by the way. I'm the team's weapons expert and everyone's favorite sarcastic bad girl."

"Glad to have a sarcastic bad girl on the team," Samuel replied.

"I'm Max Varian. I'm a field biologist and animal trainer, currently training the attack dolphins with Liz."

"You look like you belong in the gothic shop," Samuel said, looking at Max's black cargo pants and black shirt with a werewolf on it. He was surprised to learn Max was a biologist. "I just hope you're not one of those pompous types."

"Don't worry. That's already covered by someone else," Ashly cut in, looking right at Samuel.

"Glad you know yourself so well," he replied. Before Ashly could respond, Max cut in.

"How long have you been waiting for?" he asked.

"About half an hour," Ashly replied. "I had time to eat, so I'm happy."

"How did the two of you get dragged into this, anyway?" Samuel asked.

"This is why you read the briefing material beforehand," Ashly again pointed out. Before Samuel could respond, Okada entered the room caring a briefcase, followed by Saburo, who was pushing a small gray cart.

Saburo parked the cart, unlocked it, and handed everyone a personal laptop. Once the task was completed, Saburo walked over to the computer sitting on a desk in the corner of the room. The computer was hooked up to a large TV mounted on the wall near the front of the conference table. A blue screen briefly appeared; then the windows display filled the screen. Okada stood at the front of the table and gently slammed the pointer he was holding on the table. The slight pounding was enough to get everyone's attention.

"Now that I have your attention, we can begin. My name is Commander Okada Takahashi. Admiral Tetsuya Takahashi has given me command of the upcoming operation.

"He's also my wonderful boyfriend, who likes to cook, and watch Japanese game shows," Liz added. Okada turned and looked at her and gently smacked her hand with the pointer.

Well, we know who gets all the special privileges on this team, Samuel silently commented to himself.

"Not true. We never mix business with pleasure. There is a time for both," Okada replied in a correcting, but soft voice. Okada looked at everyone and continued his speech. "Most of you I have known for years." He moved the pointer towards Max, then Liz. He then moved the pointer towards Samuel and Ashly. "While others I will get to know with time." Ashly and Samuel had never met Okada Takahashi, but already they could feel the power and authority his presence gave off. "Now, I want each of you to look to the left and to the right." Everyone did as Commander Takahashi ordered. "The five of us will be working as one unit. The success of this operation will depend on our ability to work together and use our skills to become a singular force." Okada pulled a thin strip of wood out from his pocket.

"Here comes the stick example," Liz whispered to Max. He grinned as Okada held the wooden strip at eye level and snapped it. "Individually, we will fail." He then pulled out five similar strips of wood. He held them at the same level as the previous strip and tried to snap them. After a few seconds of applying pressure to the strips, they remained intact. "When combined, our skills will become a mighty force."

Liz laughed under her breath. Okada's symbolism was cheesy yet effective.

"Have they ever snapped?" Max whispered to Liz.

"Once, it was awkward," Liz replied.

"That is what we need to become. A mighty force. As of this moment, the five of us are known as Suijin squad."

"Are we supposed to be clapping?" Samuel whispered to Max.

"If you want," he replied. Samuel Richards clapped slowly. Liz started to join in, but a look from Okada that said "please don't start" ended Liz's clapping attempt.

"Suijin. That is the Japanese god of water, correct?" Ashly said to Max.

"Yes, a good name considering what we're most likely going up against."

"I'm still not convinced a sea monster is the cause of these disasters," Ashly replied. Her voice held more than a little skepticism. Max was about to reply when Okada started speaking.

"During this meeting, I wish to accomplish two goals. First, I want a solid theory formed on what is causing the disasters around the Hawaiian Islands. Second, come up with a plan of action to remove or destroy it."

"Sir," Ashly asked, raising her hand. Okada motioned it was okay to continue. "Do you have any more information on these incidents other than the information in the packets I received earlier?"

"Of course," Okada replied. He reached into the briefcase and pulled out a file folder that was nearly overflowing. He placed it on the table. "I hope you can make more sense of that information then I can." His tone was less serious this time, showing that he did have a softer side to him. "I also believe this information is available on our laptops. Is that correct, Saburo?" Saburo did not answer. He was on his phone. He had an intense look on his face as he typed on the computer.

"When did this happen?" he asked the person on the other line. A feeling of uneasiness started to fill the room. Everyone knew what he was talking about. "Yes, thank you," Saburo said and hung up. Okada was the first to ask what everyone was thinking.

"What has happened now?"

"A yacht was found drifting north of Maui with no one aboard."

"Was the yacht damaged?" Liz asked.

"No damage was mentioned. The vessel was just drifting through the water."

"Do we know who the yacht belongs to?" Okada asked.

"The boat was registered to a Dylan Patterson. An experienced boatman. He and his girlfriend were reported to have been on a week's vacation."

"What do you think, Max?" Liz added.

"I don't know. It could have been our animal," Max replied with a little uncertainty. "It could also have been an unfortunate case of kidnapping or two love birds both falling off the boat and drowning at sea."

"Was anything onboard stolen, or have any ransom demands been made?" Liz asked.

"Nothing was mentioned. The Maui police department have classified both people missing at sea," Saburo replied.

Samuel Richards spoke up. "Did the report say anything about damaged electrical equipment or portable electric devices with dead batteries?"

"Again, nothing was mentioned," Saburo replied.

Okada took a seat and said, "Ladies and gentlemen, let's get to work. I would like both goals to be completed by the end of the day."

"It will be difficult, but we can do it," Max assured.

"I feel the same way," Okada replied. He turned to Saburo and said, "Please make travel arrangements for us to get back to Hawaii."

"Wait, we're going to Hawaii? I thought our base of operations was going to be here," Ashly said.

"Our base of operations is on Niihau," Max added.

"Great, more traveling," Ashly said, annoyed, not wanting to go through the chaos again. A knock at the door stopped the conversation. Saburo opened it.

"Hi, the lab results from the claw examination are finished. Max wanted them right away," Sora said, handing the paper to Saburo, who in turn handed it to Max.

"Thanks, Sora," Max yelled as she and Saburo left. Everyone looked towards him as he read. Moments later, he said in a tense voice, "These results are rather worrisome. The DNA sample matches no DNA we have on record. It comes from an unknown species."

"So, it is a sea monster," Liz commended. Samuel snapped his fingers. He was the only one with an excited look on his face.

"Wait, the report said nothing about a claw? Where did you find it?" Ashly asked, surprised.

"The claw was found when Max and Liz investigated the Lucky Dragon wreckage. I thought you knew everything?" Samuel Richards said sarcastically.

"I said I read the information packet. There was no mention of a claw in that packet," Ashly snapped back. "How did you know about it?"

"I know when and how to ask the right questions to get important information," Samuel replied in a proud voice.

"All right, children, cease fire," Liz said, making a chopping motion between them. Ashly huffed in frustration at Samuel.

"Like it or not, we're a team now. So, let's get to work and create a plan," Max added.

"Sounds good," Ashly agreed. She walked over to the desk in the corner of the room and removed the HDMI cable from the computer and plugged it into her laptop. "I'm going to work over here so everyone can see and approve our final presentation." Ashly placed her iPad next to the laptop. "I also have some personal work I need to get done, which means I'm going to be multitasking for an hour or so. I hope that's not a problem."

"As long as your primary focus is with the team," Okada replied.

"I'm used to working on three to four programs at the same time. This will be easy."

Liz clapped her hands several times, then said in a motivating voice, "Okay, team, we need to figure out what we are dealing with and how to kill it." Liz pointed both her index fingers at Max and Samuel. "You two figure out what this creature is, and I'll come up with a way to kill it. Ashly can write down the

105

information and Okada can supervise the operation." Max smiled at his friend's enthusiasm.

"As I stated earlier, the only evidence we have is we're dealing with an unknown marine animal that is possibly between twenty-eight and forty feet long. It's a quadruped with approximately thirteen-inch-long claws."

"Don't forget it likes to eat humans," Liz added.

"Samuel, your field is studying unknown animals. Does that description seem familiar?" Max asked. Samuel got up and walked over to where Ashly was sitting. She quickly hid her iPad from view.

"Darling, I need to use the big screen. May I please borrow your laptop for a moment?"

"Since you said please, sure," Ashly said, getting up. "Just don't touch the word document or PowerPoint I have opened." Samuel sat down and opened the internet browser. A few seconds later, he went to his website. The top of the website's main page had the words "The Complete Guide to Cryptids Across the Globe." In the center a Yeti and Samuel Richards leaned against opposite sides of the words smiling and giving the thumbs up. A thunderbird flew overhead, and the Loch Ness monster swam beneath them.

"Welcome to my website. The Complete Guide to Cryptids Across the Globe. The most accurate and advanced cryptozoological site on earth," Samuel said with pride.

"Your humility is an inspiration to everyone," Ashly said with annoyed sarcasm.

"You're too kind, dear," Samuel replied.

"Back on topic," Okada added. Samuel moved the mouse to the menu bar and selected water cryptids.

"Cryptozoologists have identified eight different species of water cryptids. Based on the information we have, I believe our monster is a mystery saurian." Samuel moved the mouse to mystery saurians and clicked. Several images of giant crocodiles and plesiosaur-looking animals appeared on the screen. Samuel clicked on three different images. The first was a Machimosaurus, a type of marine crocodile. The second was a Tanystropheus, a small plesiosaur-looking dinosaur. The third was a Nothosaur; it looked like a crocodile only with smooth skin, and a head that looked more dinosaur then crocodile. It also had a long neck.

"Out of those three, the Nothosaur is my main suspect," Max said.

"What made you jump to that conclusion?" Samuel asked.

"Fossils show the Tanystropheus was only around six feet, plus the head and neck are two small to be hunting people and ramming ships. I doubt we're dealing with a Machimosaurus because marine crocodiles were ambush predators that hunt close to shore. If our mystery creature was a Machimosaurus, it would be spending quite a bit of time on land."

"What about dinosaurs like the Kronosaurus, or better yet an Elasmosaurus? It had a long neck that could... you know, pull someone from a moving ship," Liz asked.

"First off, Kronosaurus and Elasmosaurus are marine reptiles, not dinosaurs," Max corrected.

"Spare me the details," Liz replied.

"Details are important," Max added. "And the creature we are hunting could not be a Kronosaurus or Elasmosaurus."

"Because of the clawed feet. Those marine reptiles have flippers," Okada pointed out.

"Yes, the claw we found made this investigation so much easier. The Nothosaur has webbed feet, a thick skull, and a thick neck that could theoretically be used to ram ships. The only problem with the Nothosaur theory is the Nothosaur is only ten feet long; however, only one fossil has ever been found." Max added.

"Hold on," Ashly said. "Assuming this is true and we're dealing with a lost species of dinosaur, where has it been hiding all these years? Also, why haven't we had attacks like this occurring throughout history? Doesn't it make more sense that this creature is a mutation caused by radiation or pollution?"

"There have been a few attacks reported throughout history," Samuel replied. "One of the best known is the event that happened to the German U-boat SM UB-85. The U-boat that was sunk by a sea monster."

"I remember my grandfather mentioning that story to me," Okada added.

"What happened to the U-boat?" Liz asked.

Okada motioned to Samuel. "You probably know this story better than I do."

Samuel cleared his throat. "On April thirtieth, 1918, the British warship HMS Coreopsis was on patrol in the North Atlantic. It was midday when it spotted a German U-boat drifting on the water's surface. The U-boat did not try to submerge or fight the approaching British ship. What was even stranger was the Coreopsis found the U-boat's crew standing on deck trying to signal the ship, ready to surrender. Every German was frightened and just wanted to leave the area as soon as possible. Not a single man put up a fight. When the British crew explored the ship, they found all the electrical equipment was shorted out and the U-boats batteries were completely drained. Once everyone was safely on board the Coreopsis, the U-boat captain was interrogated. He claimed that the U-boat had surfaced the night before to recharge the ship's batteries. While the batteries were charging, the captain and some of his men walked on deck, getting some much needed fresh air. The captain stated that one of the men saw a large wake approaching the boat at a high speed. Shortly after, the front of the U-boat was struck and a monster emerged from the ocean. The monster brought its upper body out of the water and rested it on the U-boat. Unfortunately for the Germans, the creature was resting on the forward mounted gun. The captain ordered his crew to fire on the monster with their side arms, which seemed to only anger the monster. Now this is where the story gets strange. During the fight, several crew members started to unexplainably panic, while others started firing at what they called sea spirits flying around the monster. Finally, the creature released its hold on the U-boat and disappeared beneath the waters."

"Did the German captain describe what the creature looked like?" Max asked.

"Yes. He described the creature as an underwater cat that used its long claws to cling to the U-boat. Unfortunately for us, only the upper body of the animal was visible.

"Are you sure this is true?" Ashly asked skeptically, thinking the idea of an underwater cat was ludicrous.

"Every word," Samuel replied.

"What about the head? Did he get a good look at that?" Max asked, knowing the head was one of the most important keys to identifying an animal.

"I was getting to the head," Samuel replied. "He stated the creature had a face that resembled a panther with large horns coming out of the back of the skull."

"This WWI historical website states that the U-boat SM UB-85 began to dive when it noticed the Coreopsis. It was only forced to surface due to a new crew member forgetting to close the tower hatch," Ashly added. "No mention whatsoever of a sea monster." Everyone looked at Samuel. Their faces showed they were beginning to wonder if he was crazy or would just believe anything he heard.

"Yes, yes, that was the official account. No right-minded commander would report a captured U-boat had been disabled by a sea monster," Samuel countered. "Go to the bottom of the page and read the section titled 'other inform ation.'" Ashly scrolled down and placed both hands on the sides of her head.

"When the Coreopsis captain's personal log book was discovered in the early 1970s, it was found he had written that the UB-85 was disabled by a sea monster. Knowing how unbelievable the story was, the captain and the crew came to an agreement that no one would speak of the monster and blame the condition of the U-boat on water damage from an opened hatch."

"Ashly, are there any photos of the incident?" Okada asked. Ashly searched the website for a few moments.

"Yes, two of the German crew and five photos taken inside the U-boat." Ashly turned her laptop so Okada could see. The photos were black and white and not the clearest. He carefully looked over each one. After years of looking over old photos, his eyes had grown used to finding details in even poor quality photos.

"If the account of the ship flooding is true, then why are none of the German crew's clothes wet? The inside of the ship also appears to be dry." Ashly had to admit defeat on this one. She saw what Okada was looking at and knew he was right. There was no way the U-boat flooded. Ashly threw her hands up. Her rational thinking did not want to believe a lost dinosaur was responsible for the attacks, but her teammate's arguments were starting to convince her.

"Okay, playing the skeptic again, but if there is a population of sea monsters living in the oceans, why are people not seeing them more often? Or taking good photographs of them?"

"Those who have are dead," Liz said in a deep, evil voice.

Max gave a more solid answer. "Ninety-five percent of the world's oceans remain unexplored. So, it's possible that a large unknown species could remain hidden." Samuel snapped his finger and pointed at Max.

"Exactly. I find most biologists to be pompous pricks, but you seem to be okay."

"I don't know if I would have believed in sea monsters until a few days ago," Max admitted.

"Okay, you made your points and I can accept them. However, those explanations don't explain the sudden wave of attacks occurring around the Hawaiian Islands. In the past week we have had at least four attacks," Ashly commented.

Max had a theory for this as well. "The creature we are hunting could have been chased from its territory by a larger member of the same species. It could also be a younger or weaker animal that learned to prey on humans as an easy source of food."

"Just like how tigers and bears can become man eaters," Liz said.

"Right," Max complimented. "Many species of known animals can become man eaters. A great example of this is the Tsavo Man-Eaters attacks that occurred in 1898."

"What is the Tsavo Man-Eaters?" Ashly asked.

"The Tsavo Man-Eaters were two lions who killed an estimated one hundred people during a seven-month period," Max answered. "My point is just because several members of a species becomes man eaters does not mean the entire population will hunt humans."

"Okay, for the official report, we're going with the Nothosaur as our best guess. Correct?" Ashly asked, documenting all the important points they covered. Everyone nodded their heads in agreement.

"Ashly, pull up a map of Hawaii and mark the locations where the known attacks have taken place," Okada said. Ashly pulled up a map of the Hawaiian Islands and added markers on all known attack sites. The location marking formed a nearly complete circle around Maui.

"Our mystery saurian seems to like Maui. Max, would you agree we found the creature's hunting ground?" Samuel asked.

"I honestly have no idea," Max replied. "We're dealing with an unknown species. It could be creating a territory around Maui or it could be passing through." Max gently pounded his head in frustration. "There are still so many unknowns at the moment. It's hard to say anything for certain."

"I have an idea I know you'll enjoy, Max," Liz said.

"Let's hear it," Max replied.

"What if we talk to that Mya Kendig girl who survived the Molokini crater attack? I'm sure she can tell us something useful, and you can meet your crush," Liz suggested. Max tossed a ball of paper at her, which she caught.

"It would be a good idea to hear the story from an actual witness," Okada agreed.

"Speaking of the Mya attack, wasn't the Maui police department supposed to send us Jade Kendig's diving gear?" Liz said.

"I thought it arrived last night," Okada answered.

"It's not in Dr. Yamaguchi's lab, and none of his staff have seen it," Max stated.

"I'll go ask Saburo where it is. I want to stretch my legs anyway," Liz said. She placed her hand on Okada's shoulder. "I'm getting a soda; want anything from the vending machine while I'm gone?"

"The usual," Okada replied.

"Anyone else want anything?" Everyone else shook their heads no or said "no thanks."

"Okay, be back in a flash."

"Ashly, can you tell us at what time each attack took place?" Max asked. Ashly skimmed the folder for a moment. A look formed on Samuel's face that said he knew exactly where Max was going with this.

"I don't have exact times, just rough estimates," Ashly replied.

"Just confirm this statement. The Lucky Dragon, hotel, and yacht attacks occurred at night, while Mya's attack occurred in the daytime?" Max asked.

"Yes, that appears accurate," Ashly said. "What are you getting at?"

"The fact that only one attack occurred in the daytime," Samuel added. He looked at Max. "You believe those two girls accidently swam into the creature's layer?"

"Yes, it's possible that the area around Molokini crater is the creature's layer."

"If it was a territorial attack and the creature was not hunting, that would explain why that Mya girl got away," Samuel continued. Ashly added the text "possible monster lair" under Molokini crater.

"Okay, what did I miss?" Liz interrupted. She handed Okada his drink and lightly punched Max on the shoulder.

"We might have found the creature's lair," Max replied.

"Cool," Liz said, sitting down.

"Has the diving equipment arrived?" Okada asked. Liz burst out laughing.

"Sorry. No, it seems to be lost in the mail, and Saburo is not happy about it."

"Any idea when it will get here? I would like to examine it with Dr. Yamaguchi," Max asked. Liz shrugged her shoulders.

"No idea. All I know is Saburo has redirected it to Niihau." Max cursed in annoyance. He was hoping to examine the diving equipment while he was here.

"Well, since you're back, let's discuss how to kill the creature," he continued.

"I'm surprised you're in favor of killing it," Samuel said in a stunned voice. "I thought you would be making an argument to capture and study it."

"I would love to study an unknown animal in its natural environment, but I also know a man eater needs to be put down. The two of us can study the remains once it's dealt with or find another living one," Max replied.

Samuel was about to speak when Ashly shouted in satisfied excitement, "Okay, that's done!"

"What is?" Liz asked.

"The personal matter I was working on," Ashly replied, relaxing in her chair. "Now that it's finished, my life will be a little easier." She quickly sat up straight and got back on topic. "Okay, sorry for asking what some may find an obvious question, but this has been bothering me since I got here. Why do we need to destroy this creature? Why not just use the American or Japanese Navy?"

"The sight of Japanese subs and destroyers sailing around the Hawaiian Islands firing guns may alarm some people," Liz said.

"That, and Japan cannot conduct offensive military operations," Okada answered. "When it comes to the American Navy, I doubt they will want to conduct destructive naval operations in United States waters."

"Plus, it would ruin the tourist industry," Liz remarked.

"Enough," Okada ordered.

"Wait, I thought the American government was working with us and willing to give us any support we needed," Ashly commented.

"The Americans are assisting us in investigating the destruction of the Lucky Dragon. Asking for material aid is very different than asking them to conduct military operations," Okada explained.

"We do have seven attack dolphins. Maybe we should finally turn them loose," Liz suggested.

"I thought about that, but I don't think they're ready to complete a hunt and kill mission yet," Max replied.

"Every one of our dolphins has completed every training program we put them through," Liz countered.

"Patrolling a small area in a controlled environment." Max turned so he was facing only Liz. "As you know, we have only conducted the more advanced hunt and kill tests several times. With mixed results. Before we turn a group of attack dolphins loose in populated waters, I would like to conduct more tests and see them continually following commands."

"If we need to use them, can we?" Okada asked.

Max thought about it for a moment until he reluctantly said, "Yes, provided the snout mounted hypodermic lances can be built."

"What are those?" Ashly asked curiously.

"In simple terms, large needles with small amounts of C-4 explosives inside them are mounted to the dolphin's snout. The dolphins ram the target. The needle enters the target and the explosive is pushed inside the target's body. The force of the impact activates a detonator and five seconds later, boom!" Liz answered.

"What about underwater mines?" Ashly added.

"Darling, we just discussed the Navy cannot conduct destructive naval operations," Samuel replied.

"I know that, and don't call me darling," Ashly snapped back.

"What did you have in mind, Ashly?" Okada asked.

"I was thinking the Navy could give us small underwater mines that we rig with remote detonators that we can control from a ship. That way we can explode them when we want. The mines would be no danger to passing ships and the explosion would be small enough nobody will know anything unusual is going on."

"I honestly like that idea the best," Max commented.

"What? I thought you would want to use some sort of poisoned bait," Ashly commented. Max laughed a little.

"No way. First, we don't know what type of poison would affect this creature or how much we would need. Second, the poison bait could be eaten by native wildlife or leak out and contaminate the local ecosystem."

"Anyone else have anything to add?" Okada asked. Nobody said anything and everyone seemed satisfied.

Liz put her head on the table and said in a worn-out voice, "Thank God we're nearly done. Creating reports are so boring."

"It's not that bad. I love creating reports," Ashly said. Everyone looked up when Saburo entered the room.

"Hello, everyone. How's the brainstorming going?"

"Great! We came to a conclusion for both problems and are just finished up the final report," Ashly said proudly.

"That's wonderful to hear," Saburo said. He reached inside his business jacket and pulled out an envelope. "I have your plane tickets. Your flight leaves tomorrow at eight p.m." Saburo handed Max, Ashly, Liz, and Okada first class tickets. When he got to Samuel, he frowned slightly. "I'm afraid there was an error with your ticket. When I printed them, the airlines had you sitting in a middle seat back in the economy class."

"Wait, what! I'm an important person. I cannot be seen sitting in coach," Samuel said in a worried voice. "Just change the ticket back to first class!"

"Unfortunately, I cannot. When I tried, the airline was completely full."

Ashly laid her elbow on the table and placed her hand over her mouth to hide her evil grin.

Just wait till you get on the plane; it will only get worse, she thought.

CHAPTER 16

8:17 PM 4/12/2021 HST

Rain poured over the Maui waters. Keoni and his three high school friends Alanna, Elijah, and Sophia were traveling from Maui to Molokai. Keoni and Alanna were Hawaiian natives. Elijah had moved from California when he was five; since then, he had grown used to the area.

Sophia had only moved to Maui the previous year from Maine, and was having a hard time adjusting to the new climate and atmosphere the island life offered. She loved the year-round pleasant weather, but also missed the changing seasons. Elijah had grown fond of the new girl in school and invited her on the beach trip. The four friends planned to have a double date on Kumimi Beach.

Keoni had the idea of making the seven-mile journey in his wooden row boat. Keoni's father was a boat builder by trade. Last year he helped Keoni create a small glass bottom for the row boat. Keoni knew since it was a full moon, the bioluminescence bobtail squid would be shining brightly tonight. He hoped this would give the journey a more exciting and romantic feel. A quarter of the way through the trip was nothing like he had planned. What was supposed to be a clear, pleasant night had turned out to be a miserable, raining day. It had been raining moderately hard since they started their journey. Luckily the four of them had prepared for unexpected weather and brought rain jackets. So, despite the unpleasant conditions, the four friends decided to press on, hoping the storm would end soon. The sea had some rough waves but nothing dangerous. While he paddled, Keoni looked at the GPS on his phone.

"Good thing we don't need the stars to navigate," he said, trying to cheer the group up.

"How long until we reach Kumimi Beach?" Alanna asked, resting her head on Keoni's shoulder. She tried to hide the misery in her voice, but the continual beating of cold raindrops on her coat was really starting to get to her. The rain jacket kept her dry, but not warm.

"A little over an hour," Keoni replied. Elijah looked down into the boat's glass bottom. He looked up at Sophia, who was sitting up straight with her eyes closed. As she listened to the rain, she imagined she was in a boat back home on Webb Lake.

"You still with us, Sophia?" he asked.

"Yes," she said, opening her eyes. "I was just thinking of home."

"Did it rain a lot in Maine?" Keoni asked.

"Yes, rain in the summer, snow in the winter," Sophia answered.

"I've only seen snow a few times on top of Haleakalā volcano," Keoni replied.

"I remember the time you and I hiked up there to see it. It was cold and wet," Alanna added. She turned to Sophie. "How much snow did you get in Maine?"

"Around seven feet every winter." Keoni and Alanna could not believe what they just heard.

"I'm never visiting Maine," Alanna said.

"Hey, let's play a game," Elijah suggested to Sophia.

"What kind?" Sophia asked. Elijah placed his hand on her back.

"Let's look through the boat's beautiful glass bottom and see what type of sea life we can see in the sea," he replied, trying to sound poetic. A slight feeling of uneasiness came over Sophia when he started rubbing his hand up and down her back. This was her first time out with him, and she did not know how she felt about him yet. However, she liked the fact that someone had taken an interest in her, so she tolerated it, and soon found herself enjoying it.

"It's dark. We're not going to be able to see anything," Sophia replied, pointing at the dark water.

"You might be able to see bobtailed squid," Keoni stated. "At night they glow a faint blue. It's very pretty, very romantic."

"Okay, let's play 'spot the bobtail squid.' What does the winner get?" Sophie asked.

"The loser has to be the winner's servant for the beach trip," Elijah replied.

"It will be nice to have a beach servant. Let's play," Alanna added, inviting herself to the game.

"I'll row the boat while you kids play," Keoni said. For a while they saw nothing, but concentrating on the ocean helped lessen the unpleasant feeling brought by the rain. Sophia noticed a blue light in the water.

"Called it," Sophia said, smiling as the bobtailed squid came into view. "Oh, look, more," she continued, spotting three more. Keoni stopped paddling. Feelings of excitement filled the four friends as they watched the squid's mystical blue lights dance around as the squid hunted shrimp. The smile left Sophia's face when she noticed something swimming under the squid. The faint bioluminescence light coming from the squid only showed a faint outline of what she thought was the back and possibly the tail of a large creature.

"Guys, something else is down there," she yelled, a little startled.

"What? I don't see anything?" Alanna said.

"It's pitch black down there. Your eyes were just playing tricks on you," Elijah assured. Sophia looked again and saw nothing but blackness.

"You're right. It was probably just a fish," she agreed. Their attention turned back to the squid only to realize they were gone.

"Where'd they go?" Elijah wondered. He reached into his backpack and grabbed a flashlight.

"What are you doing?" Alanna wondered.

"Trying to attract the squid back." He looked at Sophie and shined the light on himself. "Your hero will bring the squid back," he said in a mystic voice. She pushed him into his seat. Elijah placed the flashlight beam against the glass and started moving it around. The two girls looked down, hoping Elijah's plan would work. Suddenly, the end of the light beam caught the shine of two eyes rapidly swimming towards the surface. Elijah screamed and pulled the flashlight up. Abruptly, the boat was struck hard from below. The impact broke the small boat apart, sending it flying several feet into the air. The four friends plunged into the ocean. Keoni broke the surface, gasping in shock. He tried to get his bearings as broken pieces of the boat fell into the water around him. Alanna soon came up a few feet in from him.

"What happened?" she cried.

"I don't know. Look for Elijah and Sophia." The two scanned the area around them. Alanna spotted Sophia emerge several yards to the left of them. She swam for a large fragment of wood. After grabbing on to it, she cried out in shock.

"Hello, is anybody there?"

"Sophia, we're over here," Keoni yelled, waving his hands up and down. "We're coming over to you," he said, noticing the bit of wreckage was large enough to hold all three of them.

"Is Elijah with you?" Sophia asked.

"No," Alanna replied. Sophia called out for Elijah, hoping her friend would answer. Her calls turned into a scream when a sharp pain filled both her legs just above the knees. It felt like numerous knives were piercing her skin. Amongst her screams of pain, she managed to cry out in horror.

"Something has my legs!" She felt both her kneecaps break as she was pulled under the water. Keoni and Alanna both stopped swimming.

"What happened to her? What happened to her?" Alanna asked in a panic. Keoni paused for a moment, but he knew he needed to tell her the truth.

"Alanna, I'm not going to lie. We're in the water with a shark!" Keoni stressed. He reached to the side of his pants and removed the bowie knife from its holster.

"What do we do?" Alanna asked in a tearful panic. Keoni looked in the direction opposite to where Sophia had gone under. He spotted another larger piece of wreckage. A piece large enough to climb up on.

"Swim for that bit of wreckage! Try to get on!" he said, pointing towards it. The two friends swam for the wreckage. Keoni figured they were safe since the shark had most likely swam off or was still feeding on Sophia's remains. When they reached the piece of floating wreckage, Keoni pushed Alanna onto it. He began to hoist himself onto the wreckage when his foot was struck by something. He spun his arm around and thrust the knife into the water. He felt the knife dig into living tissue. The knife was ripped from his hand when the animal fled the area. "I hit it. Whatever it was is gone," he said, proud of himself.

"Hurry! Get up here!" Alanna begged, reaching out her hand. Keoni grabbed it. She started to pull him up when she heard the sound of thunder. Instinctively she looked up, and then she heard Kenoni scream. He looked down to see him covering his left ear with his free hand.

"My ears!" he cried in pain. Alanna tried to hold on to him, but he was fighting her, wanting to get his right hand to his ear. She noticed a stream of blood starting to pour from his uncovered ear. Keoni began to fall backwards as he coughed up blood.

"What's happening?" she whispered to herself. She felt his wet hand slipping from her palm. Alanna closed her eyes and pulled with all the strength she had. Keoni's dead weight soon became too much for her. She felt his hand slip though hers. She watched helplessly as Keoni fell back into the water. Alanna wanted to jump in after him, but the fear that filled her body would not let her enter the water. Tears filled her eyes when she saw Keoni's body disappear under a wave. She waited and waited, but he never came up. Alanna broke down. Thoughts started to fill her head. Was the shark still in the area? What if a wave knocked her into the water? Almost like the ocean heard her thoughts, a large wave struck the wreckage, sending it bouncing up and down. Alanna grabbed on to the sides of the wreckage, struggling to stay on. When the wreckage stabilized, she sobbed in frustration.

"What did I do to deserve this? How long am I going to be stuck out here?" Her face lit up when she heard a splash break the surface of the water. "Keoni!" she cried. Regrettably, it was not Keoni that had surfaced. What came up from the depths paralyzed her body. The outline of the head and back of a large creature was right in front of her. The creature opened its mouth. The rain washed the fresh blood from the animal's teeth, sending it down on Alanna, who could not move or even scream. She closed her eyes as the head slowly came down biting her body in half.

***

Saburo lay back in the easy chair in his private quarters. Being Okada's personal assistant meant he needed to be available at all times during work days. He lived at the military complex during the work week and spent time with his wife Fumi and his eight-year-old son, Ichiro, on weekends. Saburo was enjoying a plate of omurice when his tablet pinged a notification. When he saw the message was from the Hawaiian coast guard with a link to a news article, he put down his plate and opened it. The heading of the message read: "Search for Four Missing High School Students Continues." After reading down a few paragraphs, he leaped from his chair and headed for the door. He turned around to grab his suit jacket, then headed for the commander's office. Saburo knocked on the door and entered. When he saw the room was empty, he called Okada. Okada was at the prime minister's office meeting with several military officers and Japanese government officials. Okada momentarily excused himself from the room when he got the call.

"Commander, sorry to disturb you, but there has been another attack. This time in the waters that separates the islands of Maui and Molokai."

"How many are dead?" Okada asked, knowing the likelihood of survivors was slim.

"Four high school students. A pleasure boat spotted the wreckage of the student's boat several hours ago. The Hawaiian coast guard and Maui police force are searching the area." Okada placed his hands together. He remained silent as he thought.

"I'm going to recommend to the Prime Minister that he issue a statement encouraging our citizens not to vacation in Hawaii at this time."

"I agree with that recommendation," Saburo said.

"Now I must go; the men inside are waiting for me."

"Understood, sir, goodbye," he said, hanging up. After dinner, Saburo arranged meeting times for matters he could handle personally. He was about to leave Okada's office when Okada's secretary peered through the door.

"Hello," Saburo said. "I'm afraid the commander will be away for some time. Is there any way I can help you?"

"A large package marked urgent material has just arrived from Maui Hawaii." Saburo slammed the table in frustration.

"I ordered the mail service to ship that package to Niihau!" Saburo pulled out his phone, then he looked at the time. "No, I can't have someone come back and pick it up." He looked at the secretary. "Have that package sent to Niihau at once, and tell the postal service this time without delays!"

CHAPTER 17

10:25 AM 4/13/2021 HST

Mya Kendig sat in the front row of seats arranged at the Makena Church Cemetery listening to the pastor's eulogy. Her eyes moved towards her parents, who were sitting next to her. They had not spoken to her since they arrived on Maui the previous night, and brushed her off at the start of the eulogy, which worried her. She saw the continuous glare her mother held in her direction. She just focused on the images of Jade in front of the empty casket and listened. Now was not the time to get into an argument. When the eulogy was over, Mya placed a pink plumeria on Jade's casket.

"I miss you so much. I'm so sorry I couldn't do anything to save you." Mya stood near the casket for a few minutes, looking at the picture displays. As she stared, relatives she was not close with and Jade's friends gave their condolences to her. When she turned around, she saw most of the guests were starting to leave the graveyard. She saw her parents driving off in their rental car. "Great," Mya said to herself. She knew what it meant; they blamed her for Jade's death. The "favorite," the one who had a successful career. *Hopefully things improve at the reception,* she thought.

The reception was held at a local church several hours later. Mya stared at the gaudy decoration and fancy food. Classical music played in the background. Jade would have hated this, she thought. She knew who arranged it, as her mother had insisted on handling the reception herself. She saw her parents sitting at the head table, and she figured she should go over and say something. Maybe they were just upset she didn't say anything to them at the funeral. Mya walked over and sat down.

"Hi," she said softly. "How was your flight?" she asked, wanting to start a conversation.

"Hi, Mya," her father said casually.

"What do you want, Mya?" her Mom said bitterly.

"I wanted to come over and see how you were doing. I know how hard Jade's death must be affecting you." Her mom didn't respond, instead pulling out her phone and starting to use it.

"Mya, maybe it's better if you leave," her father suggested.

Almost in tears, Mya said, "Mom, what did I do? Why are you angry with me?"

"You know exactly what you did," her mother replied, not even looking at her.

"No, I don't," Mya replied, starting to break down.

Finally, her mother looked up at her and said in a voice filled with distaste, "You used your sister's death as a publicity stunt to further your ridiculous cosplay occupation. Telling the news a sea monster was the cause of Jade's death. You're milking it for all it's worth, aren't you?" Mya was speechless; she couldn't believe her mom could even imagine accusing her of something like that. She looked to her father for comfort, but he had the same cold look her mother did. Before she could say anything, her mom said, "I don't know why you're upset. Jade left you everything: the house, car, and a two hundred thousand dollar life insurance policy."

"I miss my sister; that's why. I'd give up everything if it meant bringing Jade back!" Mya replied loudly but not loud enough to cause a scene. "And I didn't say a saw a sea monster to further anything. I said it because it happened. At this point, I don't care about money or my job."

Her mother cut her off. "We've known that for a while. Always having to live off someone. We had to lose the good daughter."

Mya put her head down, trying her best to hold back the tears.

"If you feel that way, why don't you just slap me in the face?" Mya said sarcastically. Mya felt a palm connect with her cheek. Mya gasped, not believing what just happened. Saying nothing, her mother and, shortly after, her father got up. Heartbroken, Mya ran out of the reception area. She found a lone bench out of sight of the reception area. She sat down and stared crying her eyes out. She didn't know how much time had passed before she heard a voice.

"Hey, are you okay?" She looked up to see a tall blonde girl standing near the bench.

"No, my life is falling apart," she said, sobbing.

"That sucks, girl. Any way I can help?" Riley asked sitting at the other end of the bench. "Wait, you're Jade's sister Mya. I'm Riley Sandall." Riley was a slim tanned beauty. She was 5'10" with long dirty blond hair.

"How do you know me?" Mya asked, just wanting to be left alone in her misery.

"Jade talked about you all the time. Called you her sister from the fantasy land. Last time I saw her, all she talked about was how excited she was her sister was coming to visit for a week." Hearing that made a brief smile form on Mya's face. "Look, I know I'm a stranger to you, but if you need to vent, I have an open ear and a closed mouth," Riley offered, seeing Mya was holding a lot inside. Mya snickered.

"How did you get to know Jade?" Mya asked, trying to take her mind off what happened with her parents.

"Me and the guy I was dating at the time decided to take some scuba lessons. Jade was our instructor. As fate would have it, we broke up shortly after the first lesson; then one day, Jade stopped by the gaming café I work at." A surprised look formed on Mya's face.

"Jade went to a gaming café?" Mya asked, cutting Riley off. Mya didn't know why but she already felt comfortable around Riley.

"She liked the special types of coffee we have. She never played any games. I was waiting on her and she remembered me. We got to talking and eventually became friends." A hurt look returned to Mya's face. "Mya, if you want to be alone for a while, I can leave," Riley offered.

"No, it's not you. I remember Jade telling me after the dive we were going to stop at a café. She said I would be in heaven there."

"Mya, sorry, I know this is none of my business, but you would probably feel a lot better if you were at the reception with your family," Riley suggested.

"That's why I'm out here," Mya huffed. "My parents blame me for Jade's death; they hate me. Jade was always the favorite. I was just the second child."

"Mya, I highly doubt that. Why don't you go talk to them?" Mya stood up with a look of hurt anger. Riley wondered if she had made a mistake by suggesting that.

"I tried. I thought I would get some comfort from my parents, but all they did was accuse me of profiting from Jade's death." Mya turned her cheek, showing a small bruise starting to form. "Then my mother slapped me."

"Girl, you can't be serious," Riley replied with a look of pity. Mya shook her head yes. Riley gave her a hug, which to her surprise made her feel better. Riley had a vibe about her that made people feel good.

"Thank you." Mya said feeling better. "I'd better get going."

"You might want to see this," Riley said, walking towards the reception area.

"Riley, what are you doing?" Mya asked. Riley's look of conflict told her she was up to something. Wanting to see what she was up to, Mya followed Riley back to the reception.

Riley picked up a glass of wine and said, "Stay back. I don't want this to blow back on you." Mya watched, concerned, as Riley walked over to her parents who were standing near the refreshments, and started a conversation. Mya tried to listen in but couldn't tell what they were saying. Suddenly she saw Riley throw the wine in her mother's face. Her father tried to grab Riley, but she gracefully moved out of the way, sending him crashing into trays of food. Riley said something else, before picking up two cupcakes. Mya placed a hand over her mouth. At first she wanted to scold Riley for her actions but as the seconds went by, the more she felt they deserved what happened. Her eyes were wide as Riley made her way through the crowd of shocked people. She handed Mya a cupcake.

"I can't believe you did that," Mya said, shocked. "No one hurts my friends and gets away with it. Want to get out of here?"

"We'd better," Mya replied.

After they exited the building, Mya said, "I'm going to head to." She paused. "To Jade's house. I need to clear my head."

"Okay, girl. I'm going to head home as well."

"It was nice meeting you, and thank you for sticking up for me. I mean it."

"No trouble." Riley pulled out her phone. "Let's exchange numbers. What's your cell?" Mya gave Riley hers and Riley sent a text that said *here's mine*. "When you feel up to it, let's go to dinner or something."

"Sounds good," Mya replied, getting into her car.

When Mya got home, she changed into jeans and a purple tank top, then went right to her gaming laptop and spent hours playing her favorite game, Legendary Quests and Creatures, killing every sea monster she could find. The gaming world was only a temporary escape from her pain.

It was now late afternoon. Mya sat at her kitchen island with a hand to her cheek, staring into space and thinking about what her mother had said.

"If only we didn't go diving," she said softly. Deep down, she knew Jade's death was not her fault, but she also knew Jade would still be alive if she had stayed in San Diego. She was so deep in thought, the ringing of the doorbell made her jump. "Who could that be?" she wondered, getting up to answer the door.

"Surprise," Riley said, holding up two plastic bags of food. She was wearing tight jean shorts and a sports jersey that said "Princess" on the back.

"Uh, hi, Riley. How did you find out where I live?" Mya asked, confused.

"I was friends with Jade, remember?" Mya pointed to the bags, still confused. "Anyway, I knew you were down, so I brought some Chinese." Mya smiled, pleasantly surprised.

"Riley, you didn't have to do that."

"No trouble at all, girl. If you want to be alone, totally understandable. I'll just give you half and be on my way."

"No, please come in. It will be nice to have some company." Mya stepped aside and let Riley in.

"Where do you want the food?" Riley asked.

"Put it on the table in the living room. We can watch TV while we eat." Riley laid the food on the table while Mya brought plates and glasses over. "What do you want to drink?" Mya asked.

"Girl, don't worry, I got that covered," Riley assured. She smiled as she pulled out a bottle of red wine. "I have tomorrow off, so let's get wasted and forget about our troubles."

"I could use a night like that," Mya agreed, sitting down. "By the way, how much do I owe you for the food?"

"Dinner's on me tonight. You can pay next time," Riley answered. "Oh, speaking of work, if you're interested, the gaming café is hiring. If you want, I can get you a job."

"I'll seriously consider it," Mya replied as Riley poured her a glass of wine. Mya took a long sip and lay back on the couch.

"Mya, just putting it out there: anytime you want to cut our night short, just say so and I'm gone with no hard feelings."

"No, it's fine. Having fun will keep my mind off everything," Mya replied, then said sadly, "I'm hoping now that the funeral's over, I can start the healing process. I just, I just won't ever feel safe in the ocean or be able to fully heal until that thing that killed Jade is dead."

"The authorities will get it. Don't worry," Riley said confidently. She chose not to say "shark," because she had heard the sea monster story and knew Mya believed it.

"The authorities don't know anything. I tried telling people what happened, and all I got was made fun of." Mya clenched her fists and bit down on her lip. "That monster is going to get off scot-free."

CHAPTER 18

Ashly and Samuel waited in the customs line at Honolulu International Airport on Oahu. Okada was in the international line. Liz and Max, due to their military status, were able to get through the line quickly, so they went ahead to the airstrip to prepare the X-7 for takeoff. Samuel stared at Ashly, who was entertaining herself by popping gum. He wanted more than anything to burst one of those bubbles in her face. He was absolutely furious. During the flight he was seated between two massively overweight people. When he walked up to first class to check for seats, despite the airline claiming every first class ticket was purchased, he counted seven empty ones. When he tried to sit in a first class seat, he was told he could not due to already paying for a seat in coach. He did not know how she did it, but he knew Ashly was somehow responsible for it. A feeling of nervousness came over Samuel as they approached the automated passport control machine. He just knew something bad was going to happen.

"Why do you look so nervous?" Ashly asked.

"I know what you did on the plane," he replied. Ashly gave him a confused look.

"What did I do? I was in first class the entire flight." She was sure to say "first class" a little slowly to rub it in.

Samuel raised his voice. "Somehow you intentionally sabotaged my plane ticket! That was the personal project you were working on in Japan."

"I have no idea what you're talking about," Ashly said innocently. She placed her passport in the machine. After getting through, she turned to Samuel and said, "I'll meet you in the baggage collection area." Samuel nervously placed his passport into the machine. He was just waiting for the machine to reject it, or worse, alarms to start going off. To his surprise, the machine accepted it. He sighed with relief and entered the airport's main terminal.

***

Liz backed a hydrant fuel dispenser truck up to the X-7. The airport staff had already delivered the team's luggage on a cart that was sitting next to the helicopter. Max attached a large black hose to the airport's underground fuel pipe. Since they frequently were using Honolulu International Airport as a refueling station, Okada had purchased a rental hangar and fuel truck for the X-7.

"Ready down here," Max said. Liz attached a smaller hose to the X-7 and started pumping the fuel.

"Max, since we're going to be here for a while, why don't you call your darling Mya and set up a meeting time."

"Samuel or I will when we get back to Niihau," Max replied. "Want me to park the fuel truck when we're done?" He continued, wanting to get Liz's mind off the current subject.

"Don't try to change the subject," Liz caught on. "Okada wants this done sooner rather than later, so get over your crush fear and call her!"

"Fine," Max reluctantly agreed. He walked away from the fuel truck and pulled out his phone. During the flight from Japan, Ashly had tracked down Mya's number and sent it to him.

"Put the call on speaker," Liz said.

"Why!" Max asked. Liz started to speak in a sarcastic love tone.

"Well, when someone is talking to a crush for the first time, they tend to get nervous. I wouldn't want you to miss something important when you're not thinking straight."

"Sometimes I just want to tape your mouth shut," Max replied. He was already uneasy about the situation. As much as he tried to hide it, he did have a slight crush on Mya, and reading the information about her Ashly had tracked down had made the feeling stronger.

"You can try," Liz replied. With lightning-fast speed, she hit the speaker and call button on his phone.

"Liz!" Max yelled, walking farther from the X-7 to get away from the noise.

***

Mya and Riley were watching TV, laughing hysterically. The glasses of wine they had drunk made the movie even funnier. Mya was still sober and could tell Riley was having a little too much to drink.

"Maybe you should slow down a bit," Mya suggested as she watched Riley down another glass of wine.

"Do me a favor and call Uber when this is over," Riley replied.

"Just crash on the couch," Mya offered. She heard her cell phone ringing and picked it up.

"Wonder who this is?" she said out loud, not recognizing the number. She set the wine glass down. "Hello," she said, expecting it to be a salesman.

"Hi, is this Mya Kendig?"

"Yes, who's calling?"

"Hi, my name's Max Varian, I'm a biologist with the Niihau wildlife center." The feeling of enjoyment Mya was feeling left her, replaced by feeling of bitter cold. She knew what this was about.

"What do you want?" Mya asked in a low cold voice.

"She's mad. Say something nice," Liz suggested.

Max thought quickly. "First off, I wanted to say sorry for your loss."

"Thanks, can you get to the point?" Mya replied. Max pulled away from Liz. She was not helping the situation, and neither was her advice.

"I heard that you may have had an encounter with an unknown species. I was wondering if you would be willing to share your experience so I can get a better understanding of what you saw and help you identify it." Max knew that sounded stupid, but it's all he could come up with in the heat of the moment.

"No, I'm not willing to share anything!" Mya yelled. "I made that mistake at the hospital and with the local police! You already know you're looking for a shark! I'm just the crazy girl that saw a sea monster remember! Don't call me again!" Mya screamed and hung up.

"Girl, remind me to never say the S-M word in front of you," Riley said, surprised by Mya's sudden mood change.

"Sorry for the outburst," Mya apologized.

"You didn't do anything to me," she replied, offering Mya some more wine, which she gladly accepted.

***

"Way to go," Max said to Liz.

"Me? What did I do?" she asked.

"You force me into this before I could think of what to say." Liz knew he was right, but how was she supposed to know Mya would respond like that?

"Why is the X-7 left unattended while refueling?" Okada asked.

"Aw, shoot!" Liz said, rushing back to it.

"We tried to call Mya Kendig and it didn't go well," Max said as he and Okada joined Liz.

"You mean Liz talked you into calling her," Okada said, knowing his girlfriend well. Max slightly shook his head yes.

"Liz, don't push your teammates to complete tasks if they're unprepared," Okada scolded. "This was neither the time nor the place for that type of conversation." He turned to Max. "And you don't give into temptation or peer pressure." Max and Liz took the criticism; they knew he was right.

"On the bright side, the chopper's ready to fly," Liz said. Max and Okada had to smile at that. Liz always had a way to brighten bad situations.

"Any new information on the most recent attack?" Max asked.

"Yes, I'll show you the full report when we get back to base, and apparently the diving equipment was shipped to the defense complex," Okada added. Liz put her face in her hands and started laughing. Okada glanced at her and shook his head, not understanding why she found the situation funny. "Saburo is resending it to Niihau. It should arrive tomorrow."

"It *should arrive*," Liz added, making air quotes.

"Oh my gosh, is that an X-7?" Ashly yelled. She dropped her carry-on bag and ran up to the helicopter. Samuel walked behind her, not nearly as impressed as his teammate.

"Yes, it's the fastest way to Island hop," Liz added. Max watched Ashly's face glow as she walked around the X-7, admiring every detail.

"I thought this was an experimental hybrid helicopter. How did you get this?" Ashly asked in a starstruck voice.

"It pays to know the right people," Liz replied.

"What's so special about this bird?" Samuel asked, not understanding what had Ashly so mesmerized.

"It's only the fastest helicopter in the world," Ashly replied in a giddy voice. "Its top speed is two hundred and ninety-three miles per hour."

"We can reach Niihau in less than an hour," Max added.

"We have a lot of work ahead of us. Let's get going," Okada ordered.

"Please, please can I ride up front?" Ashly begged.

"Go for it; just don't forget your bag," Liz said, pointing towards it. Ashly grabbed it and jumped into the front passenger seat. Liz turned to Max.

"Who's flying?"

"Rock, paper, scissors?" Max suggested. Liz agreed and lost. Max climbed into the cockpit next to a wide-smiling Ashly. The others tossed the luggage into the chopper's bottom compartment and climbed in. Max started the engine and lifted off. Ashly giggled with excitement when the chopper reached full speed. Max hardly noticed her excitement. His thoughts were on the creature. A fifth attack had just occurred, and he knew it was not going to be the last.

CHAPTER 19

10:33 PM 04/13/2021 HST

Mya turned the TV off and tossed a half-eaten pint of ice cream in the freezer. She was much more sober then Riley, only drinking about one fourth of the wine bottle. The empty wine bottle and empty Chinese food cartons were spread across the table. Riley lay on the couch, nearly asleep.

"You sure you don't mind if I spend the night?" Riley asked in a groggy voice.

"It's fine," Mya assured.

"I'll help you clean up at least." Riley grabbed some food cartons and got up. She immediately started stumbling.

"Riley!" Mya yelled, rushing over to her. "Just lay down. You're too drunk to move. I don't need you falling or throwing up over my carpet."

"You're probably right. The world's spinning in circles," Riley replied in a dazed voice. Mya walked over to the storage closet.

"Okay, here's a pillow and blanket. Do you need to use the bathroom before I go to bed?"

"No. Goodnight," Riley replied. She hugged the pillow and rested her head on the arm of the couch. Mya laughed, rolled her eyes, and shut off the light. She walked into Jade's bedroom and stared at the bed. It was hers now, but the thought of sleeping in it still felt so wrong. She knew she had to get over this feeling of guilt, which is why she was happy Riley was spending the night. That took the couch away as a sleeping option. Mya turned off the room light and moved to the side of the bed facing the wall. She closed her eyes and imagined Jade was sleeping next to her. Their friend Riley had spent the night, which is why they needed to share a bed.

"Goodnight, Jade," she said quietly. In her mind she could hear Jade softly breathing next to her as she drifted off to sleep.

***

The next morning, Mya woke up to the faint smell of cooking eggs. She walked out to the kitchen to find toast and orange juice sitting on the kitchen island.

"Morning. Hope you like egg whites," Riley said.

"Riley, you're a guest; you didn't have to do this." Riley shrugged her shoulders as she placed the egg whites on the table.

"Hey, you let me spend the night. The least I could do was make breakfast." Mya and Riley both sat down.

"Riley, last night I was thinking, if the job at the gaming café is still available, I would like to take it."

"You sure?" Riley asked. "Because at the reception I heard rumors that you're not going to be short on cash for a while."

"You're right that I don't need money. I just want something to occupy my time until I can find places to cosplay around here."

"Okay. If you want, we can talk to the owners later today. They will like the fact you're willing to work for free." Mya tossed a bit of toast at Riley.

"I never said that," she teased. Riley's phone vibrated. Mya went back to eating while Riley checked it. A wide smile formed on her face as she read the email.

"What?" Mya asked curiously.

"I just got my ticket for the Maui Diving Experience submarine tour!" Riley replied in excitement. The happy expression left Mya's face.

"What's that?" she asked. Riley did not notice the concern in her friend's voice. She was still glued to the phone.

"It's a submarine tour around Maui. I've been saving for months to go on one."

"Does it... Does it go by Molokini Crater?" Mya asked nervously.

"Yeah! The sub actually stops at the crater and serves passengers dinner on it." Riley put the phone up to Mya's face. "See, here's the path the sub makes and all the sites I'm going to see." Her excited expression changed when she saw the look on Mya's face.

"Mya, I'm sorry; I forgot," Riley said with regret, knowing she must have flooded Mya's mind with bad memories.

Mya reached out and squeezed Riley's arm with a sweat-covered palm, then said in a voice filled with fear, "Riley, you can't go in that water. Not until that thing is dead."

"Mya I'm not going scuba diving. I'm going to be in a large submarine. No sea creature would attack a sub," Riley said in a gentle voice filled with confidence.

"Riley, come here," Mya said. Riley followed Mya into the room that used to be Jade's office. A large map of the waters around Maui was pinned to the wall. Several tacks were placed on the map. Below the map were copies of internet articles and photos of different prehistoric marine reptiles.

"Um, what is this?" Riley asked, trying not to scoff at what she was seeing. Mya stood next to the map.

"Since the attack, I've looked up every sea monster sighting or strange sea disaster around Maui." Mya pointed to the four different tacks on the board. "During the past month, four unexplained disasters have occurred around Maui." Mya's arm moved down to the articles. "In total, nine different people have disappeared." A gradual sadness formed in her voice when she said, "Including Jade." Riley tried her hardest to keep a straight face, but Mya could see the disbelief on it. "Riley, just admit it. You don't believe me and think I'm going off the deep end." Mya was disappointed, but not surprised. If the situation were reversed, she probably would be thinking the same thing. Riley moved her tongue to the roof of her mouth as she thought about what to say.

"I...I believe you saw something, but I don't think it was one of those," Riley said, pointing to the photo of a kronosaurus. Mya crossed her arms and asked in an annoyed voice, "Well, what was it then? A shark? A hallucination made up by a girl suffering from shock?"

"Mya, I don't think you're crazy," Riley replied. "Do you want to know what I think you saw?" Mya shook her head yes.

"An escaped crocodile."

"What? How is that possible?" Mya asked.

"Some people get exotic animals as pets and release them when they get too big," Riley replied. A fun smile formed on her face as she tried to lighten the mood. "Just last month a tiger was running around the island."

"That does make some sense." Mya agreed. She was still unconvinced she saw a crocodile, but she supposed it could have been possible.

"Mya, you said you wanted to check out the gaming café. Why don't we head out now? Along the way I can give you a tour of the island and show you the best places to shop and eat," Riley suggested, hoping it would get Mya's mind off the sea monster and break the tension in the room.

"Sure. That sounds fun," Mya replied. She turned to the map, noticing how stupid it must look to Riley. She turned back to her and said, "I'll tear this down eventually. It's just my way of dealing with the situation."

"Girl, totally understandable. Now let's go have some fun!"

CHAPTER 20

On Niihau, Max and Liz were helping Samuel and Ashly get their private quarters in order. The two guest rooms were converted into temporary living spaces. A majority of the morning had been spent moving the bunk beds to storage and carrying in new furniture. One of the bunk beds had been disassembled and used for Samuel and Ashly's personal beds. Max helped Ashly move two tables into the position she wanted. The tables were set up to flank both sides of her desk.

"Thanks. Now I just need to set up my equipment and I'm set," Ashly said. She sat down in the middle of the H-shaped structure. She loved having all her equipment within arm's reach.

"Do you want help setting up your computer equipment?" Max offered.

"No, thanks. I kind of like to set up any electronic equipment myself. It's just a personal thing I have," Ashly replied, shrugging her shoulders.

"Hey, I'm not offended," Max replied.

"Go see if Samuel is still complaining to Okada about the sheets," Ashly said in a half-joking, half-annoyed voice. When they arrived the night before, Samuel had made a big fuss about the bed sheets not being the right brand. He needed the aristocrat brand for pure comfort and a restful sleep. That same night Liz had scared Ashly nearly to death when she told her there was only one guest room and she would be sharing it with Samuel. Max started to leave when the sound of an approaching chopper filled the room.

"Finally, maybe now I can examine the diving suit," Max said. He and Ashly exited the house. They walked next to Liz who was already standing near a clear patch of land.

"Supplies incoming," she said, turning to Max and Ashly.

"Um, aren't we going to the airfield?" Ashly asked, wondering why everyone was standing around as the supply chopper got closer.

"No. Our supply pilot Jose likes to save us time, so he always lands near the warehouse." Even though Max and Liz got basic supplies themselves, more advance or bulk supplies were brought in every other month.

"Isn't that dangerous?" Ashly said, a little worried. "I mean, what if he accidentally hits the warehouse?"

"I'd laugh," Liz replied. Okada joined his teammates as the helicopter began its descent. "How much do you want to bet the destroyed diving gear got lost again?" Liz shouted over the noise of the chopper's twin blades.

"Don't jinx it," Max replied. A brief dust cloud formed when the helicopter landed a few feet from the warehouse. Ashly sighed in relief while Max and Liz got ready to unload supplies. Okada approached the driver's window as the blades came to a stop.

"Commander Takahashi, how are you, my brother?" Jose asked.

"I am well. As you appear to be," Okada replied. Jose gave him a thumbs up. "Do you have the supplies we requested?"

"Yes, sir. A dozen underwater mines, four other boxes of equipment, and...." Jose paused and took a closer look at the manifest. "A set of bed sheets?" Jose handed Okada the cargo manifest. After looking it over, Okada motioned it was accurate. "Do you need help unloading?" Jose asked as he lowered the cargo door.

"No, my team can handle it, and then you can be on your way," Okada replied. Liz drove a forklift up the opened rear cargo door and grabbed the first box. Ashly walked up the ramp. A small sadistic smiled formed on her face as she grabbed the box containing the bed sheets. Max was already inside removing the cargo ratchet straps. He noticed a smaller box sitting on top of one of the larger boxes. He took it outside and looked at the return address, which read Maui police department.

"Did we finally get the diving equipment?" Liz asked, returning from the warehouse.

"Yes!" Max confirmed. "Liz, do you mind if I head to the lab and start the examination?"

"Go for it; it's not like I'm doing any heavy lifting," Liz answered.

"You going to need help?" Ashly asked.

"If the others can spare you. Sure, I could use an assistant."

"Go ahead," Okada cut in. "Liz and I can finish up here. Ashly." She turned to face Okada. "Make sure those bed sheets make it to Samuel intact. No funny business." He said "funny business" in an authoritative voice.

"Sure, whatever you say," Ashly replied. She then turned to face Max. "Max, I'm going to get some of my equipment, and then I'll meet you downstairs." She rushed to her quarters and grabbed her tablet and tool kit, then walked towards Samuel's room. The door was open, so she tossed the sheets on the bed. Samuel did not take notice; he was sitting on the floor surrounded by multiple circles of papers and books. "Samuel, you know your teammates are outside unloading supplies, right?"

"Ashly, I don't do manual labor or field work. I am currently using the scientific method to confirm a hypothesis I have about the creature."

"What?" Ashly replied, annoyed, giving him a blank stare.

"I don't expect a mind like yours to understand the nature of my work. Now please run along," Samuel said, looking up long enough to motion for her to go away.

"I know with a computer I could get twice as much work done in half the time," Ashly replied.

"My computer is not hooked up nor will it be anytime soon," Samuel said as he started writing something in a notebook.

"Why?" Ashly asked, confused.

"Because the only safe computer around you is one that is unplugged. I have no doubt if I hook it up, you will find a way to hack it, then use it to make my life miserable."

"Samuel, I told you I don't know anything about hacking. I am a respectable software and computer tech. Now will you please get up and do something useful?"

"I'm doing research on the creature, while you're standing there babbling about how useless I am. So think about it right now: who is more useless?" Ashly huffed in frustration.

"Forget it," she said, knowing Samuel had backed her into a corner. "I'm going to help Max examine the diving suit." She walked away.

"Be sure to bring me any data you collect," Samuel replied.

Downstairs, Max turned on the lab lights and laid the box on the research table. He had modeled the layout of his lab to be a smaller version of Dr. Yamaguchi's lab in Tokyo. A single research table was located in the center of the room. The right of the room had a small work station and a small sink. The left of the room had shelves with boxes and preserved specimens of local fish. The back wall had a fresh water fish tank and two blackboards on either side of it. Max sat down, put on a pair of latex gloves, and pulled a utility knife out from the table's concealed drawer. Ashly walked in as he started cutting open the box.

"That Samuel Richards always finds a way to get on my nerves. While everyone else is working, he's in the room doing research."

"That's kind of why we brought him on the team," Max reminded.

"And he's not even good at that," Ashly said to herself. Max opened the box and carefully laid the oxygen tank on the table. The bottom half of the tank looked fine, but the top section had a row of holes across it. The Velcro straps that connected the tank to the diving suit were torn. Out of the four hoses attached to the tank, only the pressure gage remained intact. Half of the yellow hose that once held the secondary mouth piece lightly tapped against the table. Max reached back in and pulled out three small fragments of the diving suit, the largest of which was only eleven inches long. "Is that it?" Ashly asked in a disappointed voice.

"Looks like it," Max answered, handing the box to Ashly, who placed it under the table. "From how the news story told it, I thought we were getting the entire suit."

"Where do you think it is?" she asked. Max did not even have to look at her before she realized how stupid of a question that was. The suit was with the rest of Jade Kendig's body.

"Well, at least we have the tank. Let's see what we can learn from that," Max said optimistically. Ashly opened the camera on her tablet and placed her tool kit on the table.

"You know I have plenty of tools here," Max said, wondering why she brought her own down.

"I know, but I like using my own tools." She smiled. "It's kind of a personal problem I have."

"Fine with me," Max replied. He turned the front of the tank towards them.

"Are those bite or claw marks?" Ashly asked.

"Those are definitely bite marks." Max reached into one of the drawers and pulled out a digital caliper. "Ashly, can you record the data?"

"I'll make both digital and physical copies." The front section of the tank had four eighteen-inch holes. Two were located on the bottom of the tank and two were located on the top. It looked as if someone had taken a large screwdriver and thrust it into the tank. Between the set of large holes were six smaller four-inch holes. A puzzled look formed on Max's face. "What?" Ashly asked.

"The layout of the creature's teeth is not what I was expecting at all," Max stated in a confused voice.

"What's so unusual about it?"

"One second." Max reached into his tool drawer once again and pulled out a magnifier headband. He put it on and looked at the area behind the larger holes. "This makes no sense," he said to no one in particular.

"What?" Ashly asked. Max did not answer. He just intently stared at the marks on the tank. "Um, you okay?" Ashly again asked, getting a little impatient he was ignoring her.

"Sorry," Max replied, coming back to reality. "These teeth marks disprove our Nothosaurus theory."

"What makes you say that?" she wondered. Everyone seemed to agree they were hunting a marine reptile, and it sounded like a good theory to her. She did not know what Max was seeing, but whatever it was seemed to worry him. He also had disregarded the Nothosaurus theory. A theory he had come up with.

"Ashly, can you pull up a picture of a Nothosaurus on the tablet?" Ashly laid the tablet next to the diving tank. A picture of a Nothosaurus skeleton and a CGI image of a Nothosaurus were side by side. "See what's wrong with the theory?" Max asked. Ashly examined the pictures and the marking. A feeling of frustration started to come over her because she was still not seeing what Max was seeing.

"Honestly, no," she replied. Max zoomed in on the Nothosaurus's teeth.

"See the rows and rows of jagged serrated teeth?" Ashly shook her head yes. "Okay, now look at the diving tank. Does the marking on the tank match the Nothosaurus tooth pattern?" A light bulb went off in Ashly's head. Now she understood what he was seeing.

"You're right; they don't match at all." She now looked as confused as he did. "Do you happen to know what type of dinosaur had teeth like this?"

"None that I'm aware of. These teeth patterns more closely resemble a mammalian species."

"Okay. What made you jump to that conclusion?" Ashly asked. She was beginning to feel like a student who continually needed to ask the teacher for guidance. Max closed the picture of the CGI Nothosaurus and pulled up a diagram of cat teeth.

"See, there are four canine teeth." Max pointed to the diagram and then to the marks on the tank. "Between the canines are six smaller teeth called incisors." Like before, Max pointed to the diagram and then to the sets of smaller holes. A hint of dread filled Ashly's body. Max was right: things were not making any sense. She was no wildlife expert, but she knew there were no aquatic cats swimming through the ocean. Max stared at the diving tank like it was some type of unsolvable puzzle. His thoughts were racing, trying to figure out what type of creature could have done this. The tank was supposed to help solve the mystery, but it was only adding to it. Completely stumped, he hoped that Samuel would have some idea of what type of cryptid they were dealing with.

"Could the creature be some type of giant unknown seal?" Ashly suggested. That was Max's first thought when he saw the teeth, but again the evidence they had gathered on the creature went against the theory.

"That would be a good guess, but the creature we're hunting has four feet. Seals have flippers. The only known animal I can even think of comparing this creature to would be the otter, and that has me more than a little worried." Ashly raised an eyebrow.

"You think dealing with a giant otter is worse than a living dinosaur?"

"Yes," Max answered in a voice that showed he was not joking with her. "All known aquatic mammals have flippers, while semyaquatic mammals like otters and beavers have webbed feet." A chill ran down Ashly's spine.

"You don't mean."

"Yes, it's possible this thing could come on land."

"This is a strong building, right?" Ashly asked in an uneasy voice, trying not to imagine herself walking outside and getting eaten by the creature.

"Don't worry, Ashly. We have a fence, and attack dolphins, and guns." Hearing that made Ashly feel a little better.

"So, what's next?"

"Let's pack this stuff up and report our finding to the rest of the team." A few minutes later everyone was gathered in the living room. Okada and Liz sat on the couch while the others sat in the easy chairs. The furniture was arranged in a circle with a small coffee table in the middle.

"Did your exanimation of the diving suit reveal anything new?" Okada asked.

"Actually, it only brought up more questions," Max replied. "Turns out we were wrong. We're not dealing with a Nothosaurus."

"What? I thought you said we were hunting a Nothosaurus," Liz said, surprised. Max went on to explain his finding in the lab. When he finished, everyone seemed confused. Everyone looked towards Samuel, expecting him to provide an answer.

"I'm afraid I have to admit I'm just as stumped as everyone. The only relevant cryptids I can think of are the Bunyip, the Ahuitzotl, and the Dobhar-chú, but I am convinced none of them are our creature."

"Care to explain why?" Ashly asked. Without looking at a reference link, Samuel easily stated facts about the cryptids.

"The Bunyip is an Australian cryptid often seen in swampy areas. I believe it to be a prehistoric marsupial. Which means it would not be swimming around in the ocean. There has not been a sighting of the Ahuitzotl since the fifteen-hundreds. The creature is also reported to be the size of a large dog so it would not be destroying boats. The Dobhar-chú is a large otter that hunts in packs." A feeling of concern started to creep into everyone's body.

"Samuel, are you telling us we are dealing with a pack of creatures?" Okada asked.

"No, I don't believe so. The Dobhar-chú is said to live in fresh water lakes and rivers, not salt water oceans. The Dobhar-chú also appears to be an ambush predator, attacking prey near the shorelines. All attacks by our mystery monster have been at sea, now let's examine our only surviving witness, Mya Kendig."

"Max will enjoy this," Liz teased. He and Okada both shot her a glare. Samuel continued.

"I strongly believe that if this creature were a pack hunter, she would have been killed along with her sister."

"I agree with Samuel's conclusion," Max said. Okada had a blank expression—the one he made when he was thinking or about to make a difficult decision.

"We are going to need to conduct a reconnaissance mission to get an accurate idea of what we are dealing with," Okada said. He hated having to send members of his team out hunting for something that was unknown. He could very well be sending lambs to the slaughter, but this was the price a commander had to pay. Having the responsibility and duty of sending his people out on missions he knew they may never return from.

"Um, do we even have a boat?" Ashly asked. She figured they must, but no one had mentioned anything about it.

"It's tied at the dock in the dolphin training area," Max said.

"And it's not a good one," Liz added.

"I have to see this for myself," Ashly said. After walking a short distance, Ashly stared down at the dock. "Um, what is that?" she asked, looking at an orange twenty-two-foot inflatable raft.

"That's the boat we use for dolphin training and fence repairs," Max replied.

"Guys, am I the only one who thinks we need something larger and with more firepower if were hunting a sea monster?" Ashly questioned.

"Now that you mention it, I think we are going to need a bigger boat," Liz said. Ashly pretended to laugh.

"Okay, Liz, can you hook me up with some of your military contacts?" Ashly asked.

"Sure," Liz answered.

"Great. By tomorrow I can have a proper boat here."

"What did you have in mind?" Max asked. Ashly just smiled.

"It's going to be my surprise for the team."

CHAPTER 21

"Alright, everyone. The new boat is here. Please follow me to the dock," Ashly said in an excited voice. She had just returned from inspecting the new boat and was anxious for her teammates to see it. Everyone stopped what they were doing and followed Ashly. Each of them was looking forward to seeing what type of vessel she had found in such a short period of time. Ashly had spent yesterday evening in her room talking to the contact Liz had given her. The boat had arrived from Oahu earlier that day. The early morning sun was covered by clouds, and a gentle breeze moved across the ocean. When they neared the dock area, Ashly stopped and spoke in a proud voice.

"Alright, everyone, I would like to introduce you to the team's personal monster-hunting vehicle. A forty-foot-long interceptor craft I've named the Barracuda!"

"Nice," Liz said. Everyone walked up to the boat. The front of the Barracuda had a V shape to it, which connected to a rectangular-shaped hull. A safety rail surrounded the main deck. A hatch was located at the front of the boat. At the back of the boat two light machine guns were mounted on the left and right side. A large cable spool was welded between the guns. The sun came out for a moment, allowing the black paint to sparkle. Several of the dolphins swam around it, wondering what the new object was. Seafin broke the surface and started making clicking noises.

"Nicer than the last one, right?" Max said as he touched the dolphin on the head. "We're going to start training soon. So, you and the others be ready." He then gave the command for the dolphin to go back under the water.

"Okay, everyone, climb aboard. I'll give you the grand tour." Ashly was proud she managed to acquire the boat for the team. Secretly, she felt like an outsider that had not contributed much to the team's efforts. Max, Liz, and Okada had worked together for years, and Samuel's website and knowledge of cryptids had been a great resource for the team. She was the only member who had not made an impact for the team, but getting the boat made her feel like she had finally done something productive. After a tour of the main deck, everyone walked into the cockpit. Three chairs sat in a vertical line to the left of the cabin, and two chairs were located at the right of the cabin. The three back chairs had tray tables in front of them with small monitors welded to them. Between the rows of chairs was a small hall that led to a set of stairs. Ashly sat in the driver's seat, which was the first chair on the right side. In front of her was the control panel, and a monitor was mounted on the right wall. "This baby can reach a top speed of sixty knots. More than fast enough to outrun any sea monster." She looked at Max for clarification. "Right?"

"I'd say yes, but we are dealing with an unknown species," he replied. Ashly gave him a look that said *thanks for the doom and gloom answer*, then got back on topic.

"The Barracuda also comes with state-of-the-art sonar, advanced radar, and GPS system. Each monitor has touch screen technology and is wirelessly hooked up to the internet." Samuel started to sit down. "No, don't sit down yet!" Ashly commanded. "I have assigned seats for everyone. Okada, you get the seat behind the driver's seat. It's the captain's seat. Plus, it has the most leg room. Max and Samuel, you get the seats located behind the shotgun seat. Liz, you get shotgun." Liz sat down. Her area was different from the others. It had a much larger monitor and a set of joysticks on the right and left sides.

"Is this for the torpedo launcher?" Liz asked jokingly.

"Unfortunately, no. That controls this." Ashly turned on the monitor and hit a button on the left joystick. A hatch at the front of the boat opened, revealing twin 12.7mm. heavy machine guns. Ashly moved the right joystick and the machine guns spun around. "The monitor is linked to a camera on the guns. Now to demonstrate how accurate it can fire." Ashly pointed the gun at the old raft sitting at the dock next to the Barracuda. A yellow square surrounded the vessel. Ashly squeezed the trigger on the left joystick and fired. The sound of gunfire was soon followed by a brief hissing sound.

"Ashly, our dolphins are nearby!" Max yelled.

"Like I said, the computer firing system is nearly one hundred percent accurate. Once the computer locks on to a target, it's nearly impossible to miss." Ashly pointed towards the stairs. "Those lead to a small storage area, which we can use to store tools and ammo. Right above the stairs are three gun racks that, Liz, you can fill with whatever you want." Liz cracked her knuckles. She liked her new toy.

"You created a new monster," Max said. Liz turned towards him and made a fist. Max made one of his own and banged hers.

"Oh, and I almost forgot to mention: in the event the creature manages to tip the boat, the design of the Barracuda allows it to self-right."

"What's this super cool boat made out of?" Liz asked.

"Carbon fiber," Ashly replied.

"Very impressive," Okada complimented. He was sitting in his chair, exploring the ship's systems. Hearing that made Ashly's day, because she knew Okada did not give compliments unless he meant them.

"Thank you, but I'm not done. I still have one more thing to show you." On the main deck, Ashly walked over to a smaller hatch located right in front of the main gun hatch. She pulled it opened and dragged out a small robot.

"Good pick, Ashly. I've used this model on an expedition in college," Max said.

"It's just a robot. What's it for? Cleaning the ship?" Samuel said, unimpressed.

"Just a robot? Samuel, I present to you, our Marine Surveillance Robot, or MSR-2 for short." The robot was three feet long and triangular in shape. The body frame of the robot was yellow. The front area that held the camera and the two propellers in the back were blue. "It comes with a built-in 4k camera, 3D scanner, has five hours of battery life, two dimmable lumen lights, and a rescue light for locating it in dark waters. It's top speed is four knots and has a max depth of three hundred and twenty-six feet."

"Okay, I have to ask: what happens if it runs out of batteries or gets stuck?" Liz asked.

"That's what the cable spoil in the back is for. You connect the MSR-2 to the cable, then toss it in the water. If any mechanical issues occur, you reel it in or follow the cable and bring it up manually. I can't wait to test this baby out!" Ashly said giddily. "Oh, and I almost forgot I made some special modification so it can hold a sonar system, and two light drones to try to lure the creature in."

"That's a smart move," Max complimented.

"Now that we have a boat, we are ready to begin operations. I will contact Tokyo and the Hawaiian Governor to locate an acceptable location to lay our mine trap. Max, Liz. I want the two of you to start training the dolphins for the hypodermic lance plan. In case the mines fail to stop the creature, I want a secondary plan in place. Ashly, Samuel. At dusk you will take the boat and try to locate the creature. Try to collect as much information as you can." A feeling of dread came over Ashly. Not because she was hunting the monster, but who she was going to be on the boat with.

"Can't I go with someone I actually get along with?" Ashly begged.

"For once, I agree with Ashly. I don't know if I trust her driving skills. Plus. I don't do field work," Samuel added.

"I know how to drive a boat," Ashly countered.

"Yes, darling, anyone can drive a boat. The question is can you do it well?"

"Enough," Okada said. "Ashly, you know that boat and its functions better than anyone. Once the creature is spotted, Samuel will be the best one to determine what it is and what type of behavior to expect from it."

"Fine," Ashly said reluctantly. "I'm going to go start planning for the operation." She jumped on to the dock and headed for the house.

"That is actually a good idea," Samuel said in agreement. Once Ashly and Samuel were gone, Liz put her elbow on Okada's shoulder.

"Why did you really put them together?" Liz asked. She knew Okada well enough to know he had other motives in his decision.

"I already explained it," Okada replied.

"Yes, I know, but I also know you had other reasons."

"Ashly and Samuel are the only two members of the team that do not get along. Forcing them to work together in a somewhat dangerous situation is the best way to build trust and a team bond."

"True, but they could also completely turn on each other," Liz pointed out.

"In that event, they will die."

"I hope not. I rather enjoy our new boat," Liz said, kissing him on the cheek."

Okada smirked a little. *Liz, you are too much sometimes*, he thought.

CHAPTER 22

12:14 PM 04/15/2021 HST

Mya was tense and nervous while waiting for Riley to arrive. She had suggested they have lunch before Riley left for her submarine tour, an invitation Riley happily accepted. She was putting the finishing touches on the sandwiches when she heard a tapping at the door.

"It's unlocked, Riley."

"Heyyyy, girl!" Riley said in an excited voice. She walked over and hugged Mya. "Only two more hours until I'm in the submarine." She jumped slightly in excitement. "Thanks for inviting me to lunch, by the way."

"Hey, I wanted to give you a gourmet meal before your big adventure." Mya stared down at the food. "Even if it is only turkey sandwiches, fruit, potato chips, and coffee."

"A girl could not ask for better food," Riley said, dipping a banana slice in chocolate sauce. "Hey, let's get a pre-trip picture before we eat." Riley pulled out her cell phone and placed her arm around Mya's neck and shoulder. Mya normally made the peace sign and stuck out her tongue playfully for photos, but this time she couldn't. The situation was hauntingly familiar. She only managed to smile. "Perfect," Riley said, snapping the photo. Mya picked up a plate.

"Okay, here's your food, and here, can you take mine over to the coffee table? I'll bring the drinks in." Riley laid both plates on the table. Mya walked in with two cups of coffee adorned with whipped cream and a strawberry.

"Mya, you didn't need to go this fancy."

"Fancy? All I did was throw a spoonful of whipped cream on the coffee and added a strawberry."

"It's still nice you took the time to do it," Riley said. "I'll have to make you lunch sometime when I get back." Riley caught a slight hint of concern form on Mya's face. "Yes, Mya, I'm coming back and you'll regret you didn't join me."

"I don't think I'll be doing anything water-related anytime soon," Mya replied.

"Okay, let's get back to a fun subject. Shall we?" Riley brought the coffee mug up to her face. When she brought it down, a bunch of whipped cream was on her nose. She had done that purposely to try to make Mya laugh. Mya giggled a bit, then formed a content smile. *That's right, Riley, drink up,* she thought. The two girls continued their lunch for about twenty minutes. When they were finished eating, Mya got up to put the dishes in the sink.

"You okay, Riley? You look really tired."

"It's the turkey. Everyone knows turkey makes you sleepy. That's why everyone takes a nap after Thanksgiving," Riley replied.

"You still have a good half an hour before you need to leave. Rest your eyes on the couch. It's not like you haven't done it before." Lying on the couch sounded like heaven to Riley. She laid her head against the couch's arm.

"Mya, I need more coffee," Riley said in a sleepy voice. Mya waited a few minutes, then walked over and saw Riley was out cold.

"Sorry, Riley," Mya said as she placed a box of sleeping pills on the computer table. Whatever was swimming in those waters had killed her sister. She was not going to let it kill her only friend on this island too.

Riley slowly woke up. As her eyes opened, she noticed the clock read four seventeen.

"Oh my gosh! No!" she cried out, bolting off the couch. Mya paused her game and spun her chair around. "Mya, please! Please tell me this is a prank!" Riley pulled her phone out to check the time, which read the same as the clock.

"The tour sub left two hours ago."

"Why didn't you..?" Riley paused when she noticed the box of sleeping pills on the computer table, which Mya had intentionally left out. She was not going to hide what she had done.

"You bitch! You drugged my coffee, didn't you? Didn't you!" Now it all made sense. Mya was nervous about the trip yesterday and this morning, she suddenly became all excited about it and wanted to have a pre-trip lunch to celebrate.

"Yeah, I did. I know what's going to happen to that sub and I couldn't stand it if something happened to you. Sorry, but I'd rather have you alive and hating me than dead and happy with me." Riley's face was turning red with fury. Mya started mentally preparing herself for the verbal beating Riley was about to unleash.

"It took me four months to finally save enough to buy that nonrefundable ticket! Do you know how much that ticket cost me?"

"Nine hundred," Mya replied. She reached into her purse and pulled out a brown envelope. "It's one thousand," she added as she tossed it to Riley, knowing it would change nothing. Riley scoffed as she looked into the envelope. She walked right up to Mya, who stood up. The two just stared at each other for a moment. Riley gave Mya the evil eye, while Mya managed to keep a neutral expression. Riley slapped her across the face. Mya squinted at the pain.

"Maybe your mother had a good reason to do that. You're insane! If you want to believe sea monsters exist, that's fine, but don't ruin other people's lives in the process," Riley said bitterly. She smacked Mya on the shoulder with the envelope. "And if you think this changes anything, you're dead wrong. Our friendship is over!" Riley started to walk out of the room. She paused, looked at the envelope, then turned to Mya with a smug smile. "You know what? I think I'll use this to go scuba diving at Molokini Crater." Mya managed to hide the concern she felt when she heard that. She knew if she made a fuss about it, Riley would be more likely to do it.

"Do what you want," Mya replied. Riley gave her one last angry look and walked out the door. Just as she was about to shut it, she reopened it.

"Oh, Mya. Do me one last favor and delete me from your contact list." Mya put her head down when the door slammed shut.

"You had to do it. You had to do it," Mya repeated, trying to hold back her tears.

CHAPTER 23

6:17 PM 04/15/2021 HST

The submarine Alexandria approached the wreckage of the Carthaginian II. The Alexandria was a tourist submarine that could hold forty-eight passengers. The sub was painted ocean blue to reduce its effect on the local marine life. This also made marine organisms more likely to swim near it, which made the tourists happy. Two rows of twenty-four seats arranged in a back-to-back position sat in the middle of the sub. Twelve large windows covered the sides of the submarine. Two larger windows were located at the front and back of the sub. Large floodlights were under each of the windows, allowing large areas of ocean to be lit up. The sub had a crew of four: a driver, two stewards, and a tour guide. When the Carthaginian II came into view, the tour guide Chris Sullivan picked up his microphone. Chris Sullivan was a thin man of average height. He had a small beard and short brown hair.

"Ladies and gentlemen, this will be the second to last site on the tour. We are now approaching the wreckage of the Carthaginian II on the right." Several children jumped out of their seats in excitement and glued their faces to the glass domes.

"We will get a chance to see it too, won't we?" a middle-aged man sitting in the left facing seats asked. Chris smiled at the people on the left. After seven years of doing this, he was used to people asking stupid questions.

"Those of you sitting on the left side of the sub, don't worry. We circle the wreckage multiple times. Everyone will have more than enough time to take pictures and see the local marine life." Chris paused and stretched out his free arm towards the driver. "Our driver has been giving submarine rides since we opened. The great Tom Reynolds always makes sure our guests get a good show."

"That's right, Chris," Tom replied. Tom Reynolds was a slightly overweight man in his early fifties. His hair was short and a peppery color of white and gray. Chris explained the wreck's history when the sub began its first pass.

"The Carthaginian II rests at a depth of ninety-seven feet. The Carthaginian II was a replica whaling vessel that for twenty years was a floating museum that covered the history of whaling. In two thousand and five, the vessel was sunk to create an artificial reef."

"What about fish?" a child screamed, interrupting him. He was sitting on the left side, trying to see the wreckage. His mother pulled him down and scolded him for interrupting the tour. The child was seated near Chris, who smiled at him and motioned to his mother it was okay.

"The artificial reef is home to a great number of marine life, including: orange spine unicornfish, green sea turtles, eagle rays, butterfly fish, and my personal favorite, the ornate wrasse." The passengers stared though the glass bulbs, eager to spot the many species of colorful fish. To their disappointment, almost nothing was in the area.

"Well, where are the fish?" an old woman asked in an annoyed voice.

"Don't worry; they will come out," Chris replied. Secretly, he was wondering the same thing. Normally, the area was teeming with many different species of fish. He put the mic down and walked over to the driver. "Tom, do you have any idea what's going on?"

"No idea, Chris. In fifteen years, I've never seen the wreck this deserted." Chris looked over at the two stewards, Sarah and Natasha, who looked just as confused as he was. Both girls were blonde and finishing their final year of college. Everyone stared out the windows, hoping to see some form of marine life as the sub started its second circle. A man in his mid-forties was seated in the chair second to the end. He was lucky enough to be seated next to the only empty seat on the sub, so he had the window all to himself. The lack of marine life did not bother him. The main reason he had come on the voyage was to see and photograph the shipwreck.

The photos would look better with some fish, but then again, a picture only showing the ship is unique, he thought. He placed the camera up to his eye. He aimed it at one of the two broken sail masts resting on the ship's hull. He was about to take the picture when the lights in the sub started to flicker. The sounds of frightened people started filling the sub as the lights flickered on and off a few more times, then went off entirely.

"What's happening?" one passenger yelled.

"Has this ever happened before?" another frightened person asked.

"Everyone, please remain calm. Yes, this has happened before. It's just a minor power outage. Please remain calm and stay in your seats," Chris said. Of course he was lying. Nothing like this had ever happened, but he needed to keep the occupants of the sub calm. "Natasha, Sarah, can you please bring out the emergency flashlights?" Chris went over to Tom and said, "Tom, what's going on?"

"Chris, I have no idea, and I'm afraid to say we are in trouble." There was a concern to his voice that Chris had never heard before, which made him feel very uneasy. "I don't understand it. Power is off throughout the sub, the radio is not working, and neither are the ballast tanks."

"Chris," Natasha whispered.

"Yes, what is it? Do you have the flashlights?"

"That's what I came to talk to you about. None of the flashlights are working. We tried changing the batteries several times and nothing. Chris, what's happening?" Natasha asked in a voice filled with pure fear.

"I don't know, but we have to stay calm. The last thing we need is a panic breaking out. Tom, try to get things working again. Natasha, you and Sarah provide refreshments, play games with the children on board, and try to comfort frightened passengers." She shook her head and went on with her duties. Chris stood in the same spot he did when he spoke on the tours. The microphone was out, but he could still speak loudly enough for everyone to clearly hear him. "Okay, folks, we are having technical difficulties and may be stuck here for a while." Several people started talking at once.

"What's going on?"

"Are we in danger?"

Chris answered in a calm, confident voice, "We don't know what happened, but there is no need to worry. We have plenty of oxygen and the sub has a GPS locator. People know exactly where we are and will come rescue us. So, let's remain calm and get through this together." His speech seemed to satisfy the crowd. The man with the camera looked down at the camera, planning on reviewing the photos he had taken. To his surprise, the camera was not on. He tried to turn it on and off again. The camera came to life long enough to show a dead battery icon.

"How can the battery be dead? It was full just a second ago," he said in frustration. He overheard several other people complaining about their cell phones or cameras not working. His attention was drawn away from the camera when out of the corner of his eye he saw a shadow move onto the wreckage. His full attention went to the outside world. Without the floodlights from the sub, the mid-section of the ship was nothing but a dark outline. He got out of his seat and walked right up to the glass. That's when he saw it. Standing between the two broken masts was a large creature. It was too dark to make out any details, but there was no doubt it was a living creature. It moved one of its front feet onto one of the masts, looked right at the sub, and got into a position similar to a large cat that was ready to strike.

"There's something out there!" he screamed as his body hit the floor. Several people started getting out of their seats. Some were trying to help the man sitting on the floor, while others wanted to know what he saw.

"Sir, calm down. I need you to return to your seat," Chris said. This was the last thing he needed. Everyone was frightened enough, and this was not going to help things at all.

"No, you don't understand; there's something out there! It was a sea monster or something!" The man's eyes were wide with horror and his voice was full of dread. The two stewards joined Chris in an attempt to calm the frightened man down. Chris heard a child ask his mother if there was really a sea monster outside. Chris knew he needed to handle the situation quickly. Before he could think what to do next, the sub was struck from below. The sub rocked slightly, causing several of the standing people to stumble.

"Tom, what happened!" Chris yelled.

"Something hit us!" he replied.

"There's something in here with us! I saw it!" a man screamed.

"He's right! I just saw something out of the corner of my eyes!" a frightened woman agreed with him.

"We have to get out of here!" the man with the camera cried. He rushed for the ladder at the front of the sub that led to the entrance hatch. In a panic, he started to climb. Chris and a few other passengers that were able to remain calm grabbed the man and pulled him down. As Chris tried to force the man back into his seat, several passengers started complaining about feeling sick. Natasha was checking on Sarah, who was throwing up.

What is going on? Chris thought. Just then, Tom's voice cut through the noise.

"Good news, everyone. I managed to manually open the ballast tanks. We'll be at the surface in three minutes. Everyone just hang in there." Hearing that was the beacon of hope they needed. Somehow in all the chaos, Tom managed to keep calm and discover a solution. A true veteran of the sea. The feeling of hope was broken by a loud roar coming from somewhere in the darkness. Shortly after the sound, the sub was struck hard on the right side. Cracks started to form in several of the glass windows. Now everyone was screaming in panic. The creature wrapped its bottom feet around the sub's underside and used its front limbs to force the sub to turn onto its left side, sending the sub towards the ocean floor. As the sub turned, the passenger's screams of terror continued. People were falling or clinging on to something. The stomach of the large marine creature attacking them covered several of the windows. Tom tried to control the sub, but it was useless. The sub hit the ocean floor hard. The impact from several large rocks broke portions of the glass windows, causing water to slowly start leaking into the sub.

Inside was a living nightmare. Many passengers were wounded or unconscious, several elderly people had bones broken or were killed by the impact. One of the small children on board was trying to wake his unconscious mother. The few passengers that were unharmed were fighting over the two oxygen tanks on board. Joining the sounds of crying and screaming people was the sound of the creature clawing and biting at the sub's steel body. The metallic scraping combined with the rising water had turned the once peaceful, fun-loving passengers into a mob of frightened animals. Chris lay on his back in disbelief, watching the creature's tail and back foot through a viewing window.

How was this possible? he thought. Somehow, he found the strength to grab on to the ship's ladder. He pulled himself up in a daze. Blood was flowing down from a wound on his head. He looked over at Tom, who was lying motionless at the controls. A large splatter of blood covered some of the controls on the side control panel. He looked for Sara and Natasha. Natasha was lying motionless on one of the windows. The bruise on her eye suggested she had been hit by someone. Sara was huddled in a ball, crying and screaming for help. Everything seemed to stop when the creature's head burst through the large window at the end of the sub. The horrifying sound of breaking glass filled the room. It grabbed one of the passengers and started shaking him. The other screams were soon muffled by the rising water.

CHAPTER 24

5:25 AM 04/16/2021 HST

Ashly Cross walked over to the boat's control panel. The night search had found no activity whatsoever. If they didn't find anything within the next few hours, she was going to call it quits. She was tired, and being stuck on the boat with Samuel all night did not help things. The two managed the situation by ignoring each other. Samuel was currently sleeping in the command chair, like he had been most of the night, which was fine with Ashly. She spent the night driving the Barracuda around Maui, using coffee to stay awake and her phone for entertainment. Ashly heard Samuel wake with a loud yawn. He pulled a small cereal box from his backpack.

After eating it, he asked, "How far does the sonar you're using track?"

"It was nice while it lasted." she muttered to herself, then answered his question. "At this depth it can reach the ocean floor. It can also scan a radius of one mile."

"You mean like that spot on the screen?" Samuel asked in warning. A look of shock formed on Ashly's face. The sonar screen showed a fifty-seven-foot-long object, twenty-four feet from them. The sonar reading also confirmed it was surfacing fast.

"How did I not catch that?" she yelled. She had been so bored and tired, she had gotten lax checking the sonar.

"That must be him! Ashly, what are we going to do?" Samuel yelled in a concerned voice. She was too busy trying to get the ship's weapon systems online to answer him.

"Get on the sonar and tell me how close the object is to the surface!" she ordered. Ashly sat in the ship's weapons chair and activated the main weapon. She looked out the window eagerly as the hatch on the front of the boat started to open. It took less than a minute for the ship's double heavy machine guns to appear. "Samuel, where is it? How close to the surface is it?"

"It's currently on the right side and only fifteen feet from the surface!" Ashly grabbed the joystick and turned the turret to the right side. "Of course, those guns will not do any good if he decides to ram us from the bottom," Samuel added. The thought of something breaking through the ship's hull sent a chill down Ashly's spine. Sweat started pouring down her forehead when Samuel told her the sonar reading was only ten feet from the surface. Ashly's index finger was tensely on the firing trigger. She was ready for the horror that was about to rise from the deep. She gasped when a large fountain of water broke the surface. The tension left her body as the massive body of a humpback whale appeared for a moment and disappeared beneath the water.

"It's a whale," she said softly in relief. She turned to Samuel. "It's a whale." Samuel did not say anything, and Ashly did not need him to. The look on his face said it all. He knew the whole time. Ashly did not say anything for a moment; she just glared at him with a look of fury. "Samuel, I could have shot that whale! Whaling is illegal in the United States! I could have been charged with poaching or…"

"Darling, if you're going to join me in monster hunting, you at least need to know the local wildlife. I knew right away the object on the sonar was way too large to be our monster." Ashly was not going to give him the satisfaction of hearing her yell about it anymore. She just reached into her pocket and pulled out her phone. "I'll let you know if anything important appears on the sonar," he said.

An hour had passed. The sun was now halfway up. Ashly had hooked an alarm to the sonar to alert them if anything large was in the area. Aside from the whale setting off the sonar detector a few times, things had been quiet. Samuel was busy updating his website with the latest cryptid news. Ashly was listening to an audiobook, trying to pretend he was not with her. When the chapter of her book finished, she took her headphones off and was about to say, "let's head home" when the sonar light went off.

"Looks like our friend the whale's back," Samuel said casually. He glanced at the screen. His voice soon took a more serious tone. "Ashly, I'm not kidding this time. Come here," he said. Ashly walked over to the sonar.

"This had better not be another joke," she thought to herself. The sonar showed a thirty-two-foot-long object had just entered sonar range.

"Do you think that's another whale?" Ashly asked, hoping it was.

"I don't know. It could be a smaller species of whale, but I recommend we check it out," Samuel replied. For once, Ashly agreed with him. She walked out onto the bridge, pulled the tarp off her MSR-2 robot, and attached a cable to it. She then tossed it into the water, then quickly returned to the ship's control room. She turned on a monitor that was connected to the robot's camera system. A highly detailed image of the ocean came into view. "Samuel, I need you to guide me to the target. Tell me how far away it is and at what depth," Ashly said as she started moving the MSR-2 in the object's direction. Samuel fed Ashly the information she needed and for the time being, they were actually working as an effective team.

When the robot was one fourth of a mile out, Samuel said, "Ashly, I highly recommend you turn off any light sources the robot has. The creature may see light sources as prey."

"That's what I'm counting on," she replied. She pressed a button, which released two smaller drones from the MSR-2. The drones started flashing bright beams of lights. Ashly activated the night vision and stopped the MSR-2 a few yards above them.

"I have to admit, very clever, darling," Samuel admitted. Ashly gave him only a slightly annoyed look but was pleased with the compliment. "Well, I think we can confirm this is our monster. The moment those lights started flashing, he increased his speed." Samuel's hands were becoming sweaty with anticipation as the large green dot got closer to the MSR-2 location. He moved his chair over to Ashly's screen, eager to see a cryptid. After years of research and searching, finally his moment had arrived. The next few minutes were filled with tension as a large dark object in the distance came closer and closer. Their breathing shortened when the creature finally came into view. Samuel dropped his coffee mug, which caused Ashly to flinch.

"No, it can't be!" Samuel said in a shocked voice. The creature's back and face was covered in light silvery colored fur. The rest of the creature's body had light brown fur. Some signs of scarring were noticeable across the creature's body, leaving black streaks and patches. Four webbed feet, and a thick tail propelled it through the water. A row of scales ran down the creature's tail. The head of the creature was its most unusual feature. It had the muscular skull and face of a large cat, and antlers protruded behind both otter-like ears. Four canine teeth showed from the front sides of the creature's mouth.

"Samuel, what is it? A Nothosaurus?" Ashly asked. Samuel was not listening to her. He started rambling as he stared at the screen in an almost trance-like state.

"The most powerful underwater being, the master of all marine creatures."

"Samuel, what is it!" Ashly screamed. She looked back at the monitor when she heard a crunching sound. The creature bit down on one of the light drones. It spit it out quickly and stared at it, seemingly confused by what he just ate. Finally, Samuel answered Ashly.

"A creature feared by indigenous peoples for centuries. The water panther!" Ashly had no idea what he was talking about, but from how shaken up he was, she could tell this was a dangerous animal.

"Look at those teeth!" Ashly said to herself, staring at them. She shook her head, trying to snap herself back into focus. She started taking pictures and activated the scanner. The next several minutes were full of tense amazement as the water panther destroyed the last light drone and swam off, disappearing into the dark abyss. Ashly noticed her hands slightly shaking as she uploaded the video footage and scanning data to her computer back on Niihau.

"How much data did you get?" Samuel asked. He was trying to hide it, but she could tell he was just as shaken as she was.

"I got video and audio footage. Plus a 3D image of the creature. That will allow us to accurately measure every part of the creature's body." She typed in a new command and pulled up the 3D image of the creature. Shortly after it came up, she yelled in excitement, "Oh my gosh! Samuel, look at the creature's right leg." One of the claws on the right leg was missing. She turned to him and smiled. "This proves this is our monster."

"Nice work, darling. Your skills have finally proven to be useful," Samuel said, patting her on the shoulder. His words rubbed her the wrong way. She slammed the button on the MSR-2 control panel to reel the cable in, not noticing that she also hit the button that activated the light beacon for nighttime recovery.

"Samuel, I contribute as much to this team as you do. Tell me who drove us here? Who activated the sonar to find the creature? Who came up with the plan we're using to kill this creature? Who...." Ashly was cut off when the boat shook. It was not much, but enough to notice. Both their heads turned to the back door and looked at the cable spool starting to reel more cable out to sea. "Oh, no. He grabbed the MSR-2," Ashly said. She looked at the MSR-2 camera feed, which showed nothing but static.

"Is it just me or are we moving?" Samuel asked. Ashly noticed the feeling as well. The boat was slowly getting pulled by the cable.

"He can't be pulling us! No way he's that strong!" Ashly yelled.

"Well, it's happening! You were just bragging about driving the boat. Start the engine and let's go!" Samuel screamed. Ashly regained her senses from her brief state of panic and started the boat's engine.

"I'm pulling the cable back in," Samuel said.

"And bring that creature right to us!" Ashly pushed the speed level forward. The boat started to move. The sudden movement broke the robot free from the water panther's jaws. He roared in anger and started following his prey. "Okay, we're moving. Hopefully he will stop chasing us," Ashly said, crossing her fingers. "Now reel the cable in."

"You're the boss," Samuel said in a mocking voice. He clicked the button to begin reeling in the cable, but nothing happened after pressing it several times. "The cable is not responding to any commands. It must have gotten shorted out."

"How?" Ashly asked. "Okay, we'll just keep going. We can fix it later." She glanced at the sonar, which showed the water panther was still following them. *Hopefully he tires out soon*, she thought to herself. "Samuel, how fast can this thing swim?"

"Who knows?" he replied. He continued slamming the cables reel-in button, convinced it would work eventually. Ashly rolled her eyes. Below, the water panther had caught up to the MSR-2. He bit down, clamping the robot deep within his jaws. The constant pulling from the boat increased the creature's fury. He started to swim around, yanking and clawing its prey, hoping to kill it. Ashly and Samuel were rapidly jerked forward by the boat's sudden loss of speed. The boat was still moving forward, but barely. The two were in a stalemate. "That's it. I'm cutting the cable!" Samuel yelled, trying to keep his balance on the rocking ship.

"The stainless steel cutters are in the tool box next to the weapons locker," Ashly grunted, struggling to keep the boat steady. Samuel made his way to the tool box, and started tossing the tools he didn't need on the ground. He spotted the cable cutters and grabbed them.

"Freedom!" he shouted, holding up the cable cutters. He gingerly made his way to the back deck. The ship was practically jumping through the water, gaining a small amount of ground with every thrust. He slowly and carefully walked over to the cable spool. The water jets from the boat's wake was spraying in his face. Inside the cabin, Ashly noticed the boat engine's overheating lights were starting to flash red.

"Hurry up, Samuel," she said out loud. To reduce the stress on the engine, Ashly pulled the boat's speed level back. Samuel placed the cable in the cutters' teeth, when the boat rapidly slowed down. The sudden jerk threw Samuel over the cable. He yelled in pain, as he lay on the ground. When his senses returned, he realized the cutters were not in his hand. He frantically looked around but saw nothing. He got up and walked back into the cabin. "Did you cut the cable?" Ashly asked.

"No, I'm going below to get the spare cable cutters."

"We don't have a spare!" Ashly screamed. Her mouth was wide with surprise. "I can't believe you dropped them in the water!" Against every instinct in her body, Ashly shut off the engine.

"What are you doing?" Samuel demanded. "Keep going. We need to tire that creature out!"

"If we keep fighting with that thing, our engine will overload, and then we will be sitting ducks!" Ashly screamed back. After shutting off the engine, the water panther stopped its thrashing. Satisfied his kill was dead, he started swimming with the MSR-2 still in his mouth. The boat started to move again. "Hey, if we die, at least the data has been uploaded to our teammates," Ashly said making a joke to keep herself as calm as she could. Samuel heard her and that was it. He was not about to be eaten by a cryptid or stranded in the middle of the ocean. He opened the emergency supplies and pulled out a flare gun. He walked outside. Pointing the gun up to the sky, he fired.

"What are you doing?" Ashly asked.

"Marking our location. Calling for help!" Samuel replied. Ashly smiled sarcastically, holding the radio and her cell phone.

"Well, use them!" Samuel screamed in a panicked voice. Ashly turned on the radio and was about to speak when Samuel yelled.

"Ashly! We're heading right for an oil platform!" Ashly ran outside and saw the abandoned oil platform rapidly getting closer.

"Run to the front of the ship and brace for impact!" she yelled. She put the cell phone in her pocket, grabbed Samuel by the shoulder, and ran. When they reached the front of the ship, Samuel hugged the machine gun.

"We're going to crash!" he cried. Ashly grabbed the ship's guard rail, getting her body ready for the coming impact. Samuel hugged the machine gun tighter and started screaming. A few yards from the platform, the boat came to a stop.

Ashly and Samuel looked at the massive structure right in front of them. They could hear the cable grumbling.

"The cable must be caught up in the underwater structures," Ashly said in relief. The feeling was short-lived, however.

"Oh, shit," Samuel said. The stern of the boat started to sink under the water. Ashly stood up.

"Samuel, we're going to jump for the oil rig and climb to the..." Before Ashly could finish, a loud snap filled the air. Ashly stumbled as the boat returned to a straight position.

"The cable must have snapped," Samuel observed. Breathing heavily, Ashly ran to the control room and slammed the speed level forward. Samuel entered the cabin as Ashly checked the sonar.

"He's not following us! We're good," Ashly said. She relaxed in her seat and sighed heavily. "I cannot believe how strong that thing was."

"Ashly, Samuel," Okada's voice came over the radio.

"Yes, Okada, everything is fine and dandy here," Samuel replied. Ashly looked at him in disbelief. "Well, it is."

"Return to base at once; we suspect that creature just sunk a sub."

CHAPTER 25

7:18 AM 04/16/2021 HST

The Barracuda arrived at the Niihau dock. After tying the boat down, Ashly and Samuel walked into the house.

"Hey. You two find anything interesting?" Max asked. He and Liz were sitting at the table, eating breakfast. Okada had gotten up an hour earlier and was hard at work in his office. Samuel sat down and started piling food onto his plate.

"You two have eaten, right?"

"Yep, take all you want," Liz answered. Ashly slumped down in the chair.

"Oh, yes. A lot of interesting stuff happened," she replied. Her body language showed she was visibly shaken. Inside, Samuel was the same way, but he managed to keep up the illusion that he was perfectly calm.

"You okay? What happened?" Liz asked.

"Well, we found our friend. It destroyed the MSR-2 and drug the Barracuda around for a while."

"What? Okada told me everything went fine?" Liz said, stunned.

"That's what people with big egos wanted you to believe," Ashly said, turning towards Samuel.

"Okay, enough, let's not start infighting," Max stressed, wanting to stop any bickering before it got started. "Ashly, the creature. What was it?"

"Hold on. Okada will want to hear this," Liz interrupted. While they waited, Ashly got up and put some eggs and toast on a plate. When Liz returned with Okada, Max spoke.

"Okay, Ashly, you were saying?" He wanted to finally learn what this mystery creature was.

"Turns out our friend is a creature known as a water panther."

"What is a water panther?" Okada asked sounding slightly surprised.

"If you don't mind, Samuel can explain it to you. I've been up all night, and I just want to eat and catch a few hours of sleep." She looked at Okada for approval.

"You're fine, Ashly. You did well."

"Thanks," she replied. "Before I go to sleep, I'll send the information we gathered to everyone's personal computers and to the one in the research lab." Ashly took her plate and headed for her room. She wanted to stick around and learn more about the submarine attack, but the lack of sleep won over her curiosity. Samuel was wide awake, so he remained at the table after she left. He gave them the same speech he had given Ashly on the boat concerning the water panther. Everyone was silent for a few moments, trying to process the information that had been presented. Samuel decided to break the silence.

"Could someone please explain what happened with the submarine?"

"At the moment all I know is the tourist submarine Alexandria's GPS locator stopped transmitting yesterday at six twenty-three p.m. Attempts to contact the submarine's crew proved unsuccessful. A Coast Guard rescue boat was dispatched and located the submarine near the last location transmitted by the GPS. The wreckage is being transported to the naval base at Peril Harbor," Okada answered.

"Wish we could get a look at it," Samuel mentioned.

"We can. The Hawaiian governor is growing deeply concerned about how frequent these attacks are becoming. He has given us full access to the submarine wreckage," Max replied.

"We plan on conducting the investigation tomorrow," Okada added. He opened an email on his phone and showed it to Samuel. The email was from the Hawaiian Governor David Fatu asking to set up a meeting time to be briefed on the team's findings.

"Very interesting. When are we meeting the big shot?" Samuel asked.

"After the submarine examination, we will travel to Honolulu to report our findings. As you can imagine, Governor Fatu is more than eager to learn about what has been terrorizing the Maui waters." Max, Liz, and Okada's phones all went off at once.

"Ashly just sent the information. I'm going to the lab to look it over," Max said with a hint of eagerness in his voice.

"We will join you," Okada said.

"If you don't mind, I'll retire for a bit. I've had enough excitement with the water panther for one day," Samuel said. Max walked down to the lab and quickly turned on the computer. Liz and Okada sat next to him. He opened the folder Ashly had marked "water panther." Upon opening it, there was a text document, a 3-D image file, and a four-minute video file. Max clicked on the video file first. They watched as the event Samuel and Ashly had experienced played out before their eyes.

"Just look at that thing. No wonder it has been doing so much damage," Liz said. Her voice filled with disbelief. Even though everyone knew they were hunting an unknown creature, the shock of seeing undoubtable video footage of one was nerve-racking.

"What are the other files?" Okada asked in a calm voice. Max opened the 3D image, which showed an image of the water panther against a white background. On the right side of the screen, a data tab appeared, showing the measurements of the water panther's body. Max moved the creature around, getting a good look at every side. The antlers and the lizard-like tail was particularly puzzling to him.

"How could something like this go undiscovered?" Matt muttered to himself. He would have found it easier to believe this was a hybrid that escaped from a government lab, but the fact that legends of the water panther describing this exact animal went back centuries disproved that theory.

"Our nemesis is thirty-two feet long," Liz commented. Max did not reply. His full attention was focused on the image in front of him. Liz snapped a finger in front of his face.

"It's not every day you get to discover a new species. Forgive me for being a little mesmerized." Max replied.

"Well, we're going to blow it up, so enjoy it while you can," Liz said, patting him on the shoulder.

"If there's one, there has to be another," Max countered. He suddenly found his reply worrisome. The thought no, the fact that there were more of these creatures swimming around the ocean was nerve-racking.

"What do you think those horns are for?" Liz asked, wanting to crush the nervous feeling going around the room.

"Since the horns are not pointing forward, my best guess would be some type of mating display. Hold on," he said, zooming in on the water panther's skull. It was hard to see from a distance, but up close, a slight dome shape could be made out. "Okay, look at the head. See the dome shape? The skull is very thick there. That's explains how it's been able to ram ships without getting injured. I bet the skull lines up with the spine to distribute the force from the impact. The horns may also assist with that." Liz gave him a look that said *I don't buy it.*

"Sorry to be Miss Skeptic again, but I can't believe these creatures are swimming through the ocean ramming fish with their heads."

"I never said that's how they normally hunt," Max replied. "It probably learned from trial and error that ramming boats was more effective then biting them."

"So, this creature is also intelligent?" Okada added.

"If we're corrected and it's demonstrating the ability to learn, then yes."

"How intelligent?"

"I have no idea," Max replied, putting both his arms out in an *I don't know* gesture. "Keep in mind, everything I'm saying is just theories and speculation.

This creature could be as smart as a primate or as dumb as a brick." Okada's face gained the expression that only formed when he was thinking hard.

"Using the information you do have. What would be your best guess on the creature's intelligence?"

Max showed a slight sign of frustration when he said, "Okada, I really cannot say. This creature's brain is most likely similar to species of big cats. I know several species of them are intelligent, but I cannot give you quotes off the top of my head." Okada realized at the moment he was chasing a loose end and accepted the answer.

"If you're done with the 3D image, please check the text document." Max opened the text document, which contained the same information that was in the data tab. Plus, Ashly's account of what had occurred during her encounter with the creature. Liz put both hands behind her head and stretched.

"So. What now?" Okada stood up.

"I will make preparations for tomorrow's meeting with Governor Fatu. Max, remain in the lab. Do your best to learn about the creature's intelligence or possible hunting habits. Liz, ready the X-7 and load any equipment we will need."

"Go team!" Liz shouted after Okada finished giving orders.

"Go team," Max replied, knowing they had a ton of work ahead of them.

CHAPTER 26

Mya Kendig entered the employee room of the Crescent Moon gaming café. She had gotten the position when Riley had introduced her to the owners, Mr. and Mrs. Hollinger. She was scheduled to work the cash register in the video game section and cosplay as the video game character of the week. The Crescent Moon gaming café was located in Kihei, a few miles from Keawakapu Beach. The front of the store was a café serving small lunches and game-themed coffee. The back of the store was divided into two rooms. One room was a modern video game section, and the other was the retro arcade. Dividing the two rooms was the gaming sales room where people could buy both modern and retro games. Mya handed the completed hiring form to the administrator, Mrs. Hollinger, who shared a small office in the back of the café with her husband. Mr. Hollinger handled supplies and anything store-related. Mrs. Hollinger handled the employee and book side of the business. Both were in their late fifties. Mya loved the idea of older people getting into video games and geek culture. She laughed when at their first meeting, Mrs. Hollinger told her the tales of her youth. How she would steal quarters from her parents' drawers to use at the local arcade.

"Everything seems in order, dear," Mrs. Hollinger said, looking over the papers. "You excited for your first day?" At first Mya was excited to start, but with the events that happened with Riley, she was wondering if she should quit before her first day began.

"Yep," Mya replied. She paused and thought about how to phrase what she wanted to say next. "Just out of curiosity, has Riley said anything to you about training me?" Riley had agreed to train her on register duties and even managed to convince Mrs. Hollinger to let them work the same shift. Mya had not heard from Riley since the fight. She had no idea how Riley felt, but she was pretty sure she did not want to see her, let alone train her.

"No, I have heard nothing from Riley, but she should be here in a little bit. Go ahead and punch in, dear," Mrs. Hollinger replied. Her response surprised Mya. She had pictured Riley calling in, demanding that someone else train her.

Maybe she won't show up at all, Mya thought. She started putting her password into the time clock when Riley walked in. She saw Mya and walked towards her. *Here we go*, Mya thought, expecting Riley to dish out another verbal beating. When Riley stood next to her, she focused on the time clock.

"Hey, Mya," she said. Mya turned to face her.

"Hey," she replied softly. To her surprise, Riley threw her arms around her, hugging her tightly.

"Thank you!" Riley said in a voice full of gratitude. A surprised looked formed on Mya's face. This was the last thing she expected to happen.

"Um, sure," Mya replied, not knowing what to think. Riley released her. Both of them were face to face. Riley had a wide, grateful smile, while Mya had a happy but confused look. "Why are you so happy? I thought you were mad at me," Mya continued.

"Haven't you seen the news or been on social media?" Riley asked.

"I don't watch the news, and I have not been on social media since yesterday. Did I miss something?"

"Mya, yesterday, the Alexandria sunk. Everyone on board was killed."

"What! How?" Mya asked. A feeling of fear came upon her. Unpleasant thoughts started entering her mind. She pictured Riley screaming as the water rose around her, trapped at the bottom of the ocean with no hope of escape. Then that monster, that demon, would come up behind her, smirking as it took its latest victim.

"Mya. You still with me?" Riley asked. Mya smiled and shook her head yes. Riley hugged her again. Gratitude returned to her voice when she said, "You saved my life, girl. If I would have been on that tour, I would have died." The feeling of fear was replaced with a feeling of relief. She had been right. The creature had attacked the sub. She was so glad she had listened to her instinct and prevented Riley from going. She could not imagine coming in and finding out Riley had been killed. If that had happened, she probably would have ended it. Joining her sister and new best friend in death. Fortunately for her, this time reality was sweet. Riley put both hands on Mya's shoulders. "Sorry I slapped you and said those all those mean things to you."

"Yeah, sorry I drugged you against your will," Mya replied.

"Just don't make it a habit." Both girls laughed. "Still friends?" Riley asked.

"Still friends," Mya confirmed. She was glad things were patched up between them. The two girls hugged a third time.

"Okay, enough hugging. Let's get to work. I have a lot to teach you," Riley said.

***

After work, Mya changed clothes and sat on her bed. She pulled out her phone and looked up the Alexandria disaster. The headline read that fifty-one people were feared dead in submarine sinking. Mya skimmed through the article until she got to the part stating the cause of the disaster. As she expected, it stated the cause was unknown. The leading theory was hull failure. Mya scoffed at the explanation. She knew exactly what caused it. She lay down and put her hands over her face.

What should I do? she asked herself. She remembered the pain Jade's death had brought to her, and now fifty-one more families were going through the same thing. She looked at the headline again, knowing she was going to keep seeing headlines like it. What she did not understand was why everyone else seemed oblivious to the situation. She would give anything just to talk to someone who would believe her. She got up, turned the room lights out, and fell onto the bed. She lay in the dark, staring up at the ceiling. It was her way of thinking without distractions. As she lay there, she started going over her options. She knew going to the police or Coast Guard would be useless. What about going to a newspaper or internet blog? No, at best, she would end up on some conspiracy station. At worst, she would be mocked. She quickly sat up when she remembered the call she had gotten a few days ago, from that biologist. Mya grabbed her phone and brought the call history up. She scrolled down until she saw a number that had no contact name above it. She clicked it. Her thumb was about to press the call button when she stopped. A feeling of anxiety started to move through her body. What if he did not believe her? What if he was still angry about how she treated him the first time? *Can't really blame him if he's still mad*, she thought. She took a deep breath and pressed the call button. The nervous feeling in her stomach increased as the phone began to ring.

It rang twice before a man with a deep Indian accent said, "Hello, this is the IRS." Mya hung up.

"Stupid scammer," she said. She scrolled down to the next unknown number and tried it.

"Hi, this is Max Varian."

Mya gasped. She hastily said in a nervous voice, "Hi, this is Mya Kendig." She waited for him to hang up.

"Oh, hi. I honestly did not expect to hear from you," he replied. Hearing him speak in a calm voice allowed her to calm down a bit. Max was pleasantly surprised himself that she had called. He had figured this lead had been lost. Now he had a chance to speak to an actual witness, and better yet, this time Liz was not around to torment him.

"Look, I'm sorry I was so rude when you called before. I had just gotten back from my sister's funeral and was pretty upset," Mya explained, the nervous tone leaving her voice. Max laughed, a little embarrassed.

"That's perfectly okay. I'm the one who should be sorry. I had no idea you had just gotten back from a funeral."

"It's fine. There's no way you could have known," Mya replied. She struggled for a moment to force the next words out of her mouth. "Look, if you're still interested, I'd like to share my experience with you, but first I need to know one thing."

"Okay, what's that?"

"Why do you want to hear about my encounter? Why do you believe I encountered a sea monster when no one else does?" Max stared at the computer screen. The water panther stared back at him. Jaws wide open, ready to attack one of the light drones. He knew his response could make or break the meeting. He knew exactly what she saw, but he could not tell her he was actively hunting the thing.

"I don't know if you saw, as you put it, a sea monster, but I don't believe you were attacked by a shark either."

"Again, why do you believe me? Why not think I'm a crazy girl who imagined the whole thing?"

"Okay, I'll admit it. I looked you and your sister's information up on the internet before I contacted you." He, of course, made that up on the spot. "You don't seem like a person who would lie to get attention, and you don't have any history of it. Your sister, Jade, was an experienced diver. She knew the safe areas to dive in, and I'm sure she would have noticed a dangerous shark coming. What really makes me believe the attack was not a shark is the fact that the divers found no body." He hoped mentioning that was not taking things too far.

"Okay?" Mya replied. She sounded more curious than upset, so he continued.

"When an unprovoked shark attack occurs, it normally bites once, then leaves the area. Sharks rarely bite multiple times, and I have never heard of a shark eating an entire body." Mya felt like a burden had been lifted off her. Finally, someone who might actually listen to her, but she still needed to know one thing before she was ready to trust him.

"Thank you for believing me about the shark at least, but why do you care?"

"Because I work in these waters, and if there's a dangerous unknown animal swimming around in them, I want to know about it so I don't get chopped." *Shoot, you may have just blown it*, he thought. His worry quickly disappeared when he heard Mya snicker. "And of course, for the safety of the hundreds of people who swim in these waters daily. If you need a selfish reason, discovering an unknown species would skyrocket my career."

"Okay, you've convinced me you're not out to use or make fun of me," Mya replied, hoping she was right. "I'll share what I know."

"Great," Max replied. "I'd rather do this in person than over the phone. Is there a place you would like to meet?"

"Do you know where the Crescent Moon Gaming Café is?"

"No, but I can easily find it," Max assured.

"Does tomorrow at eleven a.m. work for you?" Mya asked. Max scanned his memory for when they were examining the sub wreckage. Okada had said they were planning on arriving by two and having the meeting with the Governor Fatu at six.

"Eleven works fine. Now, if you don't mind, I'd like to ask you a question."

"Okay," Mya replied.

"What made you change your mind?" Mya thought for a moment before saying.

"To my knowledge, I'm the only one who has seen that thing and lived. One of my friends was supposed to be on the submarine that sunk. I...I just feel I have to do something before that creature kills again." Hearing that she figured out the water panther had attacked the sub so quickly surprised him.

"That's understandable. Your friend's okay, right?"

"Yes, thank God, she took a nap and missed the sub." Mya intentionally left out the drugging with sleeping pills part of the story.

"I'm glad to hear she's okay. See you tomorrow." Max was about to hang up when Mya spoke again.

"Wait. One more thing."

"Sure, go ahead."

"No cameras. I don't even want you having a phone out when we're talking."

"Okay," Max said, a little confused. "I was not planning on recording you, but I was planning on using my phone to show you some pictures."

"Can you print out the photos you were planning on showing me?"

"If it makes you feel better, sure. Man, this girl's paranoid." Max said under his breath.

"Okay, thanks for understanding," Mya replied, pleased he was willing to go along with her request.

"If you don't mind me asking. Why are you so concerned about getting filmed?" Max asked for his own curiosity. The question annoyed Mya, but she completely understood why he was asking it.

"For all I know, you could secretly be an undercover reporter for a conspiracy site. I know how crazy my story is, and I know some people would want to exploit it for a quick buck even if it means destroying what little credibility I have left."

"I promise I won't publish anything we talked about or mention your name without asking you first."

"Good to know. See you at eleven." The phone went dead before Max could reply. After hanging up, Mya tried to go about her day, but she started to question whether or not he was being honest with her. She walked over to her computer and Googled Max Varian, biologist. "You should have done this before you called him," she said out loud. The only relevant search result was the first one. She clicked on it. There were no photos of him. Just an article that detailed his work with the Niihau wildlife sanctuary and mentioned he was involved with training dolphins for marine shows. She searched a little more and found nothing that proved he was being dishonest, so the meeting was still on.

***

Max knocked on the door of Okada's office.

"You may enter," he said. Max opened the door. Okada was sitting at the desk. The office area was nothing fancy. It only had a small filing cabinet, and an office desk that held a phone and computer.

"Hey, I just got a call from Mya Kendig. You know, the girl who survived the attack," Max said as he sat down.

"I'm aware of who she is. What did she want?"

"She wanted to meet me and talk about her encounter."

"When and where?"

"Tomorrow at eleven, at some café on Maui." Okada gave him a look that said, *have you forgotten all the things we have going on that day?* "I know, with everything else going on tomorrow, it will be cutting it close," Max added, reminding him he had not forgotten. "But I feel the information she may have is worth investigating."

"I agree," Okada said. He pulled up a schedule and typed for a few seconds, then looked up at Max and said, "I wish to begin examining the submarine no later than two o'clock. Be sure to make the meeting quick."

"I can do that. I'd better get back to work," Max said and started to leave.

"Max." He turned to face him. "During your meeting, remember both our governments want the water panther's existence to remain secret. You cannot tell Mya the truth. In fact, I would encourage you to find a way to convince her she saw a known animal."

"I will," Max replied as he left; a feeling of deep guilt came over him for what he was about to do.

CHAPTER 27

The water panther swam near the ocean floor. Some time ago, he was driven from his territory by a larger male; being the runt of his litter, he was never good at fighting nor had he developed effective hunting techniques. To survive, he had found a new delicacy. The humans who traveled the water turned out to be an easy and delicious source of easy food. He had gotten weeks' worth of food from the submarine kill. Now he needed to safely store the remaining portions. He dug into the ocean floor until he felt his claw touch the soft flesh of a body. One of the many bodies he had temporarily stashed across the area.

He suddenly felt an impending feeling of danger. Before he could turn his head, two large tentacles wrapped around his body and back legs. He let out a cry of pain as the tentacles, hooks, and suction cups dug into his body, ripping and tearing his flesh. He turned to see the tentacles attached to the body of a colossal squid pulling him towards a sharp beak, and a legion of smaller tentacles. Knowing he had one shot of escaping, he reared his head to the side and bit down on the feeding tentacle wrapped around his body. After several bites in rapid succession, the tentacle came loose. The pain caused the colossal squid to release his back legs. The water panther swam to a safe distance, then turn to face his opponent.

The squid, who was twice as big as the water panther, had recovered and was jetting towards him. He remained still, waiting for the last longer feeding tentacle to reach him. When the tentacle was about to wrap around him, he jolted to the left side, causing it to miss. He latched on to it with his front limbs pinning it to the ocean floor. The end of the tentacle wrapped around his front right leg, ripping into it. Even with his tentacle pinned to the ground, the colossal squid still had the strength to pull the water panther towards him. Like before, the water panther bit down and separated the last feeding tentacle from the squid's body. With his enemy writhing in pain, it was his turn to strike. The water panther swam towards the colossal squid. Right before he was in range of the smaller tentacles, the sound of a thunderclap exited his throat. A sudden pain filled the colossal squid's body. To counter, the colossal squid released a stream of black ink and moved back rapidly. It did nothing to stop the pain, and soon the colossal squid's insides started to fail, as a feeling of pleasure filled the water panther when both the colossal squid's eyes exploded from their sockets. He had won.

The water panther swam on top of his adversary. He bite down digging into the squid's mantle and fins. The red cloud he had become so familiar with surrounded him. The squid's body went limp and hit the ocean floor. He was victorious, but he had paid for his victory. His body was covered with cuts and gashes from the tentacles. He was fortunate the first infrasound blast had done the job. He grabbed several human bodies and headed to his lair. He would need some time to recover before he hunted again.

CHAPTER 28

10:14 AM 04/17/2021 HST

The X-7 touched down on one of the helicopter landing pads at Kahului Airport. Max got out and slung a small travel bag over his left shoulder. Since the phone was off limits, Max had brought along drawing and writing material. The idea was to get Mya to draw what she had seen so they could compare it with the images they had of the water panther. Max looked down at his watch, which read half past nine.

"I'm going to head to the café. I should be back around one."

"Don't forget to stop at a florist," Liz added.

"Why?" Max asked, not picking up on the joke.

"To get flowers for your darling. Oh, and get some chocolates, maybe a bear that says 'I love you.'" Max gave her an annoyed look and started to walk away. Out of the corner of his eye, he saw Okada giving Liz a talking to, which made him smile.

"Hold on a moment," Ashly said.

Now what? Max thought, hoping she was not going to start acting like Liz. Ashly ran over to him and handed him a sliver ring. Max took it. The ring was in the shape of a wolf's head. The large eye holes were covered by bright blue stones.

"Why do I need a ring?" Max asked, confused.

"It's not just a ring," Ashly replied. She brought the ring to Max's eye level and held up her tablet with her other hand. A live video of Max was on the screen. "See, the eyes are actually small cameras, and the wolf's nose is the camera's speaker. The live video is connected to my tablet by Bluetooth. The feeling of guilt returned to Max. Not wanting to deceive Mya, he gently pushed Ashly's hand away.

"Ashly, Mya made it clear she did not want to be filmed."

"Well, that's too bad for her. We need an accurate record of the account," Ashly said in a serious tone.

"Ashly, the poor girl's been through hell. I feel bad enough I cannot tell her the truth. I don't want to go against her wishes any more than I have to," Max replied in an equally serious tone. Okada noticed an airport security officer's car coming towards them. He ordered Liz to speak to them, then walked over to Max and Ashly. Ashly quickly explained the situation to him.

"Max, we want to have her story on video record. Just in case you miss some time, or we need to revisit it." Okada said siding with Ashly. Max did not like it, but he knew he was right.

"Fine," he said, reluctantly taking the ring.

He started to leave when Ashly said with an embarrassed laugh, "Sorry, I forgot to give you the ear piece."

"Why do I need an ear piece?" Max asked, annoyed. Ashly moved her eyes to the side like she was about to say something she knew he would not want to hear.

"Along with watching, Okada and I felt it would be better if we had the ability to talk to you."

"What! Why is that necessary?" Max said as a feeling of discomfort came over him. It was no secret he found Mya attractive. That was going to make things awkward enough; the last thing he needed was Liz's voice in his ear.

"We will only speak if we need to remind you to ask her something important," Okada reassured. Max looked at Ashly.

"So, you're going to do all your surveillance work from inside the chopper?" he asked, mainly to break his current train of thought.

Ashly shrugged. "Don't act like we're spying on you."

"But that's exactly what you're doing." Max muttered.

"Anyway, I made arraignments for us to use one of the helicopter tour buildings that is closed today," Ashly added. They noticed the security car leaving the area.

"Paperwork is in order. We're good to use the building," Liz shouted and gave a thumbs up.

"How did you manage that on such short notice?" Max asked.

"She hacked the system and forged the paperwork. That's how," Samuel said, walking past them, carrying a box of equipment.

"I did not. I contacted the owner of the building and arranged for us to use it for the day," Ashly yelled back. With everything finalized, Max departed from his teammates, this time without any interruptions. He hated having to lie to Mya but saw there was no way to avoid it. So, like a good soldier, he followed orders.

***

Mya Kendig sat at a table for two at the Crescent Moon gaming café. She was wearing blue jean shorts and a black t-shirt. She was staring into the coffee cup, watching the white ring of cream disappear as she stirred.

"Girl, I thought you were leaving early today; why have you not gone home yet? You okay?" Riley asked.

"Umm, I'm meeting someone in a few minutes," Mya replied, looking up at Riley. Riley could tell by her body language she was uneasy. Riley raised an eyebrow.

"Oh, as in someone special?"

"No, nothing like that," Mya answered in a reassuring voice. "Remember when I got that call from the biologist wanting to know about my...my encounter?"

"How could I forget? You sure read him the riot act." Mya moved her eyes downward, remembering the incident. Max seemed to be a nice guy, and now she felt bad for treating him so poorly when he called the first time.

"After you told me about the submarine attack, I knew I had to do something. So, I thought it would be a good idea to share my experience with someone who actually wanted to hear about it." A man in his late fifties wearing a polo shirt and khakis walked by the window Mya was sitting by.

"This might be him," she said nervously. Both girls watched as the man walked by the door and continued on. Mya's face had a look of disappointment.

"Why do you look so nervous?" Riley asked.

"I'm just worried something will go wrong. I want him to get here so I can get this over with."

"Don't worry. I'll wait your table and when I get free time, I'll check in on you. If I see he's giving you trouble, I'll read him the riot act." Hearing that made Mya feel better.

"Thanks," Mya replied, feeling good she had an ally around if things got out of hand.

"No trouble. I have to get back to work. Catch you later." Mya put both hands over her ears and the back of her head. She was mentally preparing for the worst. Her thoughts were broken up when a voice behind her spoke her name.

"Hi, Mya Kendig?" She looked up to see a handsome young man wearing a black shirt with a skull knight—a skull knight from her favorite game, *Legendary Quests and Creatures*.

"Uh, hi?" Mya replied, not knowing who he was. This couldn't be the biologist, could it? Liz noticed the look on her face.

"Good news, Max. She's into you." *Shut up, Liz. Why are you even using the microphone?* Max thought.

"Hi, Max Varian," Max said, extending his hand. Mya slowly extended her hand and shook it. Max was just waiting for Liz to say something.

"Now that she's interested. You need to get her on the hook. Mention you like that game." Before Liz could finish, the headphones were pulled off her head.

"Hey! What da?" Okada used his free hand to grab the office chair and started wheeling it towards the door.

"Ashly," he said. She looked towards him in time to catch the headphones.

"Hey, I wasn't finished talking yet. I need to know how this plays out," Liz protested. Okada did not answer. He opened the door, then placed both hands on the head of the chair and pushed it outside.

"Start readying the helicopter or do something productive," Okada said and shut the door. He grabbed an extra folding chair and sat down next to Ashly.

"Max, Liz is gone; just act natural," Okada said. Hearing that made the butterflies in his stomach die down. The fact that he found the girl in front of him more attractive in person made it hard enough to focus.

"Um, you're the biologist I talked to?" Mya asked, trying to calm the butterflies in her own stomach.

"Sure am." Mya gave a doubtful look. "What? Were you expecting an old guy with a white beard and wearing field khakis?"

"I was not expecting a guy wearing a skull knight shirt from my favorite video game."

"Hey, I love *Legendary Quests and Creatures* too. So, I wear shirts like these when I'm off work. May I sit down?" Mya stared for a few seconds, then broke out of her trance.

"Um. Yeah. Sure. Sorry," Mya replied, already feeling more comfortable with the situation. Max sat down.

"First, I just wanted to say sorry about losing your sister. Jade seemed like a nice girl." A slight glare formed in Mya's eyes. This guy had made a good first impression, but she was in no mood for this type of suck-up.

"How would you know what she was like?" Mya asked in a rude voice.

"She's touchy," Ashly commented. She had not pressed the speaker button, so Max did not hear the comment.

"Because I talked to her once," Max said in a confident voice that showed no sign of lying.

"What? You knew Jade?" Mya said, taken back by the response. "She never mentioned knowing someone like you."

"Well, I never met her face to face. She emailed me about possibly setting up a dive with the dolphin event using the show dolphins I work with. I called her back and said that since the dolphins were owned by a third party, I could not authorize such a thing." Mya calmed down after hearing that. The response made sense. The conversation was interrupted when Riley approached.

"Hi, my name is Riley. May I get you a coffee to start?" she asked.

"Uh. Hold on a second," Max said. He picked up a menu and started skimming over it.

Riley turned her back to Max and, looking straight at Mya, softly said, "Liar." Mya made sure Max was not looking and started frantically shaking her head no.

"It's not like that at all. Go away," Mya replied, equally softly.

"I'll have the lava hot chocolate," Max said, diverting Riley's attention. "Have you eaten?" he asked Mya.

"Yes. I didn't want to waste your time, so I had lunch before you came," Mya replied. "I don't need anything," she said to Riley.

"I thought you said you were going to order dessert?" Riley said with a smile. Max gave her a puzzled look. Riley motioned a hand to Mya. "We work together; that's how I know her." She moved slightly over to the menu Max was holding. "Here, I can show you her favorite dessert." Under the table, Mya was franticly kicking at Riley.

"We get rid of Liz, and now this nonsense starts," Okada said. He looked at the clock, which read eleven-ten. He wanted Max to get the meeting over with as soon as possible. The sooner the team could get to Pearl Harbor, the more time they would have examining the submarine wreckage.

"So, can I get you one chocolate fudge rock golem cake to share?"

"Sure," Max said. Mya did not protest, but she felt like getting up and tossing Riley into the kitchen.

"Okay, be back in a bit." Riley turned towards Mya, raised her eyebrows, and said. "Enjoy." Mya tried to kick at Riley again, then put her hands over her face and moaned.

"I'm sorry about that," she said, embarrassed and annoyed.

"I know the feeling. I also have a co-worker I want to kick sometimes." Mya's face turned red with embarrassment. Had he noticed the whole thing? "Let's get back on topic, shall we?" Max asked, wanting to break the awkward feeling both of them had.

"Yes," Mya agreed. Max laid the travel bag on the table. He opened it and pulled out around a dozen photos.

"I brought several photos of prehistoric and modern-day animals, and I promise there are no sharks."

"Better not be," Mya said seriously.

"When I hold up a photo, I want you to say yes, no, or tell me what features look familiar."

"Got it," Mya said. They were briefly interrupted when Riley brought Max's drink. He held up the first photo, which was a photo of a giant squid.

"I doubt this is it, but I want to get it out of the way," he said.

Right away, Mya replied, "No." Max put the picture down and held up a picture of a plesiosaur. Mya looked at it for a few seconds. "No, the creature I saw had a clawed arm, not flippers."

"Well, that eliminates some creatures." Max removed five pictures from the list. Mya smiled as she looked at a photo of a kronosaurus. For once, someone was listening to her and not treating her like she was crazy. "What about this one?" he asked, showing her a picture of a marine iguana. Mya took the picture and looked at it.

"I don't think it was a marine iguana," Mya said like it was an obvious statement.

"I doubted it was, but are any of the features similar?" Mya looked at the photo again. She closed her eyes. A slight look of pain formed on her face like she was remembering something terrible.

"The claws were long like that, and the tail may be similar."

"Okay, here's my number one suspect," Max said. He handed her a photo of a large saltwater crocodile. "Does that look like the animal you saw?" Mya had a confused look on her face, thinking back to when Riley had suggested the same thing.

"Well, I don't remember any scales on the arm. The skin was smoother; it might have even had fur." Mya sighed in frustration. "I don't know. To be honest, I don't remember if the tail had scales, or spines, or anything."

"Well, at least you know it wasn't a shark," Max said jokingly. A stern look formed on Mya's face. Seeing it made Max worried she was going to get up and leave right then, but the look soon changed into a slight smile. He even saw her lightly laugh at the joke. Max showed Mya the remaining photos. On Okada's orders, he had intentionally left out a photo of a water panther or anything looking like it. The only photo Mya showed any interest in was the photo of the Nothosaurus.

"Okay, whatever this is?" she said, holding up the photo of the Nothosaurus. "And the salt water crocodile are the closest to what I saw. She laid both photos in front of Max. "You're the expert. What do you think is more likely?"

"Scientifically speaking, I would love to discover a living Nothosaurus, but I have to lean towards the salt water crocodile as the prime suspect," Max said, hoping that would satisfy her. Mya understood why he suspected a crocodile, but she was still not convinced. When she asked what a salt water crocodile would be doing swimming around Maui, just like Riley, Max explained that people often keep exotic animals as pets and it was very possible for a salt water crocodile to have escaped. After hearing the explanation, Mya still did not look convinced.

"If my encounter was the only one, I would believe the crocodile story, but how do you explain the other attacks that have been going on around Maui? We both know there is no way a crocodile could have sunk a submarine or destroyed an underwater hotel room."

"True, but in all honesty, we don't even know if these incidents are connected." Mya gave him a look that said: *you really believe that?*

Crap she's smart, Max thought. Personally, he admired her for it, but it also made achieving the goal of convincing her she had seen a known animal difficult. Max could tell he was going down a dangerous road, so he decided to change the subject. "How about this? To help me better understand what you saw, would you mind drawing everything you remember about the creature?" He pulled a drawing pad and pencil kit from the travel bag. An uneasy look formed on Mya's face. She did not want to relive anything about that day.

"I can..." She took a deep breath. "I can try." Before she could begin her drawing, Riley laid the cake between them. The smell of hot fudge and chocolate filled their nostrils.

"Why don't we take a break and eat?" Max suggested.

"Great idea," Mya agreed.

"Tell me when it's over," Okada said, getting up from his seat.

"You don't like listening to romantic lunches?" Ashly teased.

"I want him to wrap things up so we can continue the investigation," Okada said, looking at the clock. "He should know work and romance don't mix. Liz and I show no affection towards each other when we're on duty."

"Not everyone is that disciplined," Ashly reminded. For about half an hour, Max and Mya talked about life, work, and what video games they liked. As they talked, Mya would draw on the pad from time to time. When a painful memory surfaced, she focused on her conversations with Max. Finally, Mya said, "I'm finished. I drew every detail I could remember." Max took the drawing and looked at it. The paper had two separate drawings: a paw with claws, and a long tail. It was by no means a masterpiece, but it was good enough. At the first glance, Max could tell the drawing matched the claw and tail of the water panther.

"I don't mean to push, but did you see any other part of the creature? The body or the head, for example."

Mya's expression changed from having fun to slight sadness when she said, "Sorry, that's it. When it first attacked, I was struck by part of it, but I can't remember what it looked like." Max could tell this was painful for her; inside, he felt bad he had forced her to relive it. Ashly was casually listening in when Samuel started waving a card in front of her face.

"Samuel, he cannot hear me unless I want him to. You can speak."

"I need to remind him to ask something." Ashly handed the extra headset to him and told him what button to press.

"Max, this is Samuel. Can you hear me?" Max was slightly startled by the voice in his ear. Fortunately, Mya did not seem to notice.

"He can hear you. Just tell him whatever you need to and shut up," Ashly snapped.

"Max, try to get information on how the creature attacked, and ask if she felt any sudden feeling of fright or felt like her body was paralyzed." He turned to Ashly. "Do I need to say over?" Max tried to keep a straight face. He could just imagine what Ashly was saying. He also wondered why Samuel wanted to know the second part of his question.

"Something wrong?" Mya asked, wondering why he had not replied.

"Sorry, I was just thinking whether or not I should ask these next two questions."

"Go ahead," Mya replied. She appreciated the fact that he was thinking about how she felt and not just shooting her question after question without any thought to her feelings.

"I know this will be painful to remember, but can you tell me about the attack from start to finish?" Mya gave a quick version of what happened. She had told the story several times before, so she was used to it.

"What was the next question?" Mya asked.

"Okay, this is going to be a little odd." Max admitted

"What do you want to know?"

"Before or during the attack, did you have any unexplained feeling of dread, paralysis, or nausea?" Max asked. He knew how stupid the question probably sounded to her.

"My sister was getting torn apart in front of me! Of course I felt frightened and sick!" she yelled. "Sorry," she apologized a few seconds later. "As you can imagine, reliving my encounter is painful and I'd like to stop talking about it."

"Sure, no problem. Sorry I brought it up." For a few moments, both were silent. Mya's face formed a look like she just remembered an important detail.

"I don't know if I imagined this, but right before the attack, I thought I heard thunder."

"Thunder?" Max said, a little surprised, before disregarding it.

"Mean anything to you?" Ashly asked Samuel.

"Yes; in fact, that's the most important thing she said. It confirms my theory." Samuel pulled off the headset and walked out of the room.

"I just want to kill whatever took Jade from me so bad." She made a fist and slammed the table gently in frustration. "But I can't." She looked up at him. "I kind of wish this whole thing was a fantasy story. If it was, I would end up meeting someone who knew about the ocean and believed me when no one else did. Then we would team up, track the creature to whatever hidden cave system it's hiding in, and kill it. That's why I love video games and fantasy worlds. In the end, the hero always comes out on top. Even if something terrible has happened to them." Max understood the subliminal message she was using.

"Max, there's no way we can bring her on the team. She would be nothing but a liability," Ashly said, worrying he was going to spill the beans and recruit her.

"Please don't do anything stupid. This is the real world, not fantasy, and the ocean can be a very dangerous place," Max said seriously.

"I know that all too well," Mya replied. She highly doubted he was going to take the bait and team up with her, but it was worth a try. Max looked at his watch and saw he needed to get going.

"Unfortunately, I have an appointment at two, so I need to be heading out." Mya had been dreading this meeting and now she felt upset it was going to end. She had really taken to the young biologist.

"I understand. I hope the information I gave you was helpful."

"It was," Max replied. "Do I need to wait for a check?"

"No, you pay up front. I get ten percent off. So, I can take care of it."

"No way. Food's on me," Max said. Mya blushed. Max pulled out his wallet and handed her a business card. "Here's my contact information. Call anytime."

"Thanks." She pulled a piece of scrap paper out of her purse and wrote on it. "Here's my number and email. Promise you'll call if you find anything?"

"Sure will. Care if I call you just to chat sometime? You seem like a fun person to hang out with." Mya laid back, hoping she would melt into her seat as the butterflies returned to her stomach.

"Sure," she managed to get out. Hearing that brought a small smile to Max's face. To this point, not many girls had interested him, but this one made him not want to think about his work life. They stared at each other for a few moments before Max walked over to the register to pay. Riley slithered into Max's seat with a mischievous grin.

"So how was it?"

"Go away," Mya replied, hiding her lovesick expression with her hands. After paying, Max exited the café.

CHAPTER 29

1:47 PM 04/17/2021 HST

The short ride to Oahu felt like an eternity to Max. With Okada flying and Samuel in the co-pilot seat, buried in his notes, he was left sitting between Liz and Ashly, who for the entire trip had been watching the video recording. Both girls were more focused on how he and Mya interacted then any information on the water panther. Ashly, of course, knew where all the highlights were and was showing Liz, who was making every joke she could think of. After what felt like hours of torture, the X-7 touched down at Pearl Harbor-Hickam air base. Suijin Squad was escorted to the base commander, who was waiting for them outside the warehouse where the wreckage of the Alexandria was being kept.

"This is Captain Allen Pierce," the guard escorting them said. Introductions were quickly made.

"I'm sure your team is anxious to get to work," Captain Pierce said in a heavy Texas accent.

"Yes, we are," Okada replied. "You spoke with my assistant Saburo regarding the current situation?"

"Mr. Nakamura has brought all high-ranking base staff up to speed on the current situation regarding this." He paused for a moment as he thought of the creature's name. "This water panther."

"Does this mean the Navy is going to take action against the creature?" Ashly asked, thinking it would make their job so much easier.

"Governor Fatu has not authorized us to conduct any military actions in U.S. waters. However, to help ensure the safety of the people living on Oahu, I ordered several destroyers to discreetly patrol the island. If they get a sonar reading on the sucker, your team will be our first call."

"What if the water panther attacks one?" Liz added.

"Then the wrath of the United States Navy will be brought down on it," Captain Pierce replied as he reached towards the warehouse door and punched in a security code. He pushed the door open, which made a metallic creaking sound. The Alexandria was sitting in the middle of the warehouse held several feet off the ground by two large steel structures located on the front and back of the sub.

"Captain, can you explain what the situation was like when you located the Alexandria?" Samuel asked.

"To give you the short version, the Coast Guard vessel Titan entered the disaster area about an hour after the last known GPS signal was received. Divers entered the water and attached towing cables to the wreckage. After that, the wreckage was brought here by orders of Governor Fatu," Captain Pierce answered.

"You wrote that down. Right?" Samuel asked, looking towards Ashly.

"No, I'm not your court reporter," Ashly snapped back.

"Did the divers or sonar spot the water panther?" Max inquired.

"And how many bodies did you recover?" Liz added.

"The Titan's sonar captured no unusual activity, and we currently have re-covered no bodies," Captain Pierce replied, sounding a little surprised by the last answer.

"That might be good news," Max said to no one in particular. Ashly looked at him like he was nuts. "I'll explain later. Right now, I want to examine the wreckage." Once Suijin Squad started their examination, Captain Pierce left the area. Max walked around the Alexandria several times. The windows on the right and back side of the sub were destroyed. Claw marks created a grey stripe pattern across the ship's hull. Ashly entered the sub to check out the radio equipment. The inside of the sub was intact and surprisingly clean.

"Did they clean this already? Because I'm seeing no blood?" Ashly questioned. She was expecting to see a bloody scene from a horror movie, but there was nothing.

"No, it has not been touched. The only other people who have been in here were the rescue divers," Liz replied.

"Any fresh blood was removed by the water, Ashly," Max observed. He looked at the destroyed back viewing window. He could tell by how the remaining edges of glass were facing that the glass had been broken from the outside.

"Hey, Samuel," he yelled. Samuel was standing on top of the sub, examining the claw markings. He stopped what he was doing, climbed down, and walked over to him. "Is there any information about water panthers having a thick skull?" he asked, thinking back to the bone pattern he noticed under the creature's skull.

"It's funny you brought that up," Samuel replied, noticing the same details Max was. "There is a lesser known cryptid called the splinter cat. The splinter cat is said to ram trees to locate honey." Max gave him a skeptical look. "I don't know if I believe that," Samuel defended. "More reasonable accounts state the splinter cat is seen frequently in water and is believed to feed on fish. Some accounts even state that they steal fish from fishermen's lines."

"What does that have to do with our water panther?" Max replied.

"Some cryptozoologists have suggested that the splinter cat and the water panther are the same species—the splinter cat being the juvenile of the species."

More reports of these creatures coming on land, Max thought.

"Did you learn anything useful from my conversation with Mya?" Max asked, wondering if Samuel had picked up on something he missed. He had enjoyed the time with Mya but felt she provided no new useful information.

"Yes; in fact, her stating she heard thunder pretty much confirmed a theory I had about the creature."

"What theory would that be?" Okada asked as he and Liz joined them. Samuel did not answer right away. The look on his face said he had an idea but was trying to work it correctly.

"Let's just say this creature may have a unique ability that is rare in the animal kingdom."

"What kind?" Okada asked.

"I know what you're talking about," Max added. "Infrasound?"

"Yes, exactly. It has been suggested that some cryptozoological species have the ability to produce infrasound."

"Okay, you two, please explain to the nonscientist in the room what infrasound is?" Liz questioned.

"Okay, I'll explain it so even you can understand it," Max teased. Liz threw a slow jab, which Max blocked.

"Infrasound is simply a sound that has a frequency lower then 20 hertz a second. In nature, events like ocean waves, earthquakes, and lightning cause infrasound. It's been theorized that's how some species of animals can predict earthquakes: by hearing infrasound waves traveling through the earth."

"So, you're saying we should use cats to track this creature."

"Liz," Okada said in a voice that showed he was getting annoyed. He turned his attention back to Max. "Can known organisms use infrasound?"

"Some species of animals like whales and elephants use infrasound to communicate with one another."

"Can we hear infrasound?" Liz interrupted.

"No, humans cannot hear infrasound, but we can feel it."

"So, if we cannot hear infrasound, why is it dangerous to us? And if known animals use infrasound, why is it such a big deal that this creature might be able to use it?" Liz commented.

"Just because you cannot hear infrasound does not mean it cannot affect you. Infrasound at high intensities can be felt and even bruise internal organs. People who work with tigers at times have reported sudden symptoms of fear, hallucinations, dizziness, nausea, vomiting, and even temporary paralysis. These symptoms were caused by the tiger using infrasound. It has also been suggested that infrasound can...." Max paused and looked at Samuel.

"You want to take this, Samuel?"

"No continue, you're doing a fine job."

"Recent studies have suggested that at the right frequency, infrasound might"—he stressed the word might—"be able to drain batteries, and shut down electronic equipment."

"That sounds a little farfetched," Liz observed.

"But it makes sense," Okada added. "The Hawaiian Coast Guard reported that no distress call came from the sub."

"What about the Lucky Dragon? It sent out a distress call, and the recovered VDR was working fine," Liz added. "Too bad it didn't provide any useful information."

"Perhaps the creature did not use infrasound on the Lucky Dragon. It was the first attack, after all; maybe it learned that using infrasound makes hunting easier," Okada suggested.

"More likely, the water panther needs to directly target something with the infrasound," Max said. Liz looked at him, confused. "Think of it more like a bullet that needs to be aimed than a blast wave that hits everything."

"Okay, that makes sense," Liz said. Satisfied with the answer, Okada walked to the opposite side of the sub to check on Ashly's progress, while Liz checked the scratch marks on the sub's hulls to see if the water panther had lost a claw during the attack. Ashly was sitting in the driver's seat looking over the electronics.

"Ashly, how does the electrical equipment look?"

"Everything is completely fried," she answered.

"Can you determine the cause?" Okada inquired, thinking of the infra-sound theory.

"Unfortunately, no. I cannot say whether the damage occurred before or after hundreds of gallons of water poured into the sub."

"Didn't find anything on the hull," Liz shouted to Max. He was not surprised to hear that. Even if the water panther had lost a claw, it would have most likely been dislodged when the Alexandria was moved.

"Does anyone know if this sub had?" Samuel snapped his fingers as he tried to think of the right wording. "One of those cameras that records the tour for the passengers to purchase later?"

"I don't know," Max said, intrigued. "Ashly."

"What?" she replied in a voice that showed she was concentrating hard on her work.

"Did the Alexandria have a tour camera?"

"No, but cell phones or personal cameras may have been recovered," she replied. Max pulled out his phone and called Saburo. Saburo reported that along with several non-relevant items, eleven cell phones had been collected, none of which were working. Max looked at Ashly.

"Do you wanted to look over the damaged cell phones?"

"I can take them back to base and see if I can recover some of the data, but in all honesty, I will most likely do a lot of work for nothing. Checking the passengers cloud accounts would be a good idea though."

"Why don't we take them back to check for unusual damage? It might provide more evidence for the infrasound theory," Max suggested.

"The infrasound theory?" Ashly asked, confused.

After Max explained it to her, Liz said, "Well, I don't think there is much more we can learn here."

"Agreed," Okada said.

After the Alexandria examination, the team had about an hour of down time before the car that would be transporting them to the Hawaii State Capitol building arrived. Okada was talking with Captain Pierce, and Liz was hanging out with some naval friends she had on base. Ashly and Samuel went to the mess hall to grab a quick bite to eat. After that, Ashly examined a few of the damaged cell phones recovered from the Alexandria. As she suspected, due to the severe water damage, it was impossible to tell if the phones were damaged by infrasound, and the cloud accounts provided nothing useful. Max decided he wanted some alone time, so he found a bench under a large tree overlooking the bay. Time slipped away from him as he looked across the waters of Pearl Harbor. He was mainly thinking about Mya, about what that poor girl must have truly gone through. After seeing what the water panther had done to the submarine, he could not imagine how terrifying it must have been for a diver to randomly come across it.

"Max, we are departing soon," Okada's voice said, bringing Max back to reality.

"Right. I'm ready when everyone else is." Okada stared at the memorials of the U.S. Arizona and Missouri for a moment. He sat down next to Max, which Max found surprising.

"Strange, isn't it?" Okada said.

"What is?" Max asked, having no idea what Okada was talking about.

"Nearly a century ago on this very spot, our ancestors fought one another, and here we stand as allies united against a common enemy," Okada said with a slight hint of wonder in his voice.

"Your grandfather was stationed aboard the Akagi. Correct?" Max asked, slightly curious. To this point, neither man had ever shared any stories of what their grandfathers had done during World War II. Max knew from the photos in Okada's office that his grandfather was aboard the Akagi, but he had never found the courage to ask what his story was. Okada's face showed no sign of strain when he responded.

"Yes, he was stationed on the Akagi. He piloted a torpedo bomber. Once the Akagi was sunk, he was stationed aboard the Jun'yō. What about your grandfather? Did he fight in the Great War?" Okada asked with genuine interest. Max took a moment to think. It had been quite a while since he had accessed these memories. Towards the end of his life, his grandfather had told him about his experiences during World War II. Max had recorded the tales and kept his grandfather's personal war time journal.

"Yes, he was in the war, but he fought the Germans, not the Japanese. He was the gunner of a tank crew. His first combat mission was storming the beaches of Normandy on D-day. He was the second tank to make landfall."

"The second tank?" Okada said, amazed. "Did he survive the war?"

"I wouldn't be here if he didn't," Max answered jokingly.

"True," Okada replied, sounding like he took the statement more as a fact than as a joke. "After the Germans were defeated, why did he not go to the Pacific to fight?"

"He was in training for the Pacific, but the war ended before his training was finished. I have his complete war story in a journal if you would like to read it."

"I would. It sounds like a very interesting read," Okada replied.

"Hey, you two. Ride's here," Liz shouted from the hill above them.

"Duty calls," Okada said, getting up.

Chapter 30

5:56 PM 04/17/2021 HST

Governor David Fatu was in the middle of a phone conversation regarding a new civil law when his secretary entered the room. The governor's office was a large square room. Beautiful wood coverings enclosed the walls. Further adding to the walls' splendor was the many pictures of Hawaiian landmarks. The Governor and Lieutenant Governor's desks were placed on opposite sides of the room. A large wooden table had been placed between the desks in preparation for the meeting.

"Yes, Ms. Kelemen?" he said, covering the speaker.

"Governor Fatu, your guests have arrived." He motioned for her to wait, spoke to the person on the other line for a few moments, and ended the call.

"Send them in," he requested, pleased they were here. Okada was the first to enter. Governor Fatu stood up. He was a slightly overweight Hawaiian native in his late fifties. He had light brown skin and short balding brown hair. A small beard and mustache covered his face.

"Governor Fatu. Thank you for having us," Okada said, extending his hand.

Governor Fatu shook it and said, "Thank you for helping us with our problem." After Okada introduced the members of his team, everyone sat down. Governor Fatu was the first to speak.

"I wanted to start this meeting off by thanking the Japanese government and each of you for helping us solve this mystery. As you can imagine, many people living on Maui are becoming concerned about the growing number of deaths that have occurred around the island."

"Thank you for your help and cooperation. Remember this creature's first attack was on a Japanese fishing vessel. Your government's assistance in that matter was truly helpful," Okada replied. Both men's faces signaled a sign of respect.

"To this point, we've managed to keep feeding the media cover stories, but I don't know how much longer people will buy them," Governor Fatu said, slightly concerned. "I only know that an undiscovered animal is behind these attacks. Your team has been investigating this creature since the first attack, so I'm curious to know what your team has learned."

"We have a pretty good idea of what this creature is and what it might be capable of. Governor, if I may present our findings?" Max asked.

"Yes, please," Governor Fatu replied. The wall mounted TV was turned on. Liz turned off the lights. Ashly played the video of the water panther and showed slides of the information the team had gathered. As the slides were shown, Max and Samuel explained the information, as well as their theories on the water panther. After the presentation was over, the lights were turned back on. Governor

Fatu sat motionless for a moment, trying to comprehend the information he just received.

"I just can't believe it. An actual sea monster swimming in the Maui waters." His voice was filled with disbelief. "Do you believe other Hawaiian islands are at risk, and is it possible this water panther might come ashore?"

Max was about to speak when Samuel said confidently, "No, it cannot come ashore. The water panther is a purely aquatic creature."

"Looking at the current attack patterns, it seems this creature's primary territory is around Maui. However, I feel it's very possible that attacks might also occur around the islands of Molokai, Lanai, and Kahoolawe," Max said.

"Mr. Varian, during the presentation, you mentioned you believed the water panther has some form of intelligence. Are you saying that it can speak or build weapons?" Governor Fatu asked nervously. Max tried not to laugh at the ridiculousness of the statement.

"No, nothing like that," Max replied, managing to keep a serious tone. "It seems to be learning how to more effectively use its natural weapons to sink ships. In time it may also learn naval patterns like shipping lanes or when beaches are most active."

"Is this type of intelligence common in the animal kingdom?" Governor Fatu replied.

"Very common. In fact, if our theories are correct, this creature is by no means the smartest creature in existence." Max smiled a satisfied smile when he said, "Our dolphins appear to be much smarter." Governor Fatu closed the folder

Ashly had given him containing the information the team had gathered on the creature.

"Each of you has certainly done a good job gathering information on this creature. Now I would like to move on to the subject of destroying it." He looked towards Okada. "Commander Takahashi, when we spoke over the phone, you mentioned using underwater mines. Do you think that is still a viable option?"

"Yes, that is currently our first plan of attack," Okada replied.

"Well, that would certainly be an effective option." Governor Fatu spoke in an unsure voice when he said, "However, I must admit I'm concerned about the dangers a mine field may pose to vessels that travel the Maui waters." Ashly explained in great detail the plan she had laid out in Tokyo. How she would be able to remotely detonate the mines, so they posed no threat to local ships. Hearing her plan brought Governor Fatu's mind at ease.

"Ms. Cross, you seem confident in your plan and you managed to convince me."

"Well, thank you," Ashly said proudly.

"I will authorize you to deploy a mine field to destroy the creature. Where do you plan on deploying the mines?"

"The plan is to place the mine field near the creature's lair once we locate it," Max said.

"Do you have any idea where that is?" Governor Fatu asked.

"Our research shows that it's very possible the creature has a lair near Molokini crater. Tomorrow we plan on conducting a reconnaissance mission of the area," Ashly added.

"Now, I don't mean to play devil's advocate, but if the mine field should fail, do you have a backup plan?" Governor Fatu inquired.

"Our secondary plan is using the attack dolphins armed with hypodermic lances," Max continued. Since she had not spoken yet, Max let Liz explain the process of what the hypodermic lances were and what type of explosives they would be using. Governor Fatu shook his head in an amused way.

"I never imagined when I signed the agreement allowing the Japanese government to train attack dolphins on Niihau that they might one day be used to destroy a sea monster." He looked towards Okada and Liz. "How soon can the mine operation be ready? As you can imagine, I want this creature dealt with as soon as possible."

"We plan on conducting operations in several weeks," Okada answered.

"Several weeks!" Governor Fatu said in a shocked, surprised voice. "I'm sorry; that timeframe is unacceptable. Attacks from this creature have been occurring almost daily. In two weeks, fourteen new attacks may occur." He paused for a moment, then said softly. "God knows how many people will be killed."

"Based on new information we gathered from the submarine, I highly doubt there will be any new attacks for at least several weeks," Max said.

"What new information is that?" Governor Fatu asked, looking pleased and slightly confused at the same time.

"The submarine had fifty-one passengers on board. Based on this creature's size, I doubt it will need to hunt for some time. I believe the creature is either storing food for later or, like a snake, eating a large amount of food at one time and then becoming less active until the food is digested."

"An interesting theory, but what evidence do you have to support it?"

"The fact that no bodies were recovered; they just didn't disappear into thin air," Liz cut in. Even though Liz's comments were crude, they managed to convince Governor Fatu.

He said, "I understand your need for planning, and I agree to a two-week planning phase for the operation. However, if attacks from this monster continue, you will have to conduct immediate counter operations."

"We can agree to that. Once the creature is destroyed, we plan on taking the remains to Niihau for future study," Okada stated.

"I honestly don't care what is done with the body. I just want this creature out of my waters." A buzzing sound broke the current conversation. Governor Fatu picked up the phone to see what his secretary wanted.

"Do you think this meeting will end soon?" Liz whispered to Max in a bored voice.

"I'm guessing we're nearing the end of it," Max replied softly. Governor Fatu put the phone down.

"The final topic we need to address is what cover story do we tell the public? If the existence of this creature goes mainstream, it will cause a mass panic that the tourist industry will never recover from," Governor Fatu said, alarmed.

"Are you going to tell the surviving victim the same thing?" Max added, thinking of Mya.

Ashly looked at him and said, "Speaking of Mya. During your meeting with her, you came up with a great cover story. The escaped salt water crocodile." Governor Fatu snapped his finger and smiled.

"That's a brilliant idea!" He stretched his hand out in an excited manner. It was obvious by his facial expression, he was visualizing the newspaper heading in front of him when he said, "The cover story will be a salt water crocodile escaped from a private collector and is responsible for most of the attacks. The other events are unfortunate coincidences." He looked at everyone else. "What do you think?"

"I think it will work," Liz replied. Everyone nodded in agreement. "Is that all the information you needed from us?" Liz asked, wanting to get the meeting over with.

"Yes, you have given me more than enough information to think about. I must again congratulate each of you for discovering so much information about this creature in so short of time, and on top of that coming up with a plan to destroy it."

"No thanks is needed; we are just fulfilling our duties," Okada said.

"Not many people could have accomplished this much in such a short time-frame. Now I would be honored if you and your team would be my guests at dinner tonight."

"It would be our honor," Okada accepted. When Governor Fatu's back was turned, Liz made a gun with her finger, pointed it towards her head, and fired.

CHAPTER 31

The Barracuda drifted above the edge of the world at Molokini Crater. Sonar scans conducted earlier in the day had revealed several locations that appeared to be entrances to underwater caves. It was a clear cloudless day with a pleasant temperature of seventy-eight degrees. Ashly tossed the new MSR-2 into the water.

She walked back into the cabin and said, "Before I take her down. Everyone knows where the four pairs of cable cutters are. Right?"

"Yes," Liz replied. The tone of her voice showed she thought Ashly was overreacting.

"Hey, after what happened the first time, I'm not taking any chances," Ashly countered. Having the full team with her and a better understanding of what the water panther was overshadowed any feeling of fear that began to surface when she started to control the MSR-2.

Okada kept a watchful eye on the sonar, Liz was on gunner duty, and Max and Samuel's screens showed the MSR-2 camera feed. The idea was Ashly would concentrate on the driving while the two of them looked for anything out of the ordinary. Ashly moved the MSR-2 to the first location tagged by the sonar. The building anticipation soon diminished when the MSR-2 lights revealed the area to be nothing more than a large crack in the crater wall. Investigations of the other locations turned out to be nothing more than large holes in the reef's floors. A feeling of disappointment started to fill every member of the team.

"I hate to say it, but this trip was a bust," Ashly said, admitting defeat.

"Maybe he's just not home," Liz suggested.

"We have not found anything that even looks like it could be the water panther lair," Max added, shrugging his shoulders. "You sure these were the only possible cave sites the sonar found?"

"Yes, I checked it over twice," Ashly said, a little snappy. She sent the information to Max's computer. "Here's a copy of the scans if you want to look them over." Ashly paused for a moment, then said, "Sorry, I didn't mean to be so snappy. I just want to hurry up and find this thing's lair and get out of here." Max gave her a look that said no offense was taken.

"This area is also a tourist hotspot. So, it's highly unlikely an unknown creature could be living here without more attacks or sightings," Samuel noted.

"Are there other areas you suggest we check out?" Okada asked. Max laid back in his chair, closed his eyes, and started to think. He was sure this was the area, but it turned out he was wrong. His thoughts went to his meeting with Mya and her words.

"Track the creature down to whatever hidden cave system it's hiding in and kill it."

"Hidden cave system, hidden cave system." He repeated. Trying to figure out why he was focusing on that. Max suddenly opened his eyes when the revelation came to him. "Liz, didn't you tell me about a cave system around here that was too dangerous to dive in?" Liz's eyes grew wide with excitement.

"Yes, the Five Caves Five Graves cave system!"

"What kind of a name is that?" Ashly asked.

"The name comes from a local saying: five divers entering the cave will create five new graves. Sort of this area's haunted house," Liz replied. Ashly did not seem satisfied with the answer.

"Five Caves Five Graves is a maze of underwater caverns that connects five different underwater caves' systems. Due to the silty floor and dark conditions, divers can easily lose visibility and become disoriented," Max answered.

"Have these five cave systems ever been explored?" Samuel wondered.

"If I recall, a few years ago a scientific team conducted a mapping expedition of the cave system," Max replied. Ashly opened a web browser and pulled up a news article on the expedition. The article read: "two divers tragically lost in mapping operation. Expedition leader claims cave labyrinth too dangerous for any type of diving."

"Did they uncover how the divers perished?" Okada asked.

"Yes. Both bodies were recovered. Cause of death was drowning due to disorientation," Ashly read.

"In my book, the cave site is worth looking into," Samuel suggested. The team unanimously agreed.

***

The Five Caves Five Graves site was two miles north of Molokini Crater and three miles west from Maui's Poʻolenalena Beach Park. While traveling, Ashly tried to locate the cave diagrams the previous mapping expedition had created. Unfortunately, the only information she could locate was that due to the diving accidents, the mapping was never completed. The team had tried to scan the cave system with the Barracuda's sonar, but could not get any detailed layouts of the cave systems' connecting tunnels. Ashly held her breath as the MSR-2 once again plunged into the depths. She was heading into an unknown cave system with no information whatsoever. Some people would find this exciting; she, on the other hand, hated it. What also worried her was the fact that she never had a chance to add modifications to this new MSR-2. Which meant no sonar or light drones. The MSR-2 was at a depth of seventy feet when it reached the ocean floor. Ashly pushed the joystick forward. Moments later, the MSR-2 approached a rocky outcrop, and the entrance to one of the caves came into view. Against the ragged wall of stone, its appearance was like an open mouth, hiding God knows what horrors on the inside. Ashly opened a small window in the corner of Max's computer screen.

"Max, I need you to keep an eye on the cable gage," Ashly said in a tense voice.

"Sure. What am I looking out for?"

"That display shows the cable tension. If it starts to flash red, tell me. It means the cable's getting caught on something." Ashly turned to him and smiled a nervous smile. "The last thing we need is to lose this drone because it got snagged on a rock." She turned back to the controls and moved the MSR-2 through the underwater cave opening. The wide opening quickly started to become a narrow tube. A feeling of claustrophobia came over Ashly. She started wishing more than anything this drone had a sonar system. Max and Samuel's eyes were glued to the screen looking for anything that could be the water panther. Max, of course, kept one eye on the cable screen. The drone's light was only illuminating about ten feet in front of it, showing nothing but uneven shapes of the rock tunnel that surrounded it.

"This is very odd," Max said.

"What?" Ashly asked, feeling her body jolt. She may have been safely aboard the ship, but focusing on controlling the drone made her feel like she was the one inside the tunnel system. Max's words were unintentionally creepy when he said, "No fish. No marine life of any kind." As Ashly listened, the MSR-2 drifted to the cave bottom. The twin propellers started stirring up sediment from the bottom floor, creating a thick cloud of mud and sediment.

"Ashly, move the drone towards the top of the cave," Samuel said, giving unwanted advice.

"I'm trying," Ashly replied. The screen in front of her was showing nothing but a brown cloud. After a moment of tense driving, the MSR-2 screen became clear again.

"No wonder they call this place five graves," Liz said, thinking about how terrifying it would have been to be a diver trapped in those conditions. For several minutes, the MSR-2 traveled through the tunnel, the seemingly endless darkness and unnatural lack of marine life making the situation unnaturally eerie.

"What's that?" Ashly asked, noticing a small circle of light in the distance.

"The light at the end of the tunnel?" Liz replied as if it were obvious.

"You always find a way to get your puns in," Max said.

"Isn't that why you love me?" Liz asked.

"Only sometimes," Okada replied. Focus was returned to the screens when the MSR-2 went through the opening, which the team guessed was around thirty-five feet high.

"How much free cable do we have?" Ashly asked.

"A little over one hundred feet," Max answered. This new opening was easily as big as the mouth of the cave they entered in.

"We must have entered another cave system," Samuel stated.

Yeah, you think? Ashly thought, rolling her eyes at the comment. Max noticed something strange at the edge of the light beams.

"Ashly, I just saw something stop," he said, feeling his heart pounding in his chest. Ashly adjusted the light beam so the distance was shortened but brightened a larger area in front of them. The light beam caught the end of a large log.

"What's a log doing in a cave system?" Max remarked. He was asking himself the question as much as anyone else. Ashly moved the MSR-2's light upward, revealing a large wooden structure. As the light moved across the structure, its size and shape came into view. The structure had no uniform shape. It looked like someone had been crudely throwing large logs, bits of steel, and what looked to be pieces of ship wreckages on top of each other.

"Is that the creature's lair?" Okada asked Max.

"No way. Too small," Max replied, wondering himself what he was looking at. He guessed the structure was fifteen feet high and twenty feet long, with thirty separate pieces, many of them wooden, making up the structure.

"Anyone know what it is?" Liz asked.

A disturbed look formed on Samuel's face; then he said, "It's a food cache."

"A what?" Ashly asked, horrified.

"He's right," Max agreed. He looked at Ashly and said in a disturbed tone, "Well, there's only one way to confirm this." Reluctantly, she moved the MSR-2 closer to the structure until it was close enough to see between two of the logs. The drone's light shined into one of the spaces, revealing what they thought could have been an arm. Ashly tried adjusting the light beam, but it did not show anything new. The MSR-2 moved to the space above it. This time the light shined upon a man's head and upper body. The right side of his face was nearly gone. His left eye was hanging by threads. Small crabs were walking inside the open areas of his face. Ashly felt vomit moving from her stomach to her throat. She started coughing and ran down the stairs.

"Weak stomach," Liz commented, taking Ashly's seat. She turned to Max and Okada and said, "Knowing the two of you, I'm guessing you want me to get a count of how many bodies are in here?"

"Yes, as unpleasant as it may be, the task must be completed," Okada confirmed. After taking a moment to figure out the controls, Liz started moving the MSR-2 upward. Suddenly a stream of bubbles briefly filled half the screen, followed by the end of a large tail. Before Liz could react, the MSR-2 was shoved into the wooden structure. The screen started flickering on and off as the MSR-2 was jerked around. The final image showed what looked to be the cave floor; then the video feed went completely dead. Samuel bolted from his chair, grabbed the bolt cutters, and ran for the cable. Seconds later, a loud snap filled the air as he cut the cable.

"Let's get out of here before he decides to come up. Ashly, we're leaving!" Liz shouted.

"Why? What happened?" Ashly asked, coming up the stairs.

"The water panther got the MSR-2... Again," Liz replied. Ashly frantically turned to the cable spool. Samuel was standing near it, holding the wire cutters up in victory.

"Already on it," he yelled proudly.

"Everyone get in and sit down," Okada ordered. Ashly and Samuel quickly got into the empty seats. Liz slowly moved the speed level forward.

"We going home or what?" Liz asked.

"Let's leave the immediate area and regroup," Okada ordered.

Fifteen minutes later, the Barracuda drifted in the ocean around ten miles from the Five Caves Five Graves site. The team was going through the final moments of video transmission from the MSR-2, hoping to spot details missed in the heat of the moment. Ashly was checking the ship's engines, which everyone knew was an excuse to get out of looking at the dead bodies.

Max had a still image of the water panther's food cache up when Okada asked, "Have you seen this type of behavior before?"

Max thought for a moment and said, "I know a few species of animals store food. For example, alligators will let food rot so it's easier to eat. Or jaguars will hide a kill in a tree, slowly eating it over a period of a few days." Max then forwarded the recording to when the MSR-2 got attacked. In the heat of the moment, he thought nothing of it, but now the sight of bubbles was bothering him. He went through the video frame by frame until the MSR-2's camera was pointing towards the surface. "This could be bad," he said out loud.

"What now?" Liz asked. It seemed the more they learned about this creature, the worse things got.

"The camera's currently pointed towards the surface. It's faint, but do you notice a slight ripple pattern at the top of the screen?"

"Kinda. Why, is it important?" Liz asked.

"It means this cave might have an air pocket. The ripple pattern and air bubbles formed when the water panther entered the water from the land above." Samuel had heard enough and chimed in.

"I want to end this rabbit trail before it starts. Like I said before, the water panther cannot go on land." Everyone was looking at him skeptically, so he tried to explain his reasoning. "The rippling effect was caused by a malfunctioning camera. The air bubbles were caused by the drone's propellers."

"Still doesn't prove it can't go on land," Liz stated, mainly to see how he would respond.

"Look, if the water panther could go on land, don't you think it would have taken a stroll down Main Street by now, or attacked a local beach?" Samuel countered in an uptight critical voice. Okada spoke before Liz could get a snappy comeback in.

"We also have to acknowledge that the creature could not have entered the cave system the same way the drone did. There has to be another entrance to that cave."

"What I'm wondering is how did the water panther manage to carry fifty people twenty-seven miles in under an hour?" Liz brought up.

"I don't know if the people we just saw are all victims of the Alexandra wreckage," Max said.

"Give us your theory on what happened, professor," Liz teased, leaning back in the chair. Max softly punched her on the shoulder. Liz made a sad face and rubbed it.

"My guess would be when the water panther finishes eating, he creates a temporary hiding place near the kill site for any extra bodies, then returns to eat them later," Max theorized. He grunted in frustration and said, "The question now is does he have other lairs or food caches other than the Five Cave Five Graves site?"

Samuel snapped his fingers and said, "Okada, do you happen to know if the Coast Guard divers searched the wreckage of the Carthaginian II?"

Okada recalled the memory of that conversation and replied, "Captain Pierce stated the divers only worked on recovering the Alexandra." Hearing that caused everyone in the room to think the same thing. Liz pulled up the GPS unit and found where the Carthaginian II was located.

"It's on the way home. Let's go check it out," Liz suggested.

"I hate to point out the obvious, but the drone got destroyed," Samuel commented. Max and Liz looked at each other and sighed.

"Ugh, we're going to have to dive down there and take a look," Liz said.

"Yep," Max agreed, not liking the idea any more than she did. They both looked to Okada for his thoughts. He had the usual blank expression that he used when he was thinking over his options. If possible, he knew Governor Fatu would want the bodies recovered. He also had a good idea of where the water panther was now, and the sonar would give his teammates plenty of time to escape if needed.

"Do you believe it is worth the risk?" Okada asked.

"I do," Max replied. Liz took her turn to punch him.

"Very well; we will go," Okada said, hoping he was making the right call.

CHAPTER 32

3:48 PM 04/18/2021 HST

On route, Ashly learned about the plan and did not like it at all. She questioned why they couldn't wait a day for her to get another drone. The response was the water panther was more active at night and may move any remaining bodies from the location. Max and Liz sat on the back end of the Barracuda. Max was holding the underwater camera, and Liz had an extra bag of twenty spears slung over her shoulder. Both had spear guns.

"How far down is the wreckage, anyway?" Ashly asked, concerned.

"I thought you would be telling us. You always have the answers," Liz replied.

"I didn't have time to research the area," Ashly replied softly. Her hands were cupped, and she was moving the top hand back and forth a clear sign she was nervous.

"It's ninety-seven feet. A pretty easy dive," Liz continued.

"Ashly, relax; we'll be fine down there," Max added, noticing her nervousness.

"Guys, are you two sure about this?" Ashly asked in a final attempt to stop the dive.

"Of course not, but today's as good of a day as any to die," Liz replied sarcastically. Liz's lackluster attitude on the situation was driving Ashly crazy.

She shot back with, "If that thing is storing food down there, what if it's mad about what happened with the MSR-2 and comes back to check on it?"

"Your be on the sonar. I trust you'll give us a heads up if anything happens," Max said. Samuel wished them good luck. Liz and Okada held hands for a moment; then her and Max fell backwards into the water. Visibility was bright and clear to about fifty feet. Minutes later, they approached the wreckage of the Carthaginian II.

"Local marine life is around the wreckage. That's a good sign," Max said, noticing the many species of fish and a green sea turtle swimming around the wreck.

"Let's search around the Carthaginian II, then we can work our way inside," Liz suggested.

"Doubt we'll find anything on the outside, but it's worth a look," Max agreed. Max and Liz split up at the front of the wreckage. Liz went left. Max went right. Liz turned on her flashlight to clearly see areas blocked by shadows created by the ship's hull. She was sure to stick close to the wall of rusting metal that was the Carthaginian II hull. Above Ashly's eyes were glued to the sonar. So far, everything was clear, but she hated the fact that the water panther could show up any second with her teammates in the water.

"Jeez!" Liz suddenly screamed in alarm.

"Liz! Max!" Ashly yelled in a worried voice. A few moments later, Max's laughter filled the intercom.

"Guys, what's going on?" Okada asked.

"A white tip spooked Liz, that's all," Max replied.

"A what?" Ashly asked.

"A white tipped reef shark. It's a small species of shark." Liz pointed her spear gun at the shark resting peacefully on the ocean floor. Max quickly pulled it down with his hand. "No reason to shoot the shark. He's not doing anything to us. Find anything interesting besides this?"

"No, what about you?"

"Several pieces of the ships mast are laying on the ocean floor. I don't know if that occurred naturally or if the water panther did it," Max answered.

"Well, let's head to the top of the ship and find out," Liz suggested. The two of them swam to the top of the Carthaginian II. The first thing they noticed was the large hole that stretched across most of the ship's hull. A few feet of the ship's bow and stern were all that remained of the main deck.

"Did that thing rip the hull apart?" Liz asked. Hearing that sent a chill down Ashly's spine.

"No, this was done before the ship was sunk, to create hiding places for marine life," Max replied. He looked at the hole more closely and noticed several large logs and other pieces of debris inside. "But I know logs were not stored inside."

"Might as well go in," Liz said reluctantly. The thought of seeing dead bodies did not bother her, but the idea of going into an enclosed area that a sea monster was using to store food did. Max and Liz swam through the hole that led to the ship's insides. The debris field was located at the left end of the ship. Max and Liz immediately noticed it looked very similar to the structure in the cave.

Liz looked up at the space above them and said, "This hole is too small for that creature to fit into. How'd he get the logs inside?" Liz commented.

"My guess would be he dropped the debris and bodies in from above," Max replied. Liz noticed a small area with a seven-foot-tall doorway directly behind them. She pointed to it.

"That will be a good hiding spot if the water panther does show up." After removing a few logs, they could tell dead bodies were indeed under them.

"Okada, we found bodies," Max said. "We're taking a few photos, then heading up."

Okada looked at Ashly and said, "I'm going to report our findings to Governor Fatu. I'm sure the families will want those bodies recovered."

"Please tell me we're not bringing a dead body aboard?" Ashly asked, worried.

"The Coast Guard will handle that," Okada answered.

"Okada, before you make the call, I have an idea," Samuel added.

"I'll count. You photograph," Liz stated. Max agreed and they started working. Liz pointed her finger at each body, mentally counting as she did. "Seventeen bodies. Far less than what I was expecting to find."

"Max, you and Liz have GPS locators on your dive watches, right?" Samuel's voice crackled in their ear pieces. Max was about to reply when Samuel said, "Over."

"Yes, both our watches have them; why?" Max asked.

"Place your watches on two of the bodies that way…" Liz cut him off excitedly.

"We can track the water panther when he eats them." Max and Liz took off their watches and placed them on two of the bodies.

"Let's head back up and go home," Max said. When they emerged from the wreckage, Max noticed Liz freeze. He turned to see a large object sitting on the ocean floor.

"Max, move!" Liz cried, aiming her spear gun.

"My god," he said out loud. Liz fired and jetted upward.

"Guys, what's happening? There's nothing on the sonar," Ashly asked, starting to panic herself.

"Liz, stop. That's not the water panther; it's a dead colossal squid." Liz stopped ascending when she saw Max swimming towards the object.

"Max where are you going? Get back here," Liz begged, wanting him to come up.

"Guys, what's happening down there? Someone please tell me something," Ashly's nervous voice said over the intercom.

"Ashly, we're fine," Max assured. "I'm going to examine a carcass. It will just take a minute."

"That's what people say right before they die," Liz said, reluctantly joining him. Max hovered above the half-eaten carcass. The entire top portion of the trunk was eaten away, and inside the squid's body scavenging marine life gorged themselves on the free meal.

"Look at the claw marks across the head and sides," Max commented, staring at the deep gashes.

"Cool, can we go?" Liz asked.

"Yes, Max, please come up," Ashly begged. Max ignored them.

"I can't believe the water panther was able to bring down something this big," he said with wonder in his voice. He started to examine the severed feeding tentacles when Liz pulled on his arm.

"The science lesson is over. Let's go," Liz ordered, pulling on his arm. Knowing she was right, Max headed for the surface.

***

The next two weeks were utter chaos for Suijin Squad. The tracking system plan failed due to the Coast Guard rescue team recovering all the bodies. Okada spoke with Governor Fatu about the incident and coordinated operations, to acquire a base of operations on Maui. This proved to be challenging because the base needed a holding area for the dolphins. Governor Fatu's team was able to find an abandoned estate that had its own private beach in the town of Makena. The beach overlooked two rocky cliffs and a natural coral reef, creating a small gulf. Perfect for housing the dolphins. The only down side to the location was right across the road was a small shopping center. People coming from it enjoyed walking in the shade of the estate's trees and seeing the view the ocean offered. This would not have been a problem except the estate's boat dock was visible from the sidewalk. A major challenge for Max and Liz was getting the dolphins transported to Maui. It was decided the dolphins would make the two-hun-dred-and-fifty-mile journey to Maui by wet transit. This process turned out to be easy since the dolphins had been transported by wet transit several times in the past. The dolphins would then be transported to the airfield where a cargo plane was waiting for them. The plane would land at Kapalua Airport, and the dolphins would be transported to the estate. Workers had already placed netting at the entrance of the gulf, so the dolphins could enter their new home right away. Once the dolphins were given several days to settle into their temporary home Max had spent hours each day training them, using texts with Mya as an escape from the challenges before him. His primary challenge was the dolphins were going to be sharing the combat zone with friendly divers and vessels. This met he couldn't simply teach them to attack anything that entered the area they were assigned to patrol. To overcome this, he came up with a simple yet effective exercise. A glow stick would be attached to a spear. The spear would then be fired at an underwater target. The dolphins knew the object marked with the bright light was what they needed to attack. The snout mounted hypodermic lance system had also proven to be troublesome. A completed lance harness was a harness placed around the dolphin's front flippers and upper snout with a two-foot lance resting on top of the dolphin's upper snout. At first the dolphins resisted wearing the harnesses, not liking the feeling of the leather straps or the additional weight on the upper snout. It took time and many treats, but Max managed to get the dolphins to accept the system. Now the dolphins could be combat ready in under ten minutes.

Ashly was tasked with preparing the mines and assembling the hypodermic lances. A major problem she discovered with the lance system was there was no way to reload them after the initial use. After learning from trial and error, she created modifications so new explosives could be loaded into the lances after each usage. She also modified the ten moored mines to go off by remote control rather than on contact. The mines were going to be positioned by a new robot the C-3000. This robot was slightly larger than the MSR-2. It had a box-shaped build and two strong robot arms in the front. Samuel did the simple yet important jobs like preparing meals, unloading equipment, and helping wherever he was needed.

After two weeks of intense work, everything was ready, and a battle plan was in place. The finalized battle plan was Okada, Ashly, and Samuel would lead the first wave of the attack. Mines would be remotely placed near every entrance of the Five Caves Five Graves site. A drone would then enter the cave and lure the water panther out. If the mine attack failed, it would be immediately followed up by a dolphin attack, led by Max and Liz on a second boat. The estate was four miles from the Five Caves Five Graves site. Bottle nose dolphins having a top speed of twelve miles per hour could be at the battle zone within twenty minutes. The team had discussed with Governor Fatu the idea of taking the dolphins to the attack site right away. Governor Fatu rejected the plan, feeling that mines and dolphins with explosive lances in the water at the same time was too risky, a statement Max agreed with.

CHAPTER 33

9:10 AM 05/3/2021 HST

The nearly risen sun brought with it feelings of nervousness and tension. Today was the day. The day they had been training for since the operation started. The day they would face the water panther. Since the team was going to be split, a small repainted Coast Guard patrol craft was docked next to the Barracuda. Ashly and Samuel got aboard the Barracuda. After kissing Liz goodbye, Okada got aboard. Max could tell how nervous he must be if he was showing affection for Liz in front of everyone. Max and Liz stood on the dock as the Barracuda disappeared from view.

"Do you think they'll manage to kill it?" Liz asked. Even though she was not showing it, Max could tell she was worried about Okada.

"Have faith in our teammates, buddy," he replied. He looked at the seven dolphin harnesses sitting on the dock next to training targets. "To keep our minds occupied, let's run some training sessions with the dolphins," Max suggested, knowing it was going to take a few hours for the others to get the mines deployed.

"Better than sitting around doing nothing," Liz agreed. "I'll change into my wet suit." Max blew into his training whistle. The number and length of each whistle was different for each dolphin. When Liz returned, Max had just finished placing a harness on Seafin. Liz clapped her hands to pump herself up.

"Okay, what's the game?" Max pushed three of the human-shaped targets into the water. The targets were made of wood with five-pound weights on each foot.

"With a real operation possibly coming up, I don't want to overwhelm them. We'll start out with an hour or so of games, then we'll have each dolphin attack a target once. I'm splitting the dolphins into two groups: Seafin, Tsunami, Atlantis, Depth Charge will be the first group. Typhoon, Aquatail, and Atragon will be the second."

"Got it," Liz replied. She put her mouth piece in and jumped into the water.

***

The Barracuda drifted above the Five Caves Five Graves sight. The third MSR-2 was already inside the cave, hovering near the location of the food cache. Equipped with a sonar system, the MSR-2 had confirmed the water panther was inside. He was in a cave pocket right behind the food cache. Ashly's hand had a death grip on the joystick as she positioned the mines with the H-3000. Tunnel vision had come over her during the stressful task. Nothing else mattered or existed at that moment. Adding to the stressful situation was the fact that the water panther could emerge from his lair at any time. Ashly let out a breath of relief when the last mine was positioned in place. Four mines were placed in front of the entrance that was nearest to the water panther's current location. Two mines were placed in front of the three remaining entrances. No mines were placed by the cave entrance the MSR-2 had entered during their first trip to the site. From what they saw the first time, and later scanned, confirmed the tunnel to that entrance was too small for the water panther to fit through.

"Why are three mines sitting on the ocean floor?" Samuel asked, looking at another computer screen. The program that was running showed the location of each mine and the depth they were at. Thirteen green mines sat on a black background. Above ten of the mines were two digital buttons: a green activation button and a red deactivate button. The three mines sitting on the ocean floor had a folder titled "captor" under them.

"Those are just additional mines. Always good to be prepared," Ashly said in an innocent voice. The kind Samuel had learned she used when she was lying. "Anyway, can you come help me get the H-3000 aboard?" Okada waited at the MSR-2 controls. He heard the metallic screeching of the cable pulling the H-3000 to the surface. "H-3000 is secure," Ashly said as she and Samuel returned to the cabin. She made her way back to her chair and pulled up the mine program. Samuel paced between the two of them, looking at each screen.

"It's a shame. I finally found a cryptid and we have to destroy it," Samuel said, disappointed.

"There will be more out there. After this is over, I'll help you catch a nice one," Ashly replied in a sarcastic yet sincere voice. Okada pressed the talk button on the radio.

"Max, Liz, we are beginning operations." He drove the MSR-2 right at the food cache. The team had placed a small amount of explosives inside the drone. Ashly clicked the detonator when the MSR-2 slammed into the food cache. Okada's computer screen went blank as the drone and food cache exploded. "Now we wait," he said.

Silently, everyone hoped the small explosion would be enough to kill the water panther, but everyone knew that was a fool's dream, so no one spoke of it. Seconds felt like hours. Ashly was glued to the mine's sensors, waiting for one to detect something. A mine sensor went off at the cave entrance the team had guessed the water panther would emerge from. Ashly rapidly clicked the detonation button on the two closest mines.

Still inside the cave system, the water panther saw orange flames and black smoke briefly engulf the cave entrance. The cave wall acted as a natural shield, protecting him from most of the blast. The shockwave stunned him for a moment. He cried in pain as several small bits of shrapnel punctured his nearly healed skin. He swam in circles confused then, stopped swimming, crouched down, and slowly started crawling on the sea floor. He gazed out the cave entrance, spotting the two remaining mines. A loud thunderclap left his throat.

"What! No! No!" Ashly screamed.

"What happened?" Okada asked.

"The two mines near the water panther just went offline. I don't understand how this could have happened?" Ashly said in an alarmed voice.

"The infrasound. It must have destroyed the electronics inside the mines," Samuel added.

The water panther cautiously moved towards the two mines. He didn't know what they were. All he knew was the others like them caused him pain. He remembered hearing a small clicking sound right before the loud noise occurred. That was what he was listening for. He ventured closer and closer. The objects did not move. They must have been stunned by the roar. The strange objects somewhat reminded him of those stinging blobs of jelly he would sometimes encounter while traveling the seas. He needed to destroy them while they were still stunned. The small spine under the main body seemed like a good place to attack. He bit down and the strange object fell to the sea floor. He did the same to the other object, then went to check for more.

"He just broke the mooring cables!" Ashly said, stunned with disbelief. Moments later two more mines changed from green to red. Okada leaned back in his chair, frustrated by the results.

"Contact Max and Liz. Inform them the operation was a failure," Okada ordered.

"We're not done yet," Ashly said as a mischievous smile formed on her face.

"What have you done now?" Samuel asked.

"I've been a bad, bad girl," she smirked. She clicked on the file titled "captor." Inside were three file folders titled "captor one," "two," and "three." She clicked on the captor one folder. A camera feed appeared, which looked to be coming from the ocean floor.

"Ashly, answer the question!" Samuel yelled, worried she was going to do something dumb like set off a nuke.

"Just wait," Ashly replied. She moved the camera until it located the water panther destroying the last of the moored mines. A green targeting box surrounded it. The green box turned red, indicating the target had been locked on. "It's over," she said confidently, hitting the firing button. A torpedo shot out of one of the mystery mines sitting on the ocean floor.

"What kind of a mine has a torpedo inside!" Samuel yelled.

"Their captor mines, carrying a Mark 46 torpedo," Ashly replied.

"Ashly, since when did we get authorization to use torpedoes?" Okada asked, wondering how she managed to sneak this type of equipment past him.

"Umm, they sent us the wrong stuff," Ashly replied innocently.

The water panther noticed the torpedo heading towards him. It somewhat resembled one of those sharks or dolphins he had seen many times before. They had never bothered him, so he was not too concerned with it. As it got closer, he started to circle the incoming object, wondering what it truly was. The torpedo's tracking system followed his every move. The fact that this thing was following him made him uneasy. It seemed like it was getting set up for an attack. The water panther turned to face the torpedo. He cocked its head back and opened its mouth; thunder clapped as he released an infrasound blast. The torpedo exploded yards from its target.

"What!" Ashly screamed in shock. This was impossible. First this creature had destroyed the mines, and now it had stopped a torpedo. Samuel started to explain what happened, but she already knew: the infrasound. Ashly quickly brought the other two mines online. Both fired within seconds of each other. The water panther spotted the two incoming objects. He had had enough. He swam towards them and fired a beam of infrasound. Both torpedos exploded. The team watched the unharmed water panther treading water from the mine's cameras. His tail and feet pedaled to keep himself still. None of them could believe what had just occurred. Thousands of dollars of top military technology stopped effortlessly by an animal. The water panther looked up and noticed the boat sitting on the surface. He shot upward.

"Okay, we're out of here!" Ashly screamed. She got no complaints from her teammates as the Barracuda fled the area. The team was discouraged but not finished yet. They would be back. Hopefully, the dolphins would have better luck.

CHAPTER 34

12:17 PM 05/3/2021 HST

"Liz, the operation's started," Max said.

"Should we stop the training?" Liz asked.

"Let's finish it. We only have two dolphins left." Max knew it would be confusing to Typhoon and Atragon if their brothers got to destroy a target for a reward and they didn't. Aquatail surfaced. Max removed the lance and rewarded him with a small squid.

Riley and Mya walked from the Makena shopping plaza on to Makena Street. The two girls had the day off and were returning home from getting their hair done. Mya got her purple highlights redone. Riley thought about adding some color but decided to stick with her natural blonde color.

"Who owns the mansion?" Mya asked, looking up at the large ageing building through the black fencing.

"No one. It's an abandoned estate. Let's pool our money and buy it," Riley suggested in a non-serious voice.

"Yeah, let me get a million dollar raise and I'll be happy to," Mya replied. A distant splashing sound caught Riley's attention. She walked over to a break in the vegetation and saw Max Varian standing on the dock.

She spoke slowly and playfully when she said, "Oh, Mya. Look who it is!"

"What?" Mya asked, expecting Riley to be pulling a joke. Mya saw him and blushed. She turned away from Riley, trying to hide her smile. "Wonder what he's doing here?" she wondered. Last time she had heard from him, he was on Niihau, and he never mentioned anything about coming to Maui.

"Come on. Don't you want to go say hi?" Riley suggested.

"Umm." Mya wetted her lips then said in a fast tone, "I'm sure he's busy. Let's get going." She started playfully pushing Riley down the sidewalk. Deep down, she wanted to go over and talk to him, but like she said, she was sure he was busy. Plus, she knew Riley would make the whole situation awkward.

Riley pulled away and said, "Okay, fine. If you don't want to talk to him, I will."

"Riley, no," Mya begged. Riley started walking along the fencing, ignoring her completely. At least she can't climb the fence. Mya said softly, looking at the spear heads on top of the poles.

"Hmm." Riley thought, tapping a finger on a fence pole. "Maybe I should start shouting for him to let us in."

"Don't you dare!" Mya said seriously. Now she was getting worried, knowing Riley would do something like that. Riley walked over to the gate and pushed on it. She gasped and looked at Mya with an exaggerated look of surprise. Mya put her hands over the sides of her head as Riley pushed the gate open.

***

Frank Williams and Gary Clark drove their newly bought sport yacht across the Maui waters. The two men were tourists from New York. They had planned on spending their vacation drinking on the beach by day, then hitting up the local strip clubs by night. Yesterday evening the two men heard that a man-eating salt water crocodile was loose in the Maui water. Frank determined it would be a good idea if they killed the creature. Several beers later, Gary agreed with him. Now, here they were blazing across the Maui waters, beer cans and shotguns in hand. The two men were more of a maritime hazard than the conquering heroes they saw themselves as. Only moments ago, they had unloaded a barrage of shotgun slugs into a floating piece of driftwood.

"How do you plan on paying for this boat, anyway?" Gary asked, taking a long drink. He crushed the empty can and tossed it into the water. Gary Clark was an overweight man in his early forties. He had neck-length messy brown hair with bald patches on the top front of his head. A long ungroomed beard covered most of his face.

"With the reward money, you idiot," Frank replied, trying to keep the boat near shore. He had seen on a nature program that crocodiles lived near the shore. Frank was in his late forties. He had a slim build, short blonde hair, and no facial hair.

"What reward money? I ain't heard nothing about that," Gary replied.

"They'll give us a reward for killing that alligator or whatever it is. Just makes sense." Frank reached into the cooler. "I just sure hope we find it soon. We're nearly out of ammunition," Frank said, staring into the nearly empty beer cooler.

***

"Typhoon just destroyed his target," Liz said, watching the destroyed portions of the training dummy float to the surface. Out of the corner of his eye, Max spotted movement. He was surprised to see Mya and her friend walking towards the dock.

"Liz, we got company. Keep Typhoon and Atragon under the water," Max said, concerned.

"What! Who?" Liz asked. She pulled out her clicker trainer. She clicked twice, ordering Typhoon to come to her. Max took a few moments to reply, not wanting, to admit who it was.

"Mya Kendig and one of her friends." Liz did not make a joke or torment him about it. She knew how serious the situation was.

"How did they get in?" Liz questioned.

"I have no idea. The front gate was locked, right?" Max asked. Liz cursed, realizing her mistake. A simple mistake that could cost them dearly. Liz recalled Okada always saying that it was those types of mistakes that caused the biggest problems. She grunted in frustration.

"Max, just get rid of your girlfriend as fast as you can."

"Planning on it."

"Hello," Riley said. Max turned toward her, acting slightly surprised.

"Oh, hi," he replied. As part of the act, he took a second to remember who she was. "You're the girl who waited on me at the Crescent Moon Café. Right?"

"Yep, if you don't remember, my name's Riley, and I'm sure you remember Mya?" Mya smiled and gave a shy wave. She felt like an idiot for not speaking, but she felt so awkward intruding on him like this.

"How could I forget her?" Max replied. Hearing that made Mya blush again. She moved behind Riley, creating a wall between her and Max.

"She saw you and wanted to say hi," Riley said. She slid to the side, leaving Mya and Max face to face.

"Um. Hi," Mya said. She knew she should say more than that, but her mind was completely blank.

"How did you two get in here, anyway? I thought the gate was locked," Max asked, hoping they would get the hint.

"No, the gate was unlocked. We didn't think you'd mind if we came to say hi. I hope we're not intruding?" Riley answered.

"I don't mean to be rude, but I am kind of busy at the moment. I'm in the middle of a dolphin training session for a high-level client, and my training partner is in the water," Max said seriously.

"See, I told you," Mya whispered, gently striking Riley on the shoulder. "Max, sorry, we didn't mean to intrude. We'll get going."

Max felt guilty blowing Mya off and he really wanted to see her in person again, so he said, "Tell you what, girls. Why don't you come back in a few days? Things should be calmer then and I'll have time to introduce you to the dolphins."

"Oh my gosh, really!" Riley replied, smiling widely. "Since I was a little girl, I always wanted to touch and swim with dolphins, but never had the money. You...you just made my year!" Mya had mixed feeling about it. She wanted to see Max, but the sight of the ocean still frightened her. Riley pulled out her phone. "What's your cell? I'll text you our numbers; then we can arrange the dolphin meet."

"I already have Mya's number. She can give it to you," Max replied, not wanting to waste any more time than necessary. Below, Liz was starting to become flustered. Atragon still had a lance on and Typhoon kept swimming towards the surface.

"Oh, you do? She never mentioned that," Riley replied. Her eyes turned to Mya, who felt like pushing her into the water. Mya and Riley said goodbye and started to walk away. Max began to return the gesture when Liz started screaming.

"Typhoon is heading to the surface! Typhoon is heading to the surface!" Just then Typhoon's upper body broke the surface water. He was clicking loudly, demanding his reward for destroying the target. Max let out a breath of relief when he saw Liz had taken off his lance. Hearing the splash made Mya and Riley turn around.

"Oh my gosh! Can I please, please take a second to touch the dolphin?" Riley asked. She made a sad face. "Please?"

"Riley, he said we shouldn't be here. Now let's go," Mya said, getting annoyed. She could only imagine how Max thought of them now.

"It's okay," Max reassured. "I can't let you touch him, but you can toss him a fish." Max handed Riley a small herring. She was ecstatic when she took it and tossed it to Typhoon.

"Thank you so much," Riley said, beaming.

"All right, Typhoon, say goodbye." Max made the splash command. Typhoon turned to his side and smacked his tail several times. Mya and Riley screamed when the water struck them. Their expression of shock soon turned to smiles and laughter.

***

At the gulf entrance, Gary Clark spat his beer out.

"There's one, Frank!" he screamed, spotting a dorsal fin.

"Gary, why are you so dang stupid? Crocodiles don't have fins."

"Must be a shark then. Let's get him." Not one to let a hunting opportunity get away from him, Frank turned the boat towards the gulf entrance.

"Hey, Max, there's a boat coming," Mya said. Max turned around.

What the heck, he thought. "Liz, we have intruders. Probably just local fishermen who don't know the area is off limits," he said as he tried to make out who was in the unknown vessel.

"Great, what else is going to go wrong?" Liz replied.

Frank and Gary opened fire. Small ripples started to form in the water in front of Depth Charge. "Max, what's happening!" Liz asked. The bullets from the shotguns were raining down yards from of her.

"Hey, diver in the water!" Max yelled, waving his hands up, trying to get the boaters' attention. Riley and Mya stood motionless, not knowing what to do. Sensing he was in danger, Depth Charge let out a cry of alarm. His pod members started clicking to one another. Liz knew what those clicks met. Those were attack clicks. She tried to signal the dolphin pod to head for the dock area. Typhoon, Aquatail, Seafin, and Atlantis did as commanded. Atragon and Tsunami raced towards Depth Charge.

"Max, we have two dolphins heading for that boat!" Before Liz could finish, Atragon rammed the lance into the boat's hull. The two drunk men were still firing when the boat exploded. A fire ball and boat fragments filled the air. Both men were killed instantly. Mya and Riley's eyes filled with horror. Riley put her hands over her mouth in shock. Mya was breathing heavily as she looked at the wreckage. Nothing was left but splinters of wood. Pieces of flaming debris fell from the air, making a hissing sound when they struck the water. Her body began to tremble.

No, it couldn't be? Could it? she thought. Her mind started imagining the dolphins crying out in pain as the water turned red. A large head burst through the dock, killing Max and sending her and Riley into the water. Underwater, she opened her eyes just in time to see that monster kill Riley. He turned to her with a wide, sadistic smile.

Right before he attacked her, Riley's cry of "What happened?" brought her back to reality.

"Blast fishing, most likely," Max replied, saying the first explanation that came to mind.

"What?" Mya asked, still shaken by her thoughts.

"Some people illegally fish with explosives. One of them must have gone off in the boat." Max put his hands on both girl's shoulders. "Are the two of you okay?" Both girls shook their heads yes. "I have to report this and get the dolphins to safety. So, can you two please leave the area?"

"Anything we can do to help?" Mya asked.

"No, right now the best thing you can do is leave," Max replied. Riley started walking down the dock. Mya gently put her hand on Max's shoulder.

"Be careful," she said.

"Always am," he assured. The two exchanged an affectionate glance. Mya smiled and sprinted to catch up with Riley. Liz, who had been waiting just under the surface, came up. She started tearing her diving gear off in frustration.

"What in hell happened up here?" Before Max could reply, Okada's voice came over the radio.

"Max, the mine operation failed. Get the dolphins ready. Be here in half an hour." Max and Liz exchanged worried looks.

All Max could say was, "We can't. We have a major problem over here."

"We're both dead," Liz said seriously. Atragon broke the surface, making the clicking sound that stated he had killed his target. Max tossed him a fish. "Really," Liz asked.

"He did what he was trained to do," Max replied, shrugging his shoulders.

CHAPTER 35

4:23 PM 05/3/2021 HST

Due to the incident, the Barracuda was forced to return to base. The local authorities had arrived to recover the bodies of Frank Williams and Gary Clark. Since the men were intoxicated and trespassing on an active military base, no charges were filed. The case was closed with the official cause of the explosion being a stick of dynamite used for blast fishing exploded near the ship's fuel tank.

Max and Liz sat in Okada's office. Okada sat at his desk in front of them. For a few minutes, he said nothing. He remained completely still, just staring at them with a gaze that seemed to uncover every secret they had. Neither Max nor Liz dared to speak. They both knew they had made a mistake that cost two people their lives and disrupted the attack on the water panther. As they prepared for their commander's judgment, the total silence started to become unnerving. Finally, Okada broke the silence when he said, "I would like an explanation of the events that occurred earlier today." His tone of voice was neither angry nor pleased. The inability to read his emotion made the situation tenser. Max and

Liz would have preferred it if he just started screaming at them. Knowing it was useless to lie or make excuses, Max and Liz reported exactly what happened as they remembered it. For their honesty, Okada gave them a slight look of pleasure.

"I thank you for speaking the truth." He took a moment to take a drink. Part of Okada's disciplinary tactics was making people wait. He found the mental punishments people gave themselves was more effective than any actual punishment he could give. "Half this situation was caused by errors on your part and half was caused by factors beyond your control." His face turned towards Liz. Liz knew, despite being in a relationship with Okada, he would still discipline her, like any other person under his command. "Liz, base security is part of your duties. You should have made sure that gate was locked."

"Yes, sir. I..I understand my failure," Liz replied. Okada turned his attention to Max.

"Max, your errors were caused by the plague that causes most men to lose focus." Okada's voice gained a slightly more humorous tone when he said, "It was the affection for a woman. Am I correct?"

"Correct, sir," Max said softly. His face turning red from embarrassment. Liz put her head down, trying to hide her grin.

"Use Liz and I as an example. Separate your work and personal life." Okada slightly laughed when he continued, "If you and Mya worked together, nothing productive would ever get done." Max started to prepare himself for the judgment he knew was coming. He hoped his commander, his friend, would at least let him finish the water panther operation before releasing him. Okada's serious side returned when he said, "I must commend you for coming up with a cover story so quickly. However, you also endangered the entire operation. After looking over the report and hearing your testimonies, I have no choice but to." Okada stopped to look at his phone. For several long minutes, his fingers moved over the screen. Inside, Max and Liz started to think about their future jobs. Liz figured she would get by, but she was concerned for Max. Okada put the phone down. "As I was saying, I have no choice but to forgive the situation." Max and Liz did not know if they heard him right.

"Sorry, sir, did I?" Max started to say.

"Yes, you heard correctly," Okada replied. His words destroyed the feeling of nervousness and dread consuming Max and Liz. "However," Okada continued, lifting a finger. "In the future, situations like this must not occur."

"Yes sir!" both said in sync.

Okada looked at Max and said, "Max, are the dolphins ready for tomorrow's operation?"

"Ready as they ever will be," he replied.

"Max, sorry to do this, but speaking of dolphins." The look on Liz's face showed she was about to say something that could cause tension. "Max promised Mya he would introduce her to the dolphins when this is over." A stunned look formed on Max's face.

"How did you know about that?"

"I was under the dock trying to get Typhoon when you said it," she replied.

"That is a promise he will have to break," Okada replied casually. Before he dismissed them, he said, "Now please inform Ashly Cross I wish to speak with her about smuggling torpedo mines."

"What did she do?" Liz asked, surprised.

"She purchased and used captor mines. Despite strict orders not to use torpedoes in Hawaiian waters."

"Okada, if I may." Max thought for a moment of how to continue. "We kind of need Ashly on the team."

"She will receive the same judgment as the two of you." Max and Liz gave respectful bows and left the office area. They walked into the living area where Ashly was sitting on the living room couch.

"Are you two okay?" she asked, concerned.

"We don't know. All I know is he's really mad. My own boyfriend won't give me a straight answer on my future with him," Liz said, upset as she sat down next to her.

"Yeah, after cursing us out, he said he wanted to see you. Something about torpedo mines," Max added. A look of fear formed on Ashly's face. "Better get in there quick; he hates to be kept waiting."

"To think, this could be our last night as a team," Liz said in a worried tone. Ashly reluctantly got up and headed for Okada's office. The sound of the door closing brought Liz and Max to uncontrolled laughter. The ringing of Max's phone brought the laughter to a halt.

"Aww, your darling calling to check up on you," Liz said in a lovestruck voice.

"You don't even know who it is," Max replied, getting up.

"It's Mya. I can tell by the look on your face."

"I'm off duty," Max countered and walked outside. He pressed accept on Facetime and said, "Hello."

"Max? Hey, after what happened, I just wanted to make sure you're okay," Mya said with a hint of concern in her voice.

"I'm fine. Nothing eventful happened after you left. Mya sighed with relief.

"Okay, I was worried you got fired or something." Max smiled, pleased she was concerned for him.

"No, I got a lecture but that was it. Are you and Riley okay?"

"We were both pretty shaken up, but we're okay now. Are the dolphins okay?"

"Yep, the dolphins are fine and happily swimming around." Neither of them spoke for a moment.

"So, are you working tonight?" Max asked.

"No, just hanging out at home. Trying to find something to do," Mya replied, hoping he got the hint.

"I have a big day planned tomorrow and was thinking of going out to eat and then to a movie to get my mind off things." A nervous tone entered Max's voice when he asked, "Care to join me?"

"Yes. I'd love to," Mya replied right away.

"Does five-thirty work for you?"

"Sooner the better," Mya answered. Her voice filled with excitement when she said, "Going to get ready." Just then Max felt something jump onto his back.

"Hey," Liz said, thinking Mya had hung up. On the screen, a shocked, hurt look formed on Mya's face.

"You son of a bitch!" Mya yelled in a hurt, teary voice as memories of her past started flooding her mind. "Enjoy your other girlfriend." Before Max could respond, she hung up. Max pushed Liz off and glared at her, too angry to even speak.

"Max, I'm so sorry. I thought she had hung up. Just call her back. I'll explain everything if you want."

"Just go back inside," Max snapped. He thought about calling back but figured she would reject the call. He sent a text that said, *Mya, that was my sister fooling around. Please give me a chance to explain.* He sent it, waited a few moments, and requested a Facetime. To his surprise, Mya accepted it.

"I'm listening," she said. Max could see black streaks from her eye makeup on her face.

"Mya, that was my co-worker Liz. There is nothing going on between us."

"I thought you said she was your sister," Mya reminded, noticing the change in the story. A hint of anger grew in her voice. Max thought for a moment and said, "We're not biological siblings, but we're close, and not in a romantic way."

"Well, where is she then? If you have nothing to hide, why is she not around?" Mya asked bitterly. Lucky for Max, Liz was still standing on the porch. He motioned for her to come over.

"She'll be over in a minute," Max said. Hearing that surprised Mya and surprised her even more when Liz grabbed the phone.

"Hi, look, there is nothing going on between me and Max. I know for a fact lover boy only has eyes for you."

"Really?" Mya asked. Hearing that was sunbeams breaking the clouds around her heart.

"Yeah, believe me, if I caught my boyfriend Facetiming another girl, he would be knocked out, and as you saw, Max is still unharmed." She handed the phone back to Max. When he took it, he did not know what to say. So, he just said,

"Hey."

"Hey," Mya said back in a much happier tone. "Look, sorry for assuming the worst. I just got out of a relationship where my boyfriend used and cheated on me. So, I'm a little hesitant to trust people."

"I understand what it must have looked like. Still want to go to the movies?"

"As soon as I fix my eye makeup, sure," Mya said, a little flirtatious.

"See you soon," Max replied. He ended the Facetime and walked back inside. "Thanks," he said to Liz, giving her a fist bump. "I'm taking the rental car into town. I'll be back in a few hours."

"No trouble. Come back sober," Liz reminded.

"Planning on it," Max confirmed. He walked into his room and changed. He exited the room just as Ashly exited Okada's office.

"I hate the two of you. I was sure I was getting fired," she said in an upset, but not overly angry voice.

"We thought the same thing when we were in there," Max replied. "Liz and I were just having fun with you." Ashly's body language showed she was okay with the joke.

"Where are you going?" she asked, noticing he had changed clothes.

"Might die tomorrow. Wanted to have some fun before then." A brief look of fright formed on Ashly's face.

Max noticed it and said, "Don't worry; everyone will make it out alive. Tomorrow at this time we will be examining that creature's corpse."

"Nicely gift wrapped. Delivered to our door," she replied. Max smiled not at her comment but at something he was thinking about. "What?" she asked, confused.

"Nothing. See ya," he said. When he was in the rental car, he pulled out his phone and called Saburo.

"Hey, Saburo, I need a favor. Do you remember the claw we recovered? I need a replica."

CHAPTER 36

9:17 AM 05/4/2021 HST

Gray clouds covered the sky over the Five Caves Five Graves site. The trip had been eerily silent. No one had spoken a word along the way, not even Samuel. The seven dolphins swam around the Barracuda, investigating the new area. They were led to the site by a speaker placed at the bottom of the boat that broadcast the dolphins' follow command, which was two long whistles with a two-second pause between them. Max, Liz, and Okada were already in their diving gear. For speed and maneuverability, they were using light weight rebreathers over traditional diving tanks. For weapons, each of them had small sixty cm. spear guns equipped with double flopper spear heads. Ashly dropped the fourth MSR-2 into the water. The idea was the same as last time: explode the MSR-2 inside the water panther's lair, forcing it out into the open. She then looked at her three teammates, her friends sitting on the edge of the boat doing final equipment checks.

"Good luck," she said.

"Yes, good luck to us all," Samuel added. "Same to you," Max replied.

"It's time," Okada said. The feeling of dread and fear that filled everyone grew. Max closed his eyes and fell backwards. Samuel stood behind her as Ashly watched her three friends disappear behind the surface.

I hope I see you again, she said softly. Max, Liz, and Okada split up and headed for nearby rock formations, many of which had holes large enough to create natural hiding spots, giving the team a geographical advantage.

The water panther waited near a cave opening. He had heard the Barracuda's engine cease. It was a sound he was becoming all too familiar with. Before anyone could get into position, he burst out of the cave entrance, his claws and rapidly moving tail causing clouds of grey sediment to fill the water surrounding the cave entrance. He did not react to the divers or the dolphins. He went straight for the MSR-2. A burst of infrasound caused the drone to go offline, before Ashly could detonate the explosive. The water panther bit down on the MSR-2 where the cable attached, sending it crashing to the ocean floor. His eyes followed the remaining portion of cable to the Barracuda. He began to swim upward when Liz aimed her spear gun and fired. The water panther let out a small cry of pain when Liz's spear struck his rib area.

Okada and Max fired next. Both spears hit their target, one hitting the right front leg, while the other struck the tail. The flashing lights signaled the dolphins to attack. The sound of the dolphins clicking directed the water panther's attention towards them. He had heard dolphins make that same sound right before they attacked a pod of fish. These dolphins did not appear to be hunting fish;

they were coming towards him. Seafin, Tsunami, and Atlantis swam towards the water panther head on. Aquatail and Depth Charge went for his right side, while Atragon and Typhoon approached from the back. The water panther charged the group of dolphins in front of him. His mouth open, thunder clapped, releasing a long powerful burst of infrasound. The three dolphins sensed the incoming blast. Seafin and Tsunami quickly swam to the right and left. Atlantis was not so lucky. The blast hit him head on. The intensity and length of the blast literally broke his body apart. Max cursed while reloading his spear gun. The water panther swam through the remains. As if taking a victory trophy, he ate the head of his kill. The six dolphins let out clicks of pain, mourning the loss of their brother. The four dolphins behind the water panther caught up to him. Sensing danger, he lowered his head, causing Typhoon to overshoot. More spears struck his stomach and sides, causing him to cry in pain. The momentary stun was the opening Atragon needed; he rammed the water panther from below, striking him mid-stomach. The stabbing pain caused the water panther to rapidly move upward. A few seconds later, an explosion occurred underneath him.

"Max, what happened? The dolphin got him," Liz cried in confusion. Max was scrambling for answers himself.

Why had the explosive fallen out? Max asked, then cursed himself, realizing the mistake he had made. All the lance testing was done on hard stationary targets. The water panther's coat of fur and rapid movements were not giving the explosives enough time to enter his body, causing them to fall out and explode harmlessly in the water.

Depth Charge swam up from below, aiming for the water panther's throat. The water panther moved his head backwards, avoiding the strike, then brought his front claws together on Depth Charge's body. Massive red streaks formed on Depth Charge as his speed and momentum caused the sides of his body to be shredded. The dolphin let out a final cry of pain as he fell to the ocean floor. The water panther's victory was short-lived. He roared in agony when Aquatail and Tsunami drove their lances into his back. To counter, he swam downwards, avoiding the explosion he knew was coming. Like before, the explosives went off in the water. Both pursuing dolphins avoided the main explosion but were stunned by the shockwave. The water panther turned himself upward and fired a blast of infrasound. Aquatail and Tsunami managed to recover in time and narrowly avoided the blast. The water panther was about to fire another infrasound blast when more spears struck him. The wounds they caused were not life threatening but caused pain. The water panther scanned the area. Five dolphins were left, and those humans firing spears were hiding amongst the rocks. He had managed to kill two of the dolphins, but he was not sure he could keep fighting all of them. The small wounds his enemies were inflicting were starting to take their toll. It was only a matter of time before he would be overwhelmed. He swam away from the dolphins at full speed. Seafin clicked, ordering his remaining pod members to follow the creature.

"Guys, the water panther's heading for Maui fast," Ashly said, looking at the sonar.

"Everyone, head up to regroup and resupply," Okada ordered. Minutes later, Max, Liz, and Okada got aboard the Barracuda and went below deck to rearm.

Ashly gunned the Barracuda, Samuel sat next to her, keeping an eye on the sonar. Despite the water panther having a head start, the Barracuda's speed allowed it to catch up. Ashly and Samuel could see Maui island getting closer and closer.

"Max, what's the plan?" Ashly yelled.

Max appeared at the foot of the steps and said, "Try to keep him from getting too close to Maui. The longer we can keep him moving at this speed, the more exhausted he will become. With any luck, the dolphins will be able to finish him."

"How am I supposed to do that?" Ashly wondered.

"I honestly have no idea," Max admitted.

"Perhaps getting in front of him will cause him to change direction," Okada suggested. Ashly managed to get in front of the water panther a few times. He was undeterred by the object moving above him as he neared Maui. Normally he would have attacked the pest, but with that pod of dolphins still chasing him, he continued his retreat.

"I've got it now!" Samuel suddenly screamed, which made Ashly jump. He got up from his seat, snapped his fingers, and yelled in victory. "It's heading for the shallow waters to die. By birth, these creatures must have an instinctive desire to die in shallow waters." He put his hand on Ashly's shoulder and shook it slightly. "Victory is ours!" Samuel said triumphantly. Ashly gave him an unconvinced look. The water panther stopped when he reached a twelve-foot cliff face. In the shallow waters, he placed four feet on the ocean floor and stuck his head out of the water. He paused for just a moment, looking over the rock wall in front of him, then placed all his weight on his back legs. Then he leaped out of the water on to the edge of the cliff. Ashly slowly turned to Samuel with an angered expression. He had a look of pure disbelief. "I..I don't believe it," he said, hardly able to speak.

"Well, believe it!" Ashly yelled. It took all her restraint not to punch him. "We don't have a plan in place for this because you assured us...!"

"What's going on?" Max interrupted. Ashly brought the boat to a stop, ordered Samuel to keep an eye on the panther, and ran below deck.

"What are you doing down here?" Liz wondered.

"The water panther just went ashore, right on the edge of a housing development," Ashly said in a hasty voice. "I don't know what we're going to do now," Ashly admitted, defeated.

"We have to get him back in the water," Max said, stating the obvious.

"Ashly, get back to the controls and dock at the nearest port," Okada ordered.

The water panther remained still, looking over the strange area he had retreated to. He knew from experience that marine creatures never entered the dry areas of caves. He wanted to return to the water as soon as possible. This new area was too bright for his liking, and the heat from that yellow circle in the sky made his skin feel uncomfortable. He moved his head to look back at the ocean. That pesky boat was leaving the area. That was good, but he did not want to return to the ocean just yet. That pod of dolphins was still in the area. He took some time to remove any spears that were still lodged in his flesh. He tilted his head, confused by the strange structures in front of him. He walked up to a structure and gently touched the house siding with his paw. After several touches, the object did not make a noise or move. Convinced the object was no threat, he went forward. He walked by several structures and noticed the area was filled with them. The ground in this area also had odd streaks of black rock that felt warm to the touch. His head turned to the right when two small black and brown creatures came into view and started making barking sounds. One of them was standing on his hind legs supported by a small barrier. The water panther stared back at them. To him, these creatures were more of a curiosity than a threat. A screeching noise diverted the water panther's attention to the black ground. A red creature was a few feet from him. This creature was bigger than the others, its red hide sparkling in the light. Through the transparent front of the creature, he could see a smaller creature, which he recognized as a human. He took a step forward. The red creature started making a loud unpleasant buzzing noise as it retreated backwards.

The water panther ran forward. He fired an infrasound beam, shattering the car's front windshield. The driver screamed and instinctively slammed on the brakes. The water panther saw his chance and pounced. His front legs landed on the hood of the car. He slammed his head and neck forward, going through the broken windshield. Metal screeched as the roof bent backwards. The driver screamed as the water panther bit down on his head and tore him from the car. In four bites, nothing was left of the driver. The water panther noticed many more of those human-carrying creatures in front of most of the larger objects. He leaped onto the nearest car and started tearing into it.

The Barracuda docked at Wailea Beach. The last time they had seen the water panther, he had entered the Wailea Point housing complex, which was half a mile from Wailea Beach.

"Has anything new happened?" Liz asked Okada, who was on the phone with the Maui police chief.

"The department is receiving calls from people inside the Wailea Point housing complex. I need you and Max to drive the creature back into the water at all cost." Okada desperately wanted to go with them; however, he needed to coordinate with the police and military personnel on how to handle the situation.

"What should I do?" Ashly asked, getting up from the Barracuda's driver seat.

"Yes, how can we help?" Samuel added. Okada did not reply. He was in deep conversation with the Maui police chief. He pointed to Liz, which meant to ask her.

Before she could speak, Liz said, "Ashly. You have one of those flying drones on board, right?" Ashly shook her head yes. "Reconnaissance. I want to know every move the water panther makes." She then thought about a task for Samuel. "Samuel. You keep the people on the beach calm. They're going to panic when two people armed to the teeth storm the beach."

"I can do that. I have remarkable people skills," he said. Liz jumped on to the beach with a rocket launcher over her shoulder and a submachine gun at her side. Max threw a rocket ammo bag over his shoulder, picked up his machine gun, and joined her. Ashly stood on deck, readying her drone for flight.

"Think we should commandeer a car?" Liz asked.

"Going to take too much time," Max said. Liz agreed. Both entered into a sprint as they headed for the housing complex.

"Governor Fatu is having a press conference addressing the crocodile. He's going to have a heart attack when he hears about this," Liz said. Max shook his head and laughed. Liz always found a way to make him smile even when they were probably running to their death. His smile faded when an image of Mya entered his mind.

***

At that moment, Governor Fatu stood in front of a small crowd of reporters. He spoke with confidence and reassurance.

"I want to assure everyone that the waters around our beautiful islands are safe. The tragic events that have been occurring in the Maui waters are over." A small applause filled the room. "This morning I received word that a team of zoologists have located the man eating crocodile and will remove it from our waters by the end of the day."

Inside the Crest Moon Gaming Café, Mya and Riley were watching the broadcast. It was a weekday morning, so hardly any customers were around. Mya was sweeping around Riley's cash register. Listening to the news report was sending so many questions through her mind. Was Max part of the zoological team? Is that why he was on Maui with a pod of dolphins?

"Mya, you still with me?" Riley asked, noticing her zoning out.

"Yeah, I was just thinking," Mya replied.

"About?" Riley asked curiously.

"This might sound crazy, but do you think Max was training those dolphins to hunt the crocodile?"

"That actually makes a lot of sense," Riley agreed. Her face turned slightly worried. "Do you think he was lying about letting us swim with the dolphins?" Mya threw a plush toy at her.

"I will now take any questions you may have," Governor Fatu said.

"Governor, how can you be sure the team will capture the right animal?" a young female reporter asked.

"I have the utmost confidence in the team sent to remove the crocodile. Just as I have confidence that our waters will return to normal. In fact, I'm planning on spending the weekend visiting all the wonderful Maui beaches." A middle-aged male reporter raised his hand. Governor Fatu called on him.

"Governor, some people feel a crocodile could not have caused this much damage or killed so many people." Mya walked closer to the TV.

Are they really asking if he believes it's a sea monster? she wondered. Fears that she thought were in her past started to resurface. She felt her body break out in sweat. *No, what if they mention something about me?* She saw Governor Fatu scuffling through some papers. *Here comes my picture. He's going to start making fun of me.* Governor Fatu found the paper he was looking for and started reading.

"A report prepared by the zoological team states salt water crocodiles can grow up to sixteen feet." Mya sighed in relief. "I was also informed that the Adelaide River in Australia has a twenty-foot crocodile named Brutus." He held up a photo of Brutus jumping out of the water in front of a boat. The room filled with the sounds of awed people. "A crocodile this size could easily destroy small boats and be a danger to divers. Which is why we are working very hard to remove it."

"Wow," Riley said. She could tell Mya was upset so she asked, "Mya, is that?"

"I don't know," she answered, then gave Riley a look that said, *please don't talk about it.*

"Yesterday a boat was destroyed off Maui. Do you believe that was caused by the crocodile?" a young male reporter asked.

"No, that incident was caused by a blast fishing accident," Governor Fatu assured.

"We had a front row seat for that," Riley commented, wishing she had not seen it. The young female reporter spoke again.

"Governor, what do you say to the people that feel it would be immoral to kill this creature just for acting according to its nature?"

"It deserves the worst death imaginable," Mya answered.

"Unfortunately, this animal has become a man eater that has brought much pain to our island community. I fear we have no choice but to kill it." Governor Fatu knew that sounded bad, so he quickly said, "Just because we have a man eating crocodile does not mean all crocodiles are man eaters. I'm told Brutus is a major tourist attraction. If he wishes to visit one of our aquariums, I would be happy to have him." Governor Fatu hoped that would satisfy any animal rights groups listening. He was about to address another question when a man rushed into camera view. He placed a hand over the microphone and whispered something to Governor Fatu.

"What! It's come ashore!" he screamed. Mya and Riley looked at each other, shocked. Governor Fatu looked at the camera for a moment in horror. "I'm sorry, everyone. I must cut this meeting short!" he shouted. While he was leaving the press room, a microphone clearly caught him saying, "I was just proven to be a liar! All because that fool of a cryptozoologist assured me that creature could not come ashore!" Riley pulled out her phone.

"What are you doing?" Mya asked, still trying to comprehend what had happened.

"Searching for live streams from that area. If a crocodile is rampaging through the area, someone is sure to be filming." Mya looked at the screen over Riley's shoulder. She was getting a bad feeling. Why would the governor get so freaked out over a crocodile coming ashore? Riley found a live stream titled "Real Monster Attack not Click Bait."

"Sure it's not," Riley sarcastically said as she clicked on it. The video started in an area between two houses. "Want to go back to the start of the video?" Riley asked.

"No, leave it," Mya replied in an almost mesmerized voice. The person recording slowly started to move towards the street. Loud banging could be heard in the distance. When the recording reached the front of the houses, he started to turn the camera left. Without warning, a car came flying towards him.

"Oh my god!" Riley yelled. They heard the man curse and scream as the car hit the ground and glided towards him. The camera fell from his hand. Now it was looking towards the cloud-filled sky. Riley heard Mya's throat click. The man's screams grew louder as the head and neck of a large animal appeared on the screen. It looked down at something just beyond the camera lens. Riley's eyes were wide with disbelief. Her mouth was almost hanging open. The water panther brought its head down and lifted the screaming man into the air. Drops of blood started falling, covering most of the camera's lens. The water panther moved its head back and disappeared from view.

Riley turned off her phone and stood in shock. "That couldn't have been real? Could it?" Riley's thoughts were broken by the sound of Mya throwing up. She turned towards Mya, who had just pulled her head out of the trash can. Her face had gone sickly pale. A deep feeling of guilt came over Riley. "Mya, I'm so sorry I didn't believe you." She managed to choke out. Mya walked over and hugged Riley tightly. She started breathing normally, calmed by Riley's embrace. Her feeling of fear turned to a lust for vengeance. The creature that had taken her sister from her had finally surfaced.

"I have to go deal with a personal matter," Mya said.

"Mya, where are you going?" Riley asked as Mya walked for the door.

"Going to buy a gun," Mya said in a voice filled with determination.

"Girl, did you see that thing! Are you crazy?" Riley asked, getting between Mya and the door.

"Get out of my way!" Mya said in a voice filled with hate, not towards Riley but towards the water panther. "I finally have a chance to face that thing that killed my sister and practically ruined my life." Riley could see the fire in her friend's eyes. "This is my moment to avenge Jade's death and I'm taking it!" She gently pushed Riley aside and stormed out the door.

"So, what? You're just going to start firing a gun in the middle of the street? They'll lock you up for life, girl!" Riley yelled, desperate to stop Mya.

"Not when they see what I'm shooting at," Mya stated, not turning around. Suddenly, Riley remembered something she knew would stop Mya dead in her tracks.

"I didn't even know you had a firearms permit." Mya froze and turned towards Riley.

"What are you talking about? You don't need a permit to buy rifles. I know that much."

"Yes, you do. Here, I'll show you." Riley pulled out her phone and looked up Hawaii gun laws. The information showed that rifles required a permit and pistols required a permit and a fourteen-day waiting period.

"Curse these stupid regulations!" Mya yelled. She fell to her knees, knowing her only chance for vengeance was going to slip by her. She looked up towards the sky and screamed. A small group of people started to gather around her, wondering what was going on. Riley shook her head in disgust.

"Sorry about this, everyone. My friend here." She rolled her eyes and pointed to Mya. "Lost when she was ten points away from beating the café's Ghost Maze record. She takes gaming way too seriously and rages when she loses." Amused by Riley's answer, the crowd started to leave. Riley looked at Mya and raised her eyebrows.

"Thanks," Mya replied. She started laughing at herself, thinking about what the people must be thinking of her.

***

Detective Browner parked his patrol car in front of the Wailea housing complex. Several people had called the police station in near hysteria, screaming about a giant monster moving through the development. He figured the reports of monsters were coming from uneducated people freaking out about seeing the salt water crocodile. What he found odd was all units were informed not to enter the area until ordered to. An order he disregarded.

"I'm not going to let animal control get all the glory for this." Besides, he was a detective, not a beat cop. His thoughts were broken by a loud roar coming from inside the housing complex. He pulled out his side arm in response to the piercing sound. "This must be the largest crocodile on record." He muttered, before walking into the development. He knew the crocodile was in here and he was going to kill it. After that, Governor Fatu was sure to reward him with a promotion and perhaps the public safety officer medal of valor. Thinking about it brought a smile to his face. He glanced around the edge of a house and saw a heavily armed man and woman running down the sidewalk.

"Ashly said he should be coming down this road any minute," Liz shouted, coming to a stop at an intersection. She placed the rocket launcher on her shoulder. Max laid the rocket carrier bag down and pointed his assault rifle upward.

"Freeze! Drop your weapons now!" Browner yelled as he started walking towards them.

Max glanced over at him and said, "Look, buddy, we're U.S. Military. Get out of here before you get killed." Browner did not believe what he just heard. How dare this man order him around like that. He thought about shooting both of them, but if they really were soldiers, even firing a non-fatal shot would be the end of his career.

Both of them are looking away from me, he noticed. A scenario played out in his head. He would pistol whip the man, then overpower the girl. He started sprinting towards them when another roar filled the air. He felt the sound waves slam into his chest. He hardly had time to comprehend what was happening when a large creature came rushing towards them, shattering the stone wall of a nearby house with no effort. The falling debris slammed into a parked car. The sound of the car alarm caused the water panther to stop. Browner dropped his gun. His body filled with terror as he watched the water panther tear into the car. No way. There was no way that crazy girl from the hospital was telling the truth. Yet there a sea monster was standing in front of him. With the water panther distracted, Liz fired her rocket. The rockets flames engulfed Browner's face. He screamed, holding his face from the burns. The water panther saw the rocket screeching towards him. He reared his head back and released his infrasound. The rocket exploded before reaching him. Max started firing. His shots only seemed to anger the water panther, who was now charging them at a full sprint.

"Go!" Max cried. Liz dropped the rocket launcher and ran for the opening in the stone wall. Browner was down to one knee, moaning from the pain. He opened his eyes to see himself engulfed by a large shadow. Browner saw his pistol and reached for it. He was about to close his hand around it when a jolt of pain filled his shoulder. The water panther lifted his head high into the air and released the screeching human. Browner heard his left leg crack when he hit the asphalt. He lay on the ground screaming loudly. His left leg was broken, and blood was pouring from his shoulder. The water panther watched in amazement as his prey screamed and flopped around. He suddenly shrieked in pain when a storm of bullets struck his right back leg. A whip from his tail sent Max crashing into the wall remnants.

"Max!" Liz cried. She grabbed the back of his shirt and pulled him back though the wall opening. The water panther's right paw came down on Browner's back. His claws cutting into Browner's flesh. Browner squealed as he tried to grasp anything within reach. He gasped in relief when he felt the knives leave his back. The water panther let Browner try to get to his feet. He had no desire to eat his new prey. Right now, the game of suffering brought more enjoyment then any meal could. Browner got to his one good leg and started hobbling down the street. The water panther let him get a few feet before swatting him to the ground. His enjoyment was once again interrupted by the sound of approaching humans. He turned to see Max and Liz once again raising their guns at him. The water panther bit down on Browner's head, separating it from his body. The game was over. Now it was time to deal with these pests.

Before Max and Liz could fire the water panther charged, in response they rushed between two houses. The water panther slammed his paws against one of the houses, destroying the front portion of it. Max and Liz backed up as they continued to fire. The water panther was starting to feel the overwhelming sting of the many bullets that entered his body. Enough was enough; he ran and leaped off the cliff into the ocean.

"Ashly, the water panther's back in the water. We will be at the boat in ten," Max said.

CHAPTER 37

11:11 AM 05/4/2021 HST

Rearmed, Max, Liz, and Okada dove back into the waters of the Five Caves Five Graves site. The area was eerily quiet, neither the water panther nor the dolphins in sight. Max assumed since the water panther was injured, it would return to familiar territory. As they waited for the water panther, the Barracuda broadcast the dolphin return command. Max wondered where the dolphins had swum off to. He tried to keep his eyes away from the ocean floor, worried he would see the remains of Depth Charge or Atlantis.

"Guys, got a sonar reading the water panther should be returning to the area any minute," Ashly's voice cracked over the radio. The three divers created a triangular perimeter. Okada hid inside the mouth of the cave. The head of the triangular. Max and Liz hid amongst rock formations to the left and right of the triangle's head and waited.

The wait was not long. The water panther first appeared as a small dark spot against the blue ocean. A spot that got larger and larger until the shape and details of the water panther could be seen. The water panther cautiously searched the area for those troublesome dolphins. He swam by Max and Liz without noticing them. Max could see small red clouds coming from certain areas of the water panther's body. They had wounded him. The water panther neared the middle of the triangle. Liz pulled her spear gun up, getting ready to fire. There was no way she was letting him get inside the cave or near Okada. The water panther noticed the movement. He slammed his tail against the rocks. Liz was shielded from the impact, but the tip of the water panther's tail struck the spear gun. The gun slammed downward in a fast, hard motion. The sudden movement caused her finger to squeeze the trigger. The spear entered her left leg below the knee. Liz fell down, screaming in pain. The water panther turned. The sounds of pain filled his ears, the smell of fresh blood entering his nostrils. Before Max could fire, Okada sent a spear into the water panther's neck. Okada and Max were in sight of each other. He signaled Max not to fire, and he pointed towards Liz. Max understood the message. The water panther and Okada locked eyes. Okada calmly backed into the cave. The water panther followed. As soon as the water panther passed him, Max swam towards Liz.

"Ashly, have a medical kit ready. I'm coming up."

"What happened?" she asked, concerned.

"Liz is injured," Max replied. Okada found a break in the cave rock small enough to hide in. From his position, he could see out the cave entrance. The head and upper body of the water panther entered into his sight. Okada fired his second-to-last spear, this shot striking the water panther's lower jaw. The water panther roared in annoyance. He rammed the cave wall the shot had come from.

Inside a crack, he could see the pitiful human. He reached his left paw inside, trying to claw at Okada. Okada moved to the back until he reached the end of his makeshift hiding place. He loaded his final spear and waited.

The water panther pulled his paw out and lowered his head to see where the human had gone. Okada fired his spear. The water panther's left eye suddenly went black. Sharp unbearable pain filled his body. He backed away from the crack in the wall, spinning wildly, trying to remove the spear from his destroyed eye. Soon the pain was replaced by rage: this human was going to pay, oh, yes, pay with his life for the pain he caused him. He slammed into the rocks again, which made loud cracking sounds as they started to dislodge from their position. Now the hole was large enough for the water panther to get both limbs inside. He started to push on both sides, making the hole larger, and soon he could get his upper body through; then the human would die. Okada knew it was only a matter of moments before the water panther was upon him. A small hole was forming to his left, but it was too small for him to fit through. He closed his eyes, accepting he was trapped. There was no need to call out to his teammates; there was nothing they could do anyway. Okada reached into his pocket and pulled out a grenade. The water panther backed out of the cave and slammed his head into the ever-growing opening in the wall. More rocks fell around Okada; then total darkness filled the cave. The water panther's head and upper body completely covered the opening. He looked at Okada with a hateful grin. It was like he was saying: *It's over. I won.* Okada did not shout out a final curse nor did he show fear. He simply said, "Liz, I will always love you." Then he pulled the pin on the grenade. Hearing Okada's words sent a knife though Liz's heart. Before she could respond, she and Max heard a loud explosion from inside the cave. A sound Liz recognized. The sound of a grenade going off underwater.

"Noo!" Liz cried. She pushed away from Max and headed for the cave entrance. She ground her teeth as she swam, the spear handle agitating her wound with every kick. Max followed her, knowing what he would see. Liz was the first to the cave entrance. The water panther was lying still. His head, upper body, and front limbs were covered by fallen rock. Liz could not see Okada's body but knew where it was. She swam toward the pile of fallen rocks and started tossing the smaller ones on the ground. Under the pile of rubble, the water panther's remaining eye opened.

"Liz, wait," Max warned. Before Liz could answer, the water panther tore his head out from the rock pile. His hard skull plate had absorbed most of the damage. His left horn was broken off and most of this face was charred. He swam past Max and Liz and moved his head left to right, firing infrasound. He looked towards the surface; above him, he saw that boat. The same boat that had been tormenting him for days. In a hate-filled rage, he swam upward.

Aboard the Barracuda, Ashly was trying to contact her teammates. She knew something bad had happened, but she didn't know what.

"Does anyone read me?" she asked, hoping someone would answer. Samuel sat still. All he could do was wait.

"Maybe the equipment on the boat got damaged," he suggested.

"No, it's..."

Before Ashly could finish, the water panther burst out of the ocean. The front half of his body landed between the Barracuda's bridge cabin and gun. The falling sea water sparkled off his brown fur. Drops of blood fell from his wounds. The Barracuda started to fall forward from the increased weight. He brought one of his back legs onto the front of the boat and looked towards the bridge cabin.

"Ashly, hide!" Samuel screamed, ducking under the control panel. The water panther locked eyes with Ashly, his black pupil nearly engulfing his yellow iris. Ashly could not move; she was frozen to her chair. She wanted to get up and run, but his gaze seemed to hypnotize her. A gaze that said: *I'm going to kill you.*

The water panther pulled his head back and fired a blast of infrasound. Ashly heard a thunderclap as the glass shattered around her. She screamed in pain, placing both hands over her ears as her eardrums burst. The warm feeling of blood started flowing between her fingers. She leaned forward on the control panel, coughing intensely as she spat up blood. She managed to weakly bring her head up. Her blurred vision saw the water panther raising his front claw; then everything went black. The water panther's front paw came through the window. It was a tight fit, but he managed to get it through. He moved his claws across the control panel until he felt them get a hold of cloth. He pushed down, sinking them into flesh, then started to pull his latest victim out the window. Ashly's body was halfway out when the sound of gunfire rang out. Intense pain filled his right leg. Still in his hidden position, Samuel had his right hand pressed on the Barracuda's gun's firing button. After a roar, Samuel heard a large splash and bullets started ripping through the top of the cabin, missing Ashly by inches. He released the trigger and crawled over to her. He pulled her from her seat. Her body hit the ground harder than he intended it to.

He rushed for the medical kit when he felt his feet leave him. Before he knew it, he was falling through the air. He hit the ship's ceiling with a thud. Around him, alarms started to go off and water started pouring through the broken windows. In the overturned boat, Samuel searched for Ashly. He spotted her right before the rising water covered her. He pulled her to the ceiling, holding her above the water line as long as he could. Samuel took a breath and placed a hand over Ashly's mouth and nose right before the cabin filled with water. Moments later, he felt himself falling again. Relief filled him as the Barracuda began to right itself. After most of the water drained, he checked Ashly's pulse.

"Thank goodness," he said, feeling it. He was concerned because he had no idea how badly she was hurt or what to do with an unconscious person. So, he did the only thing he could think of. He pulled his phone from its waterproof case and asked it: "How to help an unconscious person."

The water panther spun wildly, trying to numb the pain in his back right leg. He tried to move the damaged limb, but the five large bullet holes made the limb nearly unusable. He looked up at that cursed boat. He lowered his head, getting ready to ram it. This time he would break right through the ship's hull. Just as he kicked his left back leg, Atragon struck him above the rib cage. The water panther jerked hard to the left and bit down. Atragon moved out of the way, right before the water panther's jaws closed. The water panther snarled as Atragon swam out of view. The feeling of pain was nearly gone, blocked out by his desire to kill these attackers. He noticed another dolphin heading towards him. He stared at his damaged limb, keeping the dolphin in view. When the dolphin was nearly upon him, he turned his head, biting Typhoon between the head and body fin.

Typhoon's lifeless body fell to the ground. In a bloody gulp, the water panther ate the piece of flesh in his mouth. Max slammed the ground with his fist, pained to see another one of his dolphins die. He watched the panther's gaze move across the ocean, searching for the remaining dolphins.

Are any of us going to make it out alive? he thought, wondering what it would take to kill this thing. He felt Liz's arm grip his shoulder. She raised her spear gun, using her good leg and his shoulder for balance. The water panther was about twenty-five feet above them. She aimed her spear gun at the water panther's remaining eye. Max reached for his and came to the realization he had left it at his hiding place. He looked at Liz's ammo bag and saw it was empty. *This shot has to count,* he thought.

"Just die!" Liz screamed as she fired. With a whoosh, the spear shot towards the water panther's eye. A slight tilt of his head caused the spear to strike him on the skull. Max and Liz both swore they saw the monster grin as the spear harmlessly bounced off the bony plate. Now it was his turn: he dove towards them. Thinking quickly, Max pushed Liz, then kicked his feet hard, sending him backwards. The water panther landed between them. In one motion he smacked Liz across the head with his tail and pawed Max in the face with his good limb. Liz hit the ground, unconscious. Max blinked in a daze, having fallen on his stomach. He tried to lift himself up when the water panther slammed his claws into his back. He grunted in pain, feeling the claws ripping through the diving suit and into his skin. He turned his head to see the water panther's jaws coming down on him. He knew it was the end.

Mya, sorry I couldn't kill this thing, he thought, looking up at the water panther's open mouth. Darkness enclosed his head. He could see the sharp teeth moving closer and closer together. He closed his eyes and pictured Mya's face one last time. Mya's face vanished when the water panther let out a piercing cry. Seafin dug his lance into the water panther's right shoulder. His limb remained still, refusing to release his grip on Max. The water panther twisted his neck and bit down on Seafin's body. Max was unaware of what was going on above him until he heard an explosion. He opened his eyes, feeling the crushing weight from the water panther's paw leave him. He rolled on his stomach to see a large cloud of blood coming from the motionless body of the water panther. As he backstroked away from the approaching cloud, he noticed one of the panther's limbs to the far right of the cloud.

"Max, are you okay?" He spun around and saw Liz crawling towards him.

"It's over; we won," he said in a near trance like state. Suffering from shock and intense pain from his wounds he looked around for his dolphins. He saw the front half of a dolphin lying next to the severed leg. He soon recognized it as Seafin. He swam over and, as a final goodbye, placed a hand on the dolphin that had saved him. They had won the battle, but it did not feel like a victory. Four of his dolphins were dead. As his senses came back to him the painful reality that his friend Okada was dead hit him. He fell on his stomach as a deep sorrow came over him. Max felt his eyes water as memories of Okada entered his mind. A great mentor and friend was gone from his life forever. His eyes moved towards the surface, he could see the Barracuda above him. He remembered Samuel and Ashly hoping they were ok.

"Max, please talk to me." The sound of Liz's concerned voice helped bring him back to his senses.

"I'm a little banged up," he replied. Keeping the extent of his injuries hidden for her sake. A pulsing pain traveled through his entire back. "What about you?"

"How do you think I am?" she replied sadly. Max's thoughts went to the Barracuda. He tried to contact Samuel and Ashly with no response.

He turned to see Liz crawling towards the cave. He looked at his oxygen gage, which was nearly empty. Knowing Liz's gage was most likely similar, he said, "Liz, let's head back up. Ashly and Samuel are not answering radio calls. Plus, we need medical attention."

"Not yet," she cried, grinding her teeth in pain. Every crawl sent a wave of excruciating pain through her leg.

"Liz," Max said again. He swam in front of her, grabbed her under both arms, and lifted her to his eye level. "Liz, it's over. That thing is dead."

"So is a great man," she fired back. Her words again nearly brought him to tears.

"Liz, we're both injured and nearly out of oxygen. Okada would not want us to die like this."

"I'm not going back up, not without Okada. I can't leave him down here." Max noticed the unmistakable tears running down Liz's face, a sight he never thought he would see. Max threw his arms around her, hugging her tightly. Instead of resisting, she joined the embrace. The two looked into each other's tear-filled eyes.

"Liz, we're not going to leave him, but we need to go up and take care of your leg wound." Then in a sincere voice, he said, "I will be right back in the water and won't come up until I find him." Liz shook her head; she understood. She placed an arm over his shoulder. Max looked towards the surface and saw the remaining three dolphins swimming around the boat.

"Let's go," Liz said, exhausted. Suddenly they heard the unmistakable sound of a thunderclap, and then a heavy vibration shook their bodies. In horror, Max and Liz turned to the dissolving red cloud to see the figure of the water panther slowly emerging from it. Max could not believe what he was seeing.

"He should have bled out by now!" he cried. The water panther's right shoulder and a chunk of its lower neck was missing. A hissing sound came from the neck injury. He used his back legs to thrust himself towards them. Instinctively, Max jumped back. Liz tried to follow, but her damaged leg gave out. All she could do was hold her knife out against the charging monster. The water panther bit down on her arm, engulfing it up to the elbow. Uninjured, he could have easily torn the limb from her body, but in his near death state, he could not apply the needed pressure. Max frantically searched his diving pockets for anything he could use as a weapon. All he found was an unused glow stick.

Liz yelled in pain. She could feel the water panther's teeth making grinding motions on her trapped arm. She could still move her wrist. If she was going to lose her arm, she was going to make him pay. Her eyes locked with the water panther's, both exchanged looks of anger and hatred. She moved her knife back and forth across the inside of the water panther's mouth. The water panther felt the pain, but he did not care. He was going to kill these two before he died. Max cracked the glow stick and waved it above his head. The three dolphins saw it and moved to attack it. Max swam to the water panther's missing limb and slammed the glow stick into the neck wound. The water panther screeched in pain, releasing Liz's arm. Before he could retaliate, the pod of dolphins was on him. Tsunami slammed into the water panther, followed by Aquatail and Atragon. Liz jammed her knife into the water panther's throat. New red clouds started to pour out of the water panther's mangled body.

Max grabbed Liz and started swimming towards the Barracuda. He looked at the battle occurring underneath him. The water panther weakly tried to fight back, but the nimble dolphins were easily avoiding his attacks. Tsunami, Aquatail, and Atragon continued to circle and ram their lances into the water panther until the demon of paradise collapsed for good. Max and Liz broke the surface near the Barracuda. Both were tired and shaken. Max treaded water near the boat ladder, helping his wounded friend climb. A hand met Liz's when she neared the top of the ladder. She looked up, expecting to see Samuel or Ashly, but she nearly fell back into the water when she saw Okada's bruised and bloody face.

All she managed to get out was. "How?"

"Liz, I have several broken limbs; hurry up and climb aboard," Okada said in intense pain. Liz got aboard, still not believing what she was seeing. Okada lay back down. His right arm and leg were crushed, but he was alive. Liz fell onto his good shoulder and started weeping.

"Don't ever scare me like that again," she ordered.

"I will try not to," Okada replied. Samuel walked over to the ladder and helped Max up.

"Okada?" Max said, shocked. His shocked expression soon turned to a cheerful smile. "How did you manage to get out of there?" he wondered, sitting next to him.

"When I was trapped, I noticed the water panther's pounding had widened a crack in the side of the rock that led to the ocean. Right before the grenade exploded, I wedged most of my body into it. The collapsing tunnel shielded me from the blast. I am not sure what occurred after that. The next thing I recall, I woke up on the boat."

"I saw his unconscious body come up," Samuel cut in. "Despite the great danger from the monster, I jumped into the water to save my comrade."

"You have my thanks," Okada said.

"And mine," Liz added. "Any ordinary man would have died from what you went through."

"I'm no ordinary man." Okada reminded.

Max looked to the side of the boat to see Atragon leap out of the water. His joy turned to sudden concern when he realized someone was missing.

"Samuel, where's Ashly?" Max asked, looking around the boat. Samuel led Max to the bridge. Ashly was lying on the floor, her head supported by a life jacket.

"What happened to her?" Max asked. Samuel explained what had happened.

"She should be okay. I've called for a medical chopper; it should be here soon."

"Samuel, you called for a medical helicopter?" Max said, a little surprised.

"Yes, people were wounded, plus, if the battle went south, I needed a way to escape. The Barracuda's electronics are dead if you have not noticed." A glance at the controls confirmed Samuel's claim. "The water panther is dead, right?" Samuel went on to ask. Max shook his head yes and went back outside.

"Is Ashly okay?" Liz asked.

"She's unconscious, but stable," Max confirmed. "Medevac should be here soon." Tired and injured, everyone waited for the medical chopper to arrive. When it did, Okada was loaded on first, followed by Ashly and Liz. When it was Max's turn, he looked down at the ocean as he was lifted into the helicopter. He felt guilty leaving the dolphins behind. It sucked because he had no choice in the matter. "I'll be back soon. Have fun until then," he yelled into the water. His words were more for his peace of mind than the dolphins.

CHAPTER 38

2:17 PM 05/5/2021 HST

Inside the Triple Army Medical Center on Honolulu, Max and Samuel sat near Okada's hospital bed. He had gone through emergency surgery the night before. His right arm and leg were suspended above him by slings. Liz rested on his good arm, her leg heavily bandaged. Max's back was full of stitches. Ashly was in surgery to repair her eardrums. A knock on the door drew the team's attention. Everyone hoped it was a doctor reporting Ashly's surgery had been successful. A nurse opened the door, followed by Saburo, and to everyone's shock Okada's father, Admiral Tetsuya Takahashi. The nurse exited and closed the door after the two men entered.

"Admiral!" Max said, getting up to stand at attention. Max and Liz had seen Admiral Takahashi only once when he came to visit Niihau with members of the Japanese high command.

"At ease," he replied. He walked over to Okada. Max and Liz saw a look of pain on the Admiral's face. He placed an arm on Okada's shoulder and spoke not as a military commander, but as a loving father.

"You did well, my son. I am very proud of you." His gaze turned to the rest of the team. "That goes for all of you."

"Thank you, sir," everyone replied nearly in unison. Max walked over to Saburo and quietly asked, "How are the dolphins?"

"They were located late last night. I was informed the Sea Eagle safely returned them to the estate base. The Sea Eagle is currently on route to Niihau with the remains of the water panther."

"Admiral, now that we completed our mission, may I make arrangements to transport the dolphins back to Niihau?" Max asked.

"I'm afraid they will not be returning there," Admiral Takahashi replied. Max gave a confused look. "You have turned those dolphins into valuable military assets. You have achieved the program's goal. When I return to Japan, the dolphins will be returning with me to join the Japanese Defense Force." Max had mixed feeling about what he heard. He knew the dolphins would eventually join the Japanese Defense Force, but he was going to greatly miss working with them.

"You can still visit them," Saburo said, noticing he was upset.

"I will," Max replied. He leaned closer to Saburo and whispered, "And that favor I asked you about?"

"It has been taken care of," Saburo whispered back.

"Father, how much damage did the water panther cause on the main land?" Okada asked.

"Thanks to your efforts, property damage and loss of life was minor."

"What about video footage? I'm sure there are videos all over the internet," Liz added.

"Luck was on our side," Saburo said. "Many of the homes in the area where the water panther came ashore were rental homes for tourists. Only two known recordings were made. A live stream that was quickly censored and a camera recording that was brought to the Maui police station."

"What's the cover story for the damage?" Liz continued.

"With the water panther dead, that falls to Governor Fatu," Saburo answered.

"Does he know how the battle went?" Max asked.

"Yes, when I spoke to him, he appeared happy that it's over, but he also seemed worried that new recordings or photos may surface." The conversation was paused by another knock. A doctor entered the room with, to everyone surprise, Ashly. She had a gauze strip across her head, holding two large bandages over her ears. Her long hair was down, not in the usual braid. Max was the first to speak.

"Ashly, what are you doing out of bed? You just had surgery."

"She insisted on seeing her teammates. She even refused a wheelchair," the doctor said.

"I needed to make sure everyone was okay," Ashly stressed. She brought a hand over her mouth when she saw how injured her teammates were. As the doctor left the room, Max and Samuel rushed over to hug her.

"I'd join you if I could," Liz added.

"Ow," Max said. Ashly felt the stitches in his back and released her tight hug.

"Sorry," she apologized.

"Don't worry," Max replied. "How are you feeling?"

"My insides hurt like crazy and it's difficult to hear, but I'm alive." Ashly's tone got more serious when she asked, "Did we kill the water panther?"

"Sure did. We completed our mission," Max confirmed. Ashly sat down.

"What?" Liz asked, noticing her look of sadness. Ashly breathed heavily and said, "The past few weeks have been more incredible than anything I ever imagined, and now it's over."

"Darling, that's a good thing," Samuel added. Ashly looked at him like he wasn't getting what she was talking about. Ashly tried not to get too emotional when she said,

"Now, everyone will go their separate ways." She got up and tried to smile. "It was a pleasure meeting all of you." She paused and looked at Samuel. "Even the people who annoyed me."

"On the contrary: Suijin Squads mission is just beginning," Admiral Takahashi added.

"Wait, what?" Ashly uttered, confused.

"The existence of the water panther has proven that unidentified creatures exist. It is safe to assume that in the future, more incidents like the Maui incident will occur. To study and combat possible threats from unknown species, the Japanese high command has determined a special task force should be in place at all times. I would like Suijin Squad to be this task force."

Max looked at Okada and Liz. "The three of us have been working together for years. Why stop now? As soon as both of you can walk, that is," he joked.

"We'll be up before you know it," Liz replied.

"You don't have to ask me twice. I'm in," Ashly agreed.

"To go from a laughing stock to a serious government consultant is the dream of any scientist. Of course I'm in," Samuel declared.

"We still have a lot of unused space on Niihau. We could convert most of the land to holding and studying unknown species," Max recommended.

"Why stop at unknown species? Why not go after myths and legends from across the globe?" Samuel suggested.

"It's decided then: Suijin Squad will remain," Admiral Takahashi proclaimed.

"Now all we need is the champagne," Liz joked.

"I'm calling for a bottle," Saburo offered. Everyone thought he was kidding until he pulled his phone out.

CHAPTER 39

Mya Kendig set a package down on her counter. She had spent nearly all of last night and this morning trying to find information on the creature she had seen in the live stream. She could not understand why no one in authority was talking about it. What little information she did find claimed the entire thing was a hoax. This afternoon she was going to take Riley's advice and forget about it for a while. She looked at the shipping label, which read: international one day delivery. Contains fragile material. Return address Saburo Nakamura, Tokyo, Japan. A confused look formed on her face. She had no idea who Saburo Nakamura was or why he would be sending her a package. She thought about returning it, but her curiosity got the better of her. She pulled a knife out of a kitchen drawer and opened it. Inside was a golden card on top of a smaller Styrofoam box. *This has to be a mistake,* she thought. She double checked the name on the shipping label. It was her name and the correct address. She picked up the card and started reading.

"Hey, Mya. Just wanted to let you know the dolphins performed well during their first outing. To celebrate, I got you a souvenir. Hope to see you soon. Max Varian. P.S. Sorry for lying." Reading that brought a wide smile to her face. Butterflies filled her stomach as she pulled the Styrofoam box out.

Wait. I just saw him two days ago. What was he doing in Japan, and what did he mean by sorry for lying? she wondered. Was he lying about going to Japan?" She thought some more, and the answer came to her. *He probably thought I would want to go, and felt bad so he sent me this.* She rolled her eyes. *Just hope it's not expensive jewelry.* The situation was now starting to make her feel weird. She had been out with Max once. Now from Japan he had sent an overnight package to her. *I really hope he's not one of those creepy guys who becomes obsessed with a girl after one date.* She shrugged at the thought, *No, Mya, let's see what he sent before you jump to any conclusions.* She lifted the top of the box off and reached inside. It felt like a statue or something. She pulled the object out and gasped, dropping it on the counter top. The object was a large cherry finish plaque with a large claw standing upright. Her eyes were wide and her breathing rapid as she stared at it. The events of that day started flooding her memory. She knew what this was: a claw from the creature that had killed Jade. *What does this mean? What does this mean?* she thought. She noticed in front of the claw, golden words were carved into the wood. Her heart was thumping as she moved closer to read them.

"You no longer need to worry. The depths of paradise are safe." She leaned her head back and let out a breath of relief. Everything made sense now. His willingness to believe her, he and the dolphins randomly showing up on Maui, the words *sorry for lying* at the end of the letter. He was hunting that thing the whole time. For a brief moment, she was upset that he had not told her the truth, but it was okay. She'd make him tell her everything next time she saw him. She looked at the claw again, glowing with happiness. For the first time since Jade's death, a feeling of peace and closure came over her. That thing was dead. The creature that had taken her sister from her was dead. She walked out on the balcony and looked out at the ocean, then looked towards the heavens.

"Jade, it's over. We won."

***

As Saburo poured champagne into glasses, Max felt his phone vibrate. He exited the room and accepted the call.

"Hey, Mya."

"I got your package," Mya said in a low, somewhat seductive voice.

"Cool. Did you get the meaning?"

"Yes," Mya replied, a hint of gratitude and happiness filling her voice. "Max, thank you so much. I know what you did out there, and I know you probably can't talk about it, but I need to hear it. Is it truly over?"

"Yes, it's over," Max assured. He heard Mya let out a happy sigh.

"You don't know how much hearing that means to me. I truly thought that thing would never pay for what he did."

"I'll tell you all about it someday," Max added.

"Sounds good," Mya replied. "Oh, and by the way. You may be my hero, but if I recall, you still owe me and Riley a dolphin swim."

"Hey, lover boy. Get in here for the toast," Liz yelled.

"I promise I will figure something out. Something just came up, so I have to go. I'll talk to you later."

"Better," Mya replied. Max hung up and returned to the team. Saburo handed him a full glass.

"Okay, now everyone decide on a toast. To victory and many victories to come," Liz said.

"To fallen and wounded comrades," Max declared, thinking of the dolphins who died in the battle.

"To speedy recoveries," Ashly added.

"To the many unknown species we will discover," Samuel said.

Everyone turned to Okada. He remanded silent for a moment, then said, "To Suijin Squad."

About the Author

Vance Albright has been writing in some form or another since he was five. Throughout high school he wrote several book drafts but always fell into the trap of never finishing them. During college, he temporarily gave up on fiction writing to focus on his studies. After graduating, he renewed his love for writing and started Light and Dark Novelizations to begin creating his own universe of characters.

Vance believes compelling storylines and believable characters that capture the reader's interest are the keys to a great novel. Vance graduated from high school in 2008, and in 2016 he earned a B.S. in Environmental Science and minored in Biology. He is currently working in the environmental technician and horticulturalist fields.

Vance always has been an animal lover. He currently has two cats, Luna and Nova, three parakeets, and a tropical fish tank.

Thank you for reading Depths of Paradise. If you enjoyed this book, please consider leaving a review on your favorite online book purchasing site.